Kenneth Macleay

**Historical Memoirs of Rob Roy and the Clan Macgregor**

Kenneth Macleay

**Historical Memoirs of Rob Roy and the Clan Macgregor**

ISBN/EAN: 9783337390051

Printed in Europe, USA, Canada, Australia, Japan

Cover: Foto ©Andreas Hilbeck / pixelio.de

More available books at **www.hansebooks.com**

# HISTORICAL MEMOIRS

OF

# ROB ROY

AND

# THE CLAN MACGREGOR;

INCLUDING

Original Notices of Lady Grange.

WITH AN INTRODUCTORY SKETCH, ILLUSTRATIVE OF

THE CONDITION OF THE HIGHLANDS PRIOR

TO THE YEAR 1745.

BY

K. MACLEAY, M.D.

EDINBURGH:

WILLIAM BROWN, 149 PRINCES STREET.

1881.

# PREFACE.

THE previous editions of the following interesting and authentic account of the Times, the
Family, and the Exploits of the celebrated
Rob Roy have now been out of print for many
years.

It has therefore been increasingly difficult to
obtain copies of a work which throws much
light, not only upon the romantic career of the
outlaw, but upon the state of the Highlands
prior to the Rebellion of 1745.

The present publisher has for these reasons
issued this third edition, which he trusts will
meet with acceptance alike from those interested
in Scottish history, and those who may be curious to learn more of the life, character, and

adventures of the hero of one of Sir Walter
Scott's greatest novels.

The story of the abduction of Lady Grange,
which is added, as in the previous editions,
forms an appropriate sequel to the memoirs of
Rob Roy, having all the charm of a romance,
while well illustrating the utter lawlessness at
one time prevailing within the Highland borders.

The author makes the following remarks in
his preface to the second edition of the book,
published in 1819.

The historical incidents that are introduced,
and the various anecdotes given throughout the
volume, have been collected from written docu-
ments and many sources of oral tradition, where
the concurring testimonies of different respectable individuals seemed to establish a genuine
conclusion.

To Mr Buchanan of Arden, who permitted
him to take a likeness of his hero from the only

original painting, it is believed, in existence, he must beg to offer his grateful acknowledgments. The picture has long been in the possession of his family, and proofs of its being an accurate portrait have been transmitted to the present day.

In publishing the letters of James Macgregor, the son of Rob Roy, included in this volume, the author conceives himself fully justified. He received them in a manner that did not place him under any restraint; nor does he imagine that they contain expressions that may be hurtful to the feelings of any person, as they have no allusion to the character, title, or pretensions of any one now living.

# CONTENTS.

# INTRODUCTORY SKETCH,

## ILLUSTRATIVE OF THE CONDITION

### OF THE

# HIGHLANDS,

## PRIOR TO THE YEAR 1745.

THE wild and magnificent scenery of the Highlands of Scotland, when viewed in connexion
with the peculiar habits and manners of the
inhabitants, has always been regarded as an
object of interesting curiosity to the natives of
Southern Great Britain; and, in modern times,
has excited the investigation of the natural
historian, and claimed the attention of the
moral philosopher. Secluded by the formidable
aspect of their mountains, and the dissonance
of their language, from intercourse with the rest
of the world, they formed of themselves an
original nation, regulated by customs and laws
exclusively their own.

The deep obscurity which, for a series of
ages, enveloped the Northern States of Europe,

A

affected, in a particular degree, the still more
impenetrable and cloudy regions of Caledonia.
The general rudeness of manners inseparable
from the darkness of those primeval periods,
was not calculated to restrain the irregular
propensity of fierce communities, nor to overawe the conduct of their individual members,
so that they were free to become virtuous or
vicious, as best suited their inclination or purpose. The total ignorance of domestic arts to
guide and facilitate the operations of rural
economy, rendered their subsistence precarious
and miserable, and led the way to that system
of necessary rapine and pillage, which frequently desolated their country, and added
acts of violence, injustice, and inhumanity to
the catalogue of their errors; but in the
occasional prosecution of their feuds they considered themselves guiltless, because practice
had sanctioned such enormities.

Before the Highlanders emerged from this
condition of barbarism, they were a wild and
unpolished race, destitute of political institu-
tions, and despising subordination. Their
minds being wholly unenlightened by religious
truths, or the influence of literature, they appear
to have practised scarcely any other estimable

quality than that of personal courage. Possessing neither acquired embellishments, nor useful
knowledge, they were in no respect different
from other untutored nations of the same age.

This state of ignorance will account for the
prevalence of superstition and its concomitant
prejudices among them, even to a more recent
period than could have been imagined, after the
universal progress of civilization. So late as
the breaking out of the last civil commotion in
Scotland, the Highland peasantry were held in
abject dependence by their chiefs, and kept in
dark subjection to the sanctimonious artifices of
their priesthood, for the success of whose
machinations, an unlettered mind seems to
have been an indispensable quality.

During this remote antiquity, their oral
history, for they had no other, declares an
unsettled state of society, where the passions,
unrestrained by the influence of principle or
example, did not confine the wandering inclination to moderate bounds, and where
equitable laws did not curb the indulgence of
extravagant habits. Being almost destitute of
jurisprudence, or sanctioned rules to enforce
rectitude, or repress evil practices, the Highlanders unavoidably became rapacious and

ungovernable, not considering themselves amenable to any legal authority.

The pride of family distinction which latterly infatuated the minds of many chieftains, and inclined them to arrogance, was, in older times, in a great measure overlooked, as a consideration beneath the notice of men whose consequence depended often upon more estimable, though less pacific, qualifications, than the frivolous and empty honours of a name, which some of their more distant successors attached to themselves, without the merit of obtaining or deserving such marks of superiority.

Though the Highlanders were shut up within the confines of their own country, and for many years remained separate from the other provinces of the island, they felt, like all European kingdoms, the effects of the allodial, and the feudal systems. The chiefs were generally, indeed, desirous of exerting undue powers over their followers, and sometimes did so with unjustifiable austerity ; but though they were inclined to be arbitrary themselves, they could never be induced, either by threats or by flattery, to apply for regal charters, submission to any degree to the throne being incompatible with their feelings, as they conceived that they had an unquestionable right to govern their own properties ; and that to hold them by a tenure under the king or government was dishonourable to the consequence of which they believed themselves possessed. Down to the period of the last attempt of the Stewarts, the same sentiments prevailed, and a chieftain of the Clandonell publicly declared, that such condescension was unworthy of Highlanders, and that he would never hold his lands by a sheep's skin, but by the sword, whereby his ancestors had acquired them.

In the unfruitful and stubborn soil of the Highlands, subject to a variable and rigorous climate, the benefits of agriculture were formerly almost unknown, so that their means of sub-sistence were precarious and miserable, and consisted chiefly of what hunting, fishing, and the pasturage of a few tame animals afforded them : they were thus constrained to adhere to that pastoral state to which their country is naturally more adapted. In this situation we may believe that sagacity and artifice were exerted to overcome individual hardships ; but those practices were often unavailing, as strength of arm alone determined the right of property. Associations for the reciprocal protection and safety of the members, hence became essential, to check the encroachments of rapacious tribes, or as the means of prosecuting pillage. Fidelity to each other became a sacred duty, and a violation of it was considered base, and punished with severity.

The appointment of a chief, or leader, to regulate the management of such discordant societies, early became necessary, so that in this way must have originated the system of clanship, which gradually arose to be a source of monstrous oppression in those regions, and latterly met with a just and total overthrow.

As the strength of a clan grew formidable, the power of the individual chiefs seemed also to become more extensive and overbearing, and was exercised with haughty importance, and profound arrogance; and whether they were chosen or had assumed the dignity, their vassals were equally submissive, and dared not disobey them in the pursuit of any feud, however cruel or unjust. For the security of the chief, castellated habitations were erected in the most inaccessible places, where his followers were always entertained; and the more numerous they grew, his importance increased in the same degree, so that the chief whose clan was most powerful, and capable of the most desperate achievements, was considered most exalted. By affability, by promises, by a rough hospitality, a chieftain maintained a patriarchal ascendency over his people. He was regarded as possessing the quality of declaring war and concluding peace, in his own person, without the intervention of kindred or clan ; and whether right or wrong, he usurped the privilege of distributing what he called justice, an immunity sometimes exercised with partiality, and without lenity. His vassals were considered his property, and their lives were at his disposal,—such were the barbarous practices of the times.

But if a chief became unworthy of the confidence and support of the clan, betraying cowardice, or infidelity to his charge or promise, his followers rose up against him, drove him from his station, or put him to death, and appointed another to fill his place.

Some time ago, a curious instance of this determined spirit of clanship took place, when a young Highland chief, who had been educated at a distance, went to take possession of his inheritance. Great preparations were made at his castle for his reception, as well as for entertain-

ing the clan, who were convoked on the moment-
ous occasion. The profusion of viands that
were getting ready for the feast, astonished the
young economical chief, and he expressed his
surprise at such waste, declaring that, in place
of so many bullocks, sheep, venison, and other
things, a few hens would have been sufficient.
This remark acted like lightning among the
tribe then assembled. They proclaimed him
unworthy of being their chief, instantly discarded him under the degrading title of hen
chief, and set up his nearest relation as their
head, it being considered disgraceful for a clan
to be without a chief even for one day. Soon
after this incident, the discarded chief returned
with a large force from the North Highlands, to
claim his property; but his clan under their
adopted chieftain gave battle, slew the real
chief, and routed his party, so that the person
they had chosen then became their head by indisputable right.

The person in this way to be dignified was
supposed to be deserving of the honour, and
prior to his inauguration, which often was a
ceremony of great pomp, he was required to
perform some signal action worthy the head of
a clan. In the prosecution of their hereditary

feuds, descending from one generation to another as an established custom, the chief was attended by a train of young men eager to prove their valour, and when they had signalized themselves by the execution of some hazardous exploit, they were afterwards reputed brave, and if they survived, took their proper station accordingly among the clan.

The haughty distinction of chief, with other subordinate titles equally honourable in their degree, thus acquired, were pertinaciously retained among the Highlanders, and generally descended to lineal posterity, or those who seemed best qualified for the succession, and they were frequently fixed upon by the tribe before the chief's decease ; but if he died without an heir, or the appointment of a successor, quarrels often arose among the branches of the clan for the vacant dignity. Those military associations at first formed under uncertain regulations, were feeble and insecure, they were easily broken, and admitted of much dispute, so that the appellation of Chief was sometimes taken up by enterprising and intrepid members of a clan, who supported all the violent and overweening superiority claimed by their predecessors, until finally their vassals, by long submission, became the passive instruments of their inordinate ambition, in conducting their feuds, or repelling their foes.

After the confirmation of clanship, no individual existed in the Highlands who did not place himself under the banners, and become the clansman of some chief; hence arose the disgrace attached to a man who could not name his chief; yet, though this bore the appearance of systematic arrangement, it did not remove many irregular habits, which in a great measure seemed inseparable from these confederations. The practice of vice in many flagrant forms has been attributed to the Highlanders. But although it may be allowed that many causes existed to render error congenial to their disposition, it cannot be supposed that their feelings were more repugnant to virtue, their temper more ferocious, or their lives more profligate than those of their Lowland neighbours, during the unsettled times under our review.

The whole Highland regions being composed of clans, or tribes of various patronimics or names, the members commonly lived upon the lands of their respective chiefs. If these members paid any rent, it was generally in kind, as it was denominated, which consisted of such articles as the family of the chief required ; for the use of money, until a more recent period, was but little known among them. As the political importance of a chief, besides the extent of his territory, depended principally upon the number of his followers, their services was all the rent exacted or usually expected by the chief from the chieftain, and by the latter from inferior classes of the tribe. When Macdonell of Keappoch, afterwards killed in the battle of Culloden, was asked what his rental might be, he replied, that he could bring to the field six hundred fighting men.

The titles of chief and chieftain, with some others, were anciently in use, and were attended to, as they distinguished the various gradations of a clan, and gave every man his own appropriate place in the field, or on other occasions ; but these epithets were of late indiscriminately applied as of one signification.

Besides those feudal ties which bound each clan to its own hereditary chief, many individuals were in the end connected to him by claims of consanguinity, the chief taking upon himself the authority of a parent, from whom, or from some branch of whose family, every vassal imagined he was descended. The vassal, therefore, though

retained in wretched villenage, loved and respected the chief, not merely as his superior, but
as his own connexion, did him all due homage,
and supported him as the point in which his
own personal honour was centered; and the
chief from weighty motives, found it necessary
to make a return of his kindness and protection.

A circumstance, only gone into desuetude of
very late years, though it may be regarded as a
matter of trivial importance, may nevertheless
be stated, as it likewise contributed to produce
that reciprocal attachment, which so strongly
obtained among the members of a clan:—The
children of the chiefs were, for the most part,
sent to be nursed by some of their female followers, and it was usual for them to remain
under the tuition of the nurse and her husband,
till they had nearly reached maturity, when
they returned to their father's castle, accompanied with presents, chiefly in cattle, it being
considered a great honour done to their dependants thus to have the rearing of the chief's
family. This manner of training their youth
was the most contemptible and barbarous that
can be imagined, and will serve to explain that
ignorance and abhorrence of literature, which
marked the character of many old chieftains of

the Highlands. This fosterage, however, engen-
dered some useful consequences, by attaching
the members of a clan more firmly to each
other, and formed, as it were, a family compact
which effected the union of many hostile generations, and often prevented their feuds.

. From the connections in this way framed, the
castle of the chief was always open for the reception of his people as a place of entertainment
in times of peace, and as a retreat of safety in
seasons of war. On occasions of festivity, which
were frequent and distinguished for boisterous
mirth, the whole clan was convoked, the song
and the dance prevailed, and the social cup
went round. A bard was retained by every
tribe, whose province it was at these meetings
to recite such poems and other traditionary
legends as recounted the exploits of their pro-
genitors, and inspired sentiments that cherished
the warlike spirit of the hearers. Of this description originally, it is believed, were the
poems of Ossian, which, from this mode of
recital and oral transmission, must have been
improved at the will of each succeeding bard,
until they latterly received the polished form in
which they have recently been given to the
world.

The principle which then regulated the usages of war, as well as the political economy peculiar to the mountains, was founded on this system of clanship, every tribe forming a distinct and separate community, subject to its own local rules, each chief being in effect an independent prince, who acknowledged no law but such as he himself had constructed, or as had been in use among his ancestors. Regardless of statutes promulgated by the government of the kingdom, a chief protected his vassals against them, though guilty of their infringement, so that they disdained any other control than that which he imposed. He, of consequence, directed their conduct, and they willingly opposed the regal power, on any emergency of danger, as he judged proper. To the solidity of this alliance is to be attributed the difficulty with which the daring spirit of clanship was ultimately subdued.

Habituated to violent bodily exertion from their unsettled mode of life, which led them to constant exposure in a changeable atmosphere, they were a muscular and hardy people, living in the enjoyment of health to advanced age ; and though constitutionally disposed to indolence, they went forward to battle with a fearless heart and a destructive arm.

The incitements to war, while they gratified
either public or private revenge, held out other
inducements in the spoils of the conquered, no
less flattering to their ostentation than acceptable to their wants.  From almost every district
plundering parties were sent off, once a year, as
a regular service during the Michaelmas moon,
no doubt with the view of providing winter
stores.  Every young man who accompanied
these enterprises received the countenance of
his favourite fair one, according to the spoil he
brought back, which chiefly consisted of cattle ;
and the dowry of the chief's daughter was made
up by a share of the booty collected in such expeditions.  Though it was considered shameful to commit this species of theft on any one of
the same clan, it was avowedly no disgrace to
attack the property of distant or unfriendly
septs, against whom this spoliation was carried
as a custom established by long practice ; and
cattle being always their most valuable com-
modity, the loss was often severely felt as the
most cruel privation which, in the neglected
state of the soil, could have been endured.

But such nefarious practices led to a remedy
no less replete with mischief.  This was the
compulsory levy denominated black-mail, a tax

extorted from the inhabitants of the Lowland
borders and others, under promise of protecting them from the depredations of marauding
hordes, who infested them from different quarters.  This tax was sometimes also a voluntary
tribute, the party binding themselves, for a
specific consideration, to keep the subscribers
"skaithless of any loss to be sustained by the
heritors, tenants, or inhabitants, through the
stealing or taking away of cattle, horses, or
sheep, and either to return the cattle so stolen
within six months, or pay their value." These
predatory forays were either directed against
other hostile clans or the frontier inhabitants,
who were considered a different race, and, as
such, were held on the footing of enemies, particularly when latterly an armed force was kept
up to repel these attacks.  This species of warfare often called forth the decrees of different
monarchs,—"to prevent the daily hiershippes of
the wicked thieves and limmers of the clannes
and surnames inhabiting the Hielands and
Isles," accusing, "the chieftains, principal of
the branches, worthily to be esteemed the very
authors, fosterers, and maintainers of the wicked
deedes of the vagabonds of their clannes and
surnames."    And such depredations were often

retaliated and adjusted by making reprisal, or decided by the sword, which frequently terminated in sanguinary contest, and laid the foundation of future deadly feuds.

Being from habit an independent and turbulent race, full of their own personal rights and dignity, jealousies continually existed among them, and frequent disputes arose, which commonly were settled in the field.   Hence sprung their quarrels ; an injury done to an individual being resented by the whole clan, which led to the practice of wearing arms, a fashion which made them enter more readily into a brawl, while it must have accustomed the mind to horrors inseparable from civil war.

The Highland costume was well adapted to their athletic avocations, and the exigencies of their warfare.   Each clan had its own colours of the variegated cloth which formed their garb ; their bonnets being also of appropriate colours, in which, besides, were worn branches of oak, heath, or other distinguishing marks, while in former ages, they had likewise various war-cries.

Breaches of faith, when individual interest was in question, seem to have been considered no disgrace, as in many engagements that

B

ought to have been held sacred, we find abominable violation of promise among the clans, to a very recent era :—About the beginning of the sixteenth century, a terrible feud subsisted betwixt Macdonald of Kintyre, and Maclean of Duart, who were brothers-in-law, in consequence of promises mutually broken, which occasioned frequent assaults on the properties of each, wherein many of their followers were sacrificed ; and the murder of the Macdonalds at Dunavartich, by the Campbells, was no less perfidious. Numerous instances of the bloody feuds of the clans might here be narrated ; but they are generally known, and only exhibit instances of outrage, injustice, and cruelty, which were practised, without regard to the ties of consanguinity or friendship, during the existence of that irregular jurisdiction which their chieftains exercised. Several of those quarrels, however, led to important effects in the system of vassalage, and produced changes in the state of property, or rather possession, of salutary influence, even though municipal jurisprudence was wholly unknown, and sovereign edicts disregarded by the chief and his followers.

From the inaccessibility of their mountains,

they long continued ignorant of the arts
and customs of other nations, which they
were as unwilling to adopt, as they were
inimical to the introduction of strangers to
instruct them; yet they were of a social
disposition, unbounded hospitality being a
trait in their character, and constituting one
of their most prominent virtues. Accordingly
it was always practised, it being considered an
insult if a traveller passed a house without
going in to partake of such fare as it could
afford.

The important introduction of roads, however,
of which those regions stood so long and so
much in need, was totally overlooked till after
the troubles of 1715; and then, though it might
be supposed that more enlightened and liberal
ideas would have influenced the proprietors,
the formation of roads was looked upon as
an innovation, calculated to spread Lowland
habits and manners, to which the native
chieftains were always averse. In the rude
policy, and plenitude of their ignorance, they
supposed that, as roads would expose their
country to the inspection of strangers, notions
of liberty would be suggested to their vassals,
which would weaken or alienate their attach-

ment, while their fastnesses being thus laid open, and their hills rendered accessible, they would be deprived of their former security against invading foes. But, happily, both considerations have now ceased to operate.

The mental qualities of the old race of Highlanders incapacitated them for patient perseverance in any determinate line of thought. The desultory manner by which they provided for their wants, required only corporeal exertion, and to this cause, partly, is to be attributed their deficiency in useful knowledge, and their dislike to every handicraft occupation; the concerns of rural life being more congenial to their nature. Their country having been allowed to continue long in a state of insubordination and ignorance, and in itself containing so few advantages, the store of human information, and sources of comfort, were very limited. Its indigenous productions were never so abundant as to rouse a commercial spirit among the people, nor to convince them of the advantage that might arise from the culture even of these limited resources. Unaccustomed to the researches of science, and regardless of, as they were entirely unacquainted with, those elegant accomplishments which reform the heart, and soften the wayward passions, the lives of the natives were a series of vicissitudes from active rapine or tumultuous contention, to wretched indolence or insecure repose ; so that in this state of society, it was difficult to reclaim their habits, or smooth the asperity of their manners.

For a long period, their devotion was clouded with visionary horrors, transmitted from a remote and barbarous antiquity, which cast a gloom over the imagination, and induced a belief in miracles, witchcraft, and the second-sight. Supernatural agency was credited, and believed to influence their actions, and they consulted the disk of the sun, the phases of the moon, and the motion of the clouds, together with the noise of the sea, and the dashing of the mountain cataract, as ominous of their fate. The gift of prophecy likewise, was not long since generally reverenced in those regions, owing to the gloomy in-fluence of their religion, which gave sanction to the belief of charms, ghosts, and the performance of superstitious rites ; so that, whether from the inattention of their priest-hood, or from their own unrestrained dis-position, and the negligence of their superiors, their faith did not counteract their loose and irregular morals ; and they remained careless of those qualities of justice and equity, so essential to human happiness, which bind mankind together, and produce an equable union of parts in the system of civilized society.

But, though the Highlanders contemned these endowments, they possessed other embellishments which we admire, and which they themselves considered as their brightest ornaments. Faithful to the chief whose fortunes they followed, they never deserted his cause, and in the hour of danger it was their glory to evince the sincerity of their attachment, and rather than betray trust, they would suffer the most painful and ignominious trials.*   In their deportment

---

* After the defeat of Prince Charles Stewart at Culloden, a reward of £30,000 was offered for his detection.   He had taken refuge for some time in the hut of a John Macdonald, among the wilds of Lochaber.   This man knew the Prince, and sheltered him with the utmost care, making frequent journeys to Fort Augustus for provisions to his guest, where he often heard the reward proclaimed ; yet this man had a soul to resist the temptation, though he had a numerous starving family.   He was afterwards hanged at Inverness for stealing a cow, and when on the scaffold, he thanked God that he had never broken his word, injured the poor, nor refused a share of his means to the stranger or the needy.

While the sanguinary troops of the conqueror, at this time, deluged the Highlands with blood, a Captain Mackenzie of the fugitive army, with a few followers, still wandered among the

they were respectful to superiors, and unassum-
ing to their equals. Their valour was the effect
of that native hardihood for which they were
always distinguished and esteemed. To the
most severe privations they submitted without
repining ; and they died for their country or
their chief, without a sigh. Inflexible in faith,
their friendship was steady, as their hatred was
unextinguishable ; and it was an invariable
rule, never to turn their back to a friend or
an enemy.

Remote from busy scenes of commercial intercourse, the rural labours of the mountaineers,
even in modern times, were of a species which
gave a cast to the character, and formed the
mind to sentiments as well as habits peculiar to
themselves. The majestic features of the High-

hills near Loch Ness. They were overtaken by superior numbers. Some of them fled, and some threw down their arms,
but Mackenzie, convinced from his former activity in the cause,
that he could not escape, stood on the defensive. He had a
strong resemblance to Prince Charles, and by the eagerness of
the soldiers to take him alive, he believed they had mistaken
him for the Prince. The desperate bravery with which he
fought, convinced them it was Charles, and in order to make
sure of the reward, they shot him, and he expired, saying
—" Villains ! you have killed your Prince ;"—uttered no doubt
that his enemies might relax in their pursuit. Mackenzie's
head was cut off, triumphantly carried to the Duke of Cumberland's camp, and occasioned great rejoicing, until some one re
cognised the head, and undeceived the Duke.

land scenery, though combining a variety of grand and beautiful subjects which render the country picturesque and interesting, yet carries in its aspect, a complexion so sombre and gloomy, as greatly to have contributed in giving a corresponding tinge of melancholy to the mind and temperament of the inhabitants. Accustomed to contemplate this bold display of objects which compose the outline of their country, it was natural for them to acquire that characteristic impression of sadness with which their poetry and music are so highly tinctured.

In former times, much obstruction was given to the promulgation of knowledge and education, even after the influence of prelacy, the ancient enemy of learning, was removed ; as the chieftains believed that if their vassals were allowed to become informed, they would shake off the yoke of servility in which they had long been retained. The Highlanders, consequently, to a late period, were extremely illiterate, as no means had been taken for their improvement.

From the most distant and barbarous times, the fair sex held a conspicuous part in the different scenes of pastoral life and social intercourse, and though females who possessed beauty and virtue had not a champion at their service, as was the practice of knight-errantry in other contemporary nations, yet the sex was no less respected and adored by their heroes, nor less praised in the national melodies of their country.

The ancient natives had a perfect disregard to an obligation enjoined by oath, because they probably did not comprehend the serious import of it. The asseveration of a chieftain, however solemn, was often broken, while the more simple objuration of swearing by his honour on his naked sword or dirk, was held sacred, and never violated. But though progressive civilization and improvement overturned such ideas, it was only coercion, shortly before the last civil war, that prevented the frequent and open infraction of the laws.

At different periods of Scottish history, various measures were tried to crush the furious spirit of the Highland chiefs, and they were said to have been rendered submissive to different kings, giving pledges for good conduct. An Act of the Scottish Parliament was passed, July 1587, "anent the wicked inclination of the disorderly subjects in the Hie-lands and isles, deliting in all mischieves, and maist unnaturally and cruelly waistand, herriand, slayand, and destroyand, their awen nichtboures; and the chiefe of the clanne in the boundes, quhair broken men and limmers dwellis, and committes any waisterful riefe, theft, depredations, open and avowed fire-raising, upon deadly feeds, sall be charged to finde caution and soverty under pain of rebellion: and all clannes, chieftains, and branches of clannes, refusand to enter their pleges, to be esteemed publick enemies to God, the king, and all his trewe and faithful subjectes." Then follow the names of a hundred and twenty-five clans, on whose lands dwelt the lawless crowds, who came under the cognisance of this and similar statutes. But their distance from the seats of sovereign authority prevented a continuance of obedience thus imposed, and they revolted as often as they had opportunities. From this precarious submission which they yielded, they were often subjected to penalties; though it frequently happened that the clan of a refractory chief was too powerful for the then feeble hands of Government, so that the decrees of fire and sword issued against them were disregarded, and they slighted such denunciations until 1725, when an act for disarming the Highlands was declared, and garrisons planted in different parts to check their disorderly courses.

Many extraordinary transitions had taken place among the great clans of the Highlands, which as often occasioned important changes in the policy of their country. The Macdonalds, lords of the isles, were at one time the most powerful, and from them branched off many others, who afterwards became distinct clans, assuming separate designations; but the Macdonalds being overthrown in the battle of Harlaw, 1410, several other tribes laid hold of their lands under various pretences. By the disunion of the Macdonalds, and their consequent reduction, clanship began to decay and to lose its former stubborn bravery; and this being the cordial wish of the Government, they encouraged the disjunction of the clans, and sanctioned every action which favoured this object, though attended with disastrous consequences to the Highlands.

In later times the influence of a chieftain seems to have depended on the small rent exacted for his lands; but the different civil wars in which his people were engaged, with his own introduction and residence in the Southern countries, gradually removed the causes of mutual support; and though their rents were inconsiderable, the payment of them was often resisted, so that, within the last century, it was not unusual for a proprietor to carry with him an armed force to compel his tenantry to pay. This, in particular, was the case with the island of Islay and the extensive districts of Ardnamurchan and Sunart in Argyllshire. The former was sold, not sixty years ago, for a sum which is now* its yearly rental, viz., £12,000 ; and the latter, about the same period, was given in lease for 999 years for a rent of £300, which lands now pay about £7000 a year. Both these valuable estates were thus disposed of because the proprietors could get no rent from the occupiers, and one of these gentlemen was shot in going to uplift his rent.†

The doctrines of the Reformation were not considered of such importance by the Highlanders as for some time to change their creed. They had never owned the supremacy of monarchical power until a late period, and they regarded not the degrees enacted by the lords of the congregation. But from events which followed, and which agitated and distracted other parts of the kingdom, they were not free. They experienced sundry deeds of atrocity equally obnoxious to justice as they were to humanity ;

* In 1819.            † See Note, page 193.

but neither justice nor humanity were regarded
in the religious controversies of that time, which
would have dishonoured the most savage nations of antiquity. The reformed faith was enjoined throughout the mountains with rigorous
frenzy, the usual accompaniment of enthusiastic proselytes ; and the Highlanders, always
obedient to the will of their superiors, and
naturally prone to novelty, readily became con-
verts to the precepts of the Reformation, with
the exception of the remote and distant Northern islands, whose situation precluded the
means of information, and in some of which the
Reformation was not heard of for upwards of
twelve months after it was effected, when it
was told as a dispute that had taken place betwixt the laird of Macdonald and the king.

Soon after the junction of the two kingdoms
under the sixth James of Scotland, the still unsettled and obstinate situation of the Highland
districts demanded the notice of the legislature.
The state of seclusion in which their inhabitants
had lived, seemed, in the opinion of that monarch, to have disqualified them for improvement
or civilization, as they were placed beyond the
limits of regal power, so that they were still
esteemed as objects more to be dreaded by the

sovereign than to be desired as subjects. The hereditary unlimited jurisdictions enjoyed by their chieftains gave those personages a command dangerous in such hands, lest it might still be exerted, as it had formerly been, in hostility to royal authority.

King James, though a man of puerile parts and degenerate mind, foresaw, or at least was persuaded by others to see, the hazardous consequences of permitting the exercise of such privileges by any of his subjects, and jealousy awakened him to oppose the evil. He sanctioned many fruitless trials for restraining those immunities, for reforming the condition of the natives, and for reclaiming the waste and uncultivated surface of their country; but it was not until 1748 that this desirable end was accomplished, and the power of *Pit and Gallows*, as it was called, wholly wrested from the hands of the chieftains. But so tenaciously were these hereditary jurisdictions adhered to in Scotland, that, previous to their abolition by Act of Parliament, a compensation was demanded for giving them up, and one hundred and sixty persons received various sums, according to the supposed right they relinquished, amounting to several thousand pounds.

In the reign of Charles the First, the Highlanders, gradually assimilating with the inhabitants of the Low Countries, were not only im-
proving themselves by the association, but were
also receiving attention as useful auxiliaries for
supporting the crown when need should require.
Of the solemn league and covenant framed in
this reign, and forming a bond of amity and
junction of faith, much happiness was predicted.
Many chieftains sanctioned this union in the
constitution of the church ; but a large proportion of their countrymen were hostile to the
articles it contained, as they imposed restric-
tions which neither their religion, unfixed and
wavering as it was, nor their inclination would
permit ; and their defection soon appeared
when Montrose led forward the adherents of
the king against the conventiclers.  But in the
usurpation and severities of Cromwell they suffered for their loyalty.  The exertions which
they made for the monarch, and the support
which in former instances they had given to
royalty, prior to their departure from vassalage,
along with their attachment, after this period, to
the person and interest of the sovereign, how
unworthy soever he was of it, rendered the

Highlanders favourites with each succeeding prince of the Stewart family.

The bigoted principles of that house, which eventually led to its overthrow, were not calculated to sway the sceptre of a great nation, when the light of reason began to dawn with an effulgence too brilliant for the absolute power which the Stewarts contemplated. Those acts of cruelty which James the Second authorized against his Protestant subjects before his abdication, gave ample proofs to the nation of the fetters he intended for them had he remained their king, and his departure from the throne excited new hopes, though the previous influence he had acquired over the chiefs of some powerful Highland clans, gave no anticipation of speedy tranquillity.

Though James was bound, by his coronation oath, to renounce Popery, and to support the Reformed Church, he was yet at heart a steady votary of the Romish faith ; and satisfied, that upon this fascinating basis alone, he could support his declining importance, he prevailed upon many of the Highland chieftians to apostatize from the national church.  Among several others of lesser note was the family of Gordon, by whose influence in the division of Badenoch and Lochaber, Popery made great progress, and in four years, nine hundred people of those countries renounced Presbyterianism. At the accession of James, the people of Abertarf were wholly Protestants; but Macdonald of Sleat, descendant of the lord of the isles, having also relinquished his principles to gratify James, up-wards of forty families, chiefly Macdonalds in Skye, and the adjacent districts of Knoydart, Morar, Arisaig, Sunart, and Ardnamurchan, followed the example of their chief, and had the same power, it would appear, over the con-sciences, as they possessed over the services of their vassals :—a proof of the ignorance and slavery in which those miserable creatures were retained. At this time, the last earl of Perth, who, from his official situation as chancellor, had acquired great power in Scotland, likewise became a convert to the Church of Rome, at the instigation and by the connivance of the king. Perth used every means to pervert the tenets of the Highland chiefs, by promises which were never meant to be realised ; and he was successful in a manner which does not reflect much honour on their memory.

The machinations of James having failed to enthral the kingdom, he had not courage to

make another effort ; yet his retreat was considered a sacrifice of his right, and a conscientious zeal for the religion he wished to establish.
At the epoch of the Revolution, the house of
Stewart had reigned for eleven successive generations, or three hundred and eighteen years, so
that its title to the crown was considered as
indefeasible hereditary right ; and the Highlanders, who were devoted to this ancient race,
were unfriendly to any other than the Popish
succession, and beheld the Prince of Orange
assume the reins of the state, with sensations of
sorrow and regret.   Happy had it been, if the
exile of the Stewarts was the measure of suffering which the Highlanders were to undergo ;
but the acrimonious policy of the government,
added to the vindictive and peevish temper of
the monarch, carried a profusion of cruelty to
their country, and they seemed a race destined
for destruction, with whom neither faith, honour,
nor humanity were to be held sacred.

William, who was a prince at once vain and,
illiterate, no sooner set his foot on British
ground, than he believed that he had the good-
will and hearty regard of all men ; but he found
that time would be required to conciliate the
mountainous districts, whose inhabitants he

considered of a refractory temper, and the firm friends of the expatriated family. He was also persuaded by some of their unprincipled countrymen, that lenient treatment would never render them obedient, although many thousand pounds had been distributed among them for that purpose :—But, in this interested and false account of the Highlands, those persons who received the money which the Highlanders should have got, took care to conceal that they appropriated it to their own use, and pretended that the Highlanders, though thus paid to be quiet, were yet irreconcilable to William. This shameful duplicity, which was easily practised on the willing credulity of William, along with the conscientious part the Highlanders had acted under Dundee, at the affair of Killie-crankie, speedily brought about the bloody plan of exterminating the Northern clans ; and we have to deplore a dreadful instance of this diabolical intention, from which the mind must turn with horror, in the shocking massacre of Glencoe. This infamous transaction leaves an indelible stain on the memory of William, who sanctioned it. His instructions for the accomplishment of this foul murder, to Colonel Hill, the Governor of Fort-William, and dated 16th

January 1692, say, " If M'Ean, of Glencoe, and
that trybe can be well separated from the rest, it
will be a proper vindication of public justice to
extirpate that sect of thieves." This was followed by consequent orders from different officers to execute the massacre, and "allow none
to escape." But this execrable deed and disgraceful breach of hospitality, though meant to
diffuse terror and inculcate obedience among
the clans, operated in a different way; and the
equivocal as well as cowardly measures that
were adopted by the king and his ministry to
blindfold the eyes of the country on this barbarous occasion, only tended to render them more
odious, not only in Britain, but all over Europe ;
while the effect on the Highlanders may perhaps be imagined, but cannot faithfully be described.

The accession of Queen Anne at first inspired the friends of her discarded family with
favourable expectations, yet the proposed articles for the junction of the kingdoms soon
gave cause of apprehension, as these articles
purported to debar their future succession.

The Highlanders, in particular, dissatisfied
with the projected Union, and highly imbued
with sentiments of liberty, were greatly exas-

perated at the prospect, and deprecated every idea that tended to exclude the Stewarts from the throne. Nor were these antipathies diminished by the many oppressive acts which followed the Union, and which in their operation seemed to keep up national animosities that long before ought to have been laid aside.

In Scotland the pursuits of literature and the exertions of commerce had not yet overcome the fanaticism of theological controversy, nor the factions of party spirit ; and the inhabitants, almost to a man, disapproved of a union which apparently deprived them of the rights and privileges their ancestors had enjoyed as an independent nation.

Though the violent measures, which agitated the new Government on the succession of George the First, produced alarming sensations for the domestic quiet, his subjects were still disposed to be loyal, and the clans of the Highlands tendered a submissive acquiescence in his coronation.   But, unfortunately, this pacific address was rejected with contempt and contumelious disrespect from the throne.   This disdainful treatment greatly irritated the chieftains, and, with feelings natural to a proud and warlike race, not accustomed tamely to brook an offence,

they felt the insult with a degree of poignancy
which inflamed their national spirit, and prompted
them for many years thereafter to give such opposition to George and his successor as had
nearly shaken the foundation of their throne.

Upon every succeeding effort, therefore, to
overturn the Hanoverian Government, the Highlanders were the first to step forward ; and the
severities they suffered after those trials served
only to embolden rather than to intimidate them.
With these, and the recollection of former coercive measures that had been pursued against
them, the Highlanders continued obstinate, and
were always ready to descend from their fastnesses on any appearance of commotion ; and
although promises were made them at different
periods, these never appeared sincere, and were
never carried into effect, so that, to a very late
period, they remained almost wholly neglected.
In England and the South of Scotland, indeed,
their country was considered as an ungracious
and forbidding tract, hardly deserving notice,
because the people of those parts were totally
ignorant of the condition of the mountains or
the character of their inhabitants ; and it was
only when any of their bold forays were particularly remarkable that a momentary impulse

to check their daring spirit, and give them habits of industry was manifested by the councils of the state.

This essential change was not to be accomplished without the interference and exertions of their native chiefs, many of whom began to see the errors of their clans, and were anxious to reform them. Of these, Macdonald of Keapoch, one of the most accomplished men of his day, was the first who attempted to stop the depredatory expeditions of his clan ; and by uniting his influence with Cameron of Locheil, another powerful chief, they ultimately succeeded in putting an end to such practices in Lochaber. Many clans followed their example in other parts of the Highlands ; but the people still wanted the means of becoming industrious, as agricultural pursuits were not encouraged, and no resources of commerce had yet been opened up in the country to occupy their attention.

During the reign of George the Second, some of the Highland leaders were beginning to be more favourably disposed toward the house of Brunswick, and repeatedly proffered their obedience and attachment. But a shameful breach of faith, practised upon some of their military countrymen, who had been enlisted under express agreement not to leave Scotland, yet were ordered to Flanders, some of them shot, and nearly a hundred and fifty of them transported for life for daring to remonstrate, together with the disrespect which was paid to the above mentioned duteous offers of their chiefs, nearly set the Highlands in a blaze of open revolt. At all events, it crushed their growing allegiance, and thoroughly offended the undaunted spirit of the clans, as the chieftains regarded the insult discreditable to the consequence they had long possessed, and wished to maintain in their own country. From the properties which they inherited, and the numerous followers who crowded around them in support of their dignity, and who were always ready to avenge an injury done to their honour, the chieftains naturally imbibed such notions of their own power and influence as they judged sufficient to entitle them to some share of royal notice. But slighted by the king and his ministry, principally, indeed, at the sinister instigation of a nobleman of their own country, they were thus provoked; and this impolicy must be blamed as one of the causes which produced the last ruinous commotion in the kingdom, and the consequent proscription of the clans.

Such was the condition of the Highlands, prior to the civil war of 1745 and '6, into which contest a large proportion of Prince Charles Stewart's army was allured from the hope of success ; from motives of principle ; or intuitively to gratify a feeling of revenge that had been stimulated by real or imaginary aversion to the reigning government.

Since that period the manners of the Highlanders have undergone a very important change. They are now a quiet and subordinate people, no longer accustomed to fierce and desultory habits, nor possessing that impatient spirit for war, that led their ancestors to bleed in the wilds of Killiecrankie, or the muirs of Culloden.

Their unconquered and resolute courage, latterly guided by moderate and judicious regulations, has become the firm and steady support of the reigning family ; and the important deeds the Highlanders have achieved, during the last long and harrassing war, must rank them high among the heroes of their country, and among the other astonished and admiring nations of the world, who have felt and witnessed their extraordinary bravery.

# HISTORICAL MEMOIRS

OF THE

# CLAN MACGREGOR.

---

THE numerous clans who formerly inhabited the lofty regions of the Scottish mountains, rested their claims of superiority on the antiquity of their origin.

The clan Gregor, or, as they were anciently known, the clan Alpin, one of the most distinguished tribes of that country, could date their beginning from a very distant epoch. They were the descendants of Alpin, a Scottish king of the ninth century ; or, with more probability, they assumed that name at an earlier age, from the circumstance of their being in possession of the extensive range of mountains then denominated Albyn, which form a considerable portion of the Grampian chain. This, by evident analogy, constituted the appropriate name of clan Albyn or Alpin.

Various Celtic annals are favourable to the extreme antiquity of this race ; and an ancient chronicle in that language, relating to the genealogy of the clan Macarthur, declares that there is none older excepting the hills, the rivers, and the clan Alpin.

The fierce and disorderly state of society which prevailed among the clans for many ages, affected the clan Gregor in no greater degree than it did others ; but to the peculiar situation of their country may be attributed the horror with which they were regarded, and that marked them as the most unruly and violent members of the state.

Placed on the confines of the Highlands, and protected by the bold and almost inaccessible mountains that surrounded them, inducements were continually presented for exerting those lawless habits which they had acquired. But in those days the system of depredatory war that they pursued, was looked upon as venial, because it obtained among all the clans, who were equally prone to spoliation :—The opposition usually given to the Macgregors on such occasions, was the cause of many sanguinary deeds of which they were guilty.

The extensive boundaries originally occupied

by this clan, stretched along the romantic wilds of the Trosachs and Balquhidder to the more northerly and westerly altitudes of Rannach and Glenurchy, comprehending a portion of the counties of Argyll, Perth, Dumbarton, and Stirling, which appropriately were denominated the country of the Macgregors. The stupendous aspect of these rugged acclivities, the deep retirement of their woods, and the security of their valleys, rendered those regions difficult of access, and sheltered the inhabitants from the sudden and desultory intrusion of other marauding and ferocious bands, while they were equally safe from the immediate cognition of the law, and the consecutive infliction of the military.

Tradition fixes the primeval residence of one great branch of the clan Gregor, among the fastnesses of Rannach, the central part of Druim Albyn. At all events, it is certain that their chief, Alister Macgregor of Glenstrae, lived in that district before the year 1600. But, several centuries prior to that date, they were an important race, connected with many of the most distinguished families of the time ; and from the early house of Alpin descended the long unfortunate line of Stewart princes,

who, for so many generations, swayed the
Scottish sceptre, and from whom have come
down the succession of British sovereigns to
the present day :—Hence their crest and motto
are denominative of their origin—A crowned
lion, with the words, " *Sriogal mo dhream*,"—
my tribe is royal. This continued to be the
clan motto until a later period, when the chief
attended the king on a hunting expedition.
His majesty having attacked a wild boar, found
himself no match for the animal, and was
nearly worsted, when Macgregor observing the
king's danger, asked his liberty to assist him
against the ferocious beast. His majesty
assented, and said, " *E'en do, bait spair nocht*,"
whereupon Macgregor having torn up a young
oak by the root, kept off the boar with one
hand, until he got an opportunity of using his
sword, and killing him with the other. This
expression of the king's was afterwards adopted
on the shield of the Macgregors.

In the eleventh century, this clan appears to
have been in favour with the monarch, as their
chief received the honour of knighthood, and
accompanied Macduff, the thane of Fife, in an
expedition to the North Highlands to quell
some commotions among the refractory clans

of those districts. Nor does it seem that the Macgregor of that period was inattentive to the duties of religion, for his son became abbot of Dunkeld, and as such, held unlimited control over the spiritual concerns of his clan.

By such marks of superiority the power and ambition of the clan were gradually extending, and when they were farther dignified by a title of nobility, and become lords Macgregors of Glenurchy, their consequence appeared so well established, and their vassals so numerous, that they could cope with the most elevated families of the kingdom. If we except the clan of Macdonald, the territories occupied by the Macgregors, for some centuries, were more considerable than those of any other tribe ; and in order to secure their inheritance in various quarters, a lord Macgregor of the thirteenth century, built the castles of Kilchurn on a peninsulated rock in Lochawe, the castle of Finlarig at the west, and that of Ballach, since named Taymouth, at the east end of Loch Tay, together with the old castle in the lake of Lochdochart, and other strongholds. The original appearance of these fortresses, during the violent contentions of the different clans into whose hands they successively fell, was varied by additions or mutilations, suitable to the wild taste of the occupiers, or sombre architecture of the times.

It was at a very remote period that the district of Rannach became the property of the Macgregors ; and that in a manner which shews the barbarous character of the age :—It chanced that the then laird of Appin, whose name was Stewart, a branch of the primeval lords of Lochawe, was travelling with his lady and their usual retinue of walking attendants, from the city of Perth to their property in Argyllshire. In passing through Rannach they were interrupted and plundered of their baggage, and otherwise maltreated, by a certain tribe of the natives, now only known by the patronymic of " *Clan-ic-Jan-bhui*,"—the grand-children of yellow John. In order to revenge this injury, Stewart collected a body of vassals, and marched with them to Rannach. On his way, at Loch Tuille, a small lake at the head of Glenurchy, near the present road through Glencoe, he was joined by a son of the chief of Macgregor, who resided in a castle on a small island in that lake. The devoted clan of " *ic-Jan-bhui*," with their wives, their children, and their kindred, were cruelly put to the sword ; and Stewart, in return for the services rendered him by Macgregor,

placed him in the possessions of the exter
minated race, where he remained, and was the
founder of a new family, which afterwards became chief of the name.

During the variable fortunes, and severe
struggles of Robert the Bruce for the independence of his country, the chief of Macgregor
supported him at all hazards; and after the
defeat of the Scottish army at Methven, occasioned by their negligent security, Macgregor,
whose clan was present, conducted Bruce with
his followers and their ladies, to the fastnesses
of his own country, where they encountered
many hardships, though treated with all the
native hospitality of those regions.

The slaughter of the red Cumyn of Badenoch
in the cloisters of the monastery of Grey-Friars,
at Dumfries, drew many enemies on Bruce;
and from its being executed on a spot deemed
holy, as the confessional of monks, it was considered an impious offence on the sanctity of
the place.

Alexander, lord of Argyll, being married to
the aunt of Cumyn, became the declared foe of
Bruce, and was eager to revenge the death of
his friend. Learning that Bruce and some of
his fugitive patriots had taken shelter among

D

the hills of Braidalbane and Balquhidder, he
assembled twelve hundred of his vassals, in
order to pursue the royal party. Not aware
of his intention, and scattered in different places
among the mountains, only four hundred of the
latter could be collected to give a hasty opposition to the men of Argyle. They met near
the site of the present inn of Tyndrum in Braidalbane, and at the separation of the roads to
Glencoe, Glenurchy, and Glendochart, which is
still called Dalreigh, or the King's field. The
contest was fierce ; but so unequal, on the side
of Bruce's army, that a precipitate retreat for
their safety became necessary ; and the singular
escape of Bruce from three of his enemies, who
overtook and assailed him, is known to every
one. On this occasion Macgregor appeared
with a body of his clan, repulsed the king's pursuers, and relieved him from his perilous situation. The men of Lorn, amazed at his extraordinary bravery, and terrified at the known
fierceness of the Macgregors, withdrew to their
own country.

After this the forces of Bruce dispersed and
left the mountains ; and he having placed himself under the guidance of Macgregor, was conducted to the borders of Loch Lomond, and

there lodged in a cave at Craigcrostan (afterwards frequented by Rob Roy), secure from all his enemies, till an opportunity took place of his being conveyed across the lake.

In the subsequent battle of Bannockburn, that glorious exertion for Scottish freedom, the army of Bruce was principally composed of Highlanders. His undaunted prowess had gained him their esteem, and his title to the throne called forth all their support. The chief of Macgregor appeared on that day at the head of his people ; and a circumstance, of which he was the cause, though purely superstitious, yet consonant to the notions of the age, contributed to inspire the whole army with that enthusiastic valour which proved so successful :— A relic of St Fillan had long been preserved in the family of Macgregor, and this saint, being, from some traits in his history, a favourite with the king, the chief carried it, enshrined in a silver coffer, along with him to the field the day before the battle, and committed it to the care of the abbot of Inchaffray, who, in case of defeat, secreted the relic, and exhibited the empty casket as containing it. The king, while at his devotion over the precious shrine, and particularly imploring the aid of the saint, was startled by its suddenly opening and shutting of its own accord.  The priest hastening to know the cause of alarm, was astonished to find that the arm of the saint had left its place of concealment, and had again occupied the casket that belonged to it.  He confessed what he had done ; and the king immediately caused the story to be proclaimed through the whole army, who regarded the miracle as an omen of future success.  From the victory which crowned the Scottish patriots on that memorable occasion, and the supposed influence of St Fillan, Bruce caused a priory to be erected in Strathfillan in 1314, which, in grateful respect, he dedicated to his favourite apostle.

The population of the clan Gregor had often increased so much as to become too great, even for the wide domains which they occupied, and this produced frequent migrations to other districts, where various patronymics were assumed by the different septs, who in this way had branched off from the parent stem.  Even so late as the year 1748, the Grants, Mackinnons, Macnabs, and Mackays, and others who had departed from the Macgregors, held several conferences with them (during a meeting which lasted for fourteen days in Athol), for the purpose

of petitioning Parliament to repeal the attainder
that hung over them ; but some disagreement
having taken place among their chiefs, as to the
general name under which all of them should
again be rallied, their meeting and resolutions
were broken off, and no farther notice taken of
the proposal.

But the Macgregors were early marked as a
prey to the rapacity of their neighbours.  The
power and consequence they had acquired, excited the jealousy and envy of different inferior
chieftains in their vicinity, who exerted every
address to render them odious in the eyes of
Majesty, which alone could attempt to curb the
fierce and independent spirit of this clan ; and a
stratagem no less wicked than dastardly was
practised, and brought upon them for the first
time the displeasure of Government :—Prior to
the battle of Harlaw, formerly noticed in our
Introduction, the Macdonalds, Lords of the
Isles, besides other extensive boundaries, possessed and ruled over the provinces of Lorn and
Argyll ; but their frequent opposition to the
royal prerogatives gradually reduced their importance as well as their lands, and after the
defeat they sustained at that time, their domin-

ation scarcely reached beyond the limits of their native isles.

This reduction of the Macdonalds was the signal for many needy inferiors and desperate adventurers of various tribes, under sanction of the Crown, to subdue their vassals, and take forcible possession of their lands ; and in that manner the Campbells speedily grasped at those districts just named, which surround the fine lake of Lochawe. Still desirous of farther extending their arms, a knight of that name, about the year 1426, instigated the subordinate clan of Macnab to insult and commit outrages on the Macgregors. Incensed at such treatment, the Macgregors hastened to chastise them, and a battle ensued at Glendochart, wherein the Macnabs were cut off to a man. This affair was represented to the king in so false and aggravated a form, to suit the purposes of the knight of Lochawe, that he obtained letters of fire and sword against both parties, and procured a large military force to assist his own martial adherents in reducing them. But although both clans now found it necessary to combine their efforts for mutual defence, and fought the Campbells in several bloody trials, they were unsuccessful, and lost part of their estates, which were seized upon by the knight and his friends.

In the reigns of James the Third and Fourth, the prejudices that had undeservedly been excited against them, continued with unabated virulence ; and as the enactments of those monarchs permitted the execution of cruel and unjust measures, the Macgregors were perpetually exposed to the attacks of other hostile clans, who gradually deprived them of considerable portions of their lands. Thus situated, they were often led to punish their enemies, and in particular the Macnabs, who being the hirelings of the laird of Lochawe, were often incited to continue their depredations. But the Macgregors, though persecuted with increasing barbarity, were still loyal, and regarded the severities of the king as arising from the insidious machinations and advice of his courtiers.

In the faction stirred up against James the Third, headed by his unnatural son, the laird of Macgregor (for they had now lost the title of nobility) espoused the cause of his king, which, after his death, so incensed James the Fourth, that he took every means in his power to oppress and annoy the clan, and deprive them of their property, which he portioned off to his favour-

ites in lots suitable to their rapacious desires.
A natural son of the Duke of Albany laid hold
of Balquhidder, and a large share of the surrounding country; a second son of their enemy
of Lochawe seized the lands of Glenurchy;
and betwixt the years 1465 and 1504, they were
also bereaved of the great countries round Loch
Tay, Glenlyon, Rannach, Taymouth, and of
many others.

In order to conciliate family feuds, which, in
those days, was a matter of no easy accomplishment, a chief of the Macgregors married a lady
of the house of Lochawe, or Glenurchy; but
the tranquillity thus obtained was of short duration, for the chief when on a hunting party, and
not thinking of danger, was basely murdered on
the hill of Drummond in Braemar.

During the tumultuous and distracted mon-
archies of James the Fifth, and his unhappy
daughter, the Macgregors, still a powerful tribe,
were their firm adherents, and repeatedly went
forth to chastise the insolence of different clans
who were inimical to them; but their attachment to their sovereigns brought upon them the
enmity of the Regent Murray, who pursued them
with ordinances peculiarly inhuman; and had
he not fallen a just expiation of his crimes, they

would have had cause to dread the total extir-
pation of their race.

About this period, the chief of the Macgregors
entered into bonds of agreement with the heads
of several clans, for their mutual defence and
support,—"for the speciall love and amitie between them faithfully to serve ane anuther in all
causes with their men and servants, against all
wha live or die, and to maintain ane anuther's
quarrel, *hinc inde*, for behoof of all our kinsfolk,
and ablise us to abyd firm and stable under all
hazards of disgrace and infamy." Subscribed
" with their hands led to the pen."

The outrageous contentions of factious and
aspiring men in power, which at this time, 1570,
involved the kingdom in all the miseries of civil
war, seemed fully to justify the Macgregors in
resorting to such arrangements, and in adopting
measures that tended to secure them from the
tyrannical attacks of a disorderly and profligate
government.

At this time was published,—"Ane admoni-
tion to the Trew Lordis maintenaris of Justice,
and obedience to the King's Grace,"—written
by the celebrated George Buchanan, the Scottish
historian and poet, who was then lord privy-
seal ; but dictated in such homely and barbar-

ous terms as do not correspond with the elegance
of his Latinity, or give a favourable impression
of his taste, and encourage no other belief,
than that the court at which he lived, was as
unpolished as it was licentious. Of this long
address, we shall only transcribe that part in
which the Macgregors are noticed, Buchanan
being their inveterate enemy. It follows:—
" And howbeit the bullerant blude of a king
and a regēt about yair hartis, quhairof ye lust
in yair appetite, genis thame lytill rest, daylie
and hourlie making new prouocatioun, zit yat
small space of rest quhilk yai haue, besyde ye
execution of yair crueltie, thay spend in dcuy-
sing of generall vnquyetnes throu the haill
coūtrie, for not cōtent of it yat yai yame selfis
may steill, brybe, and reif, thay set out ratches
on every syde, to gnau the pepillis banis, efter
that thay haue consumit the flesche, and hountis
out ane of thame the clan Gregour, ane vther
ye Grantie and clan Chattan, &c., and sic as
wald be haldin the halyest amāgis yame, scheu
plainlie ye affectioun yai had to banies peice
and steir vp troublis, quhē thay bendit all thair
fyne wittis to stop the regent to ga first north,
and syne south, to puneis thift and oppressioun:
and quhē they sau, that thair counsall was not

authorisit, in geuing impunitie to all misordour, thay spend it in putting downe of him that would haue put all in gude ordour."

Though this clan had often experienced the undue coercion of the government, for crimes of which they were only supposed to have been guilty, they were not yet remarkable for the commission of any glaring act of atrocity; and in various edicts issued from the councils of the state for the suppression of misdemeanour, and the repulsion of the inroads of the Highlanders, the Macgregors were not individually pointed out as a sept more to be dreaded than others of their countrymen; and the decree put in force against them, near the close of the sixteenth century, appears to have been called up for an offence in which they had no share; but which, notwithstanding, involved them in greater ruin than the actual perpetrators.

In those times, many of the great landholders of the Highlands had large portions of their properties occupied as deer forests; and though game laws, of the present form, did not then exist, there were yet rules in force for the protection of such forests, setting them apart for the private use of the owners; but from the quantities of game which abounded over all the

Highland hills, it was not considered any crime for the natives to kill a deer or a hare wherever they were found, so that it was common to encroach on the boundaries of the forests with impunity.

Some young men of the clan Donald of Glencoe, from the North Highlands, having, about 1588, wandered from the recesses of their own mountains, were found trespassing in Glenartney, an extensive deer forest belonging to the king, or nominally his. They were seized by the under forester and his men, when carrying off a deer. As a punishment for this offence, those guardians of the forest, cropped their ears, and then allowed them to depart.

This being considered a disgraceful chastisement, the Macdonalds soon returned with some of their clan, and killed Drummond of Drummondernoch, the man who had so treated them. Having cut off his head, they went, with savage assurance, to the house of his sister, Mrs Stewart of Ardvorlich, situated on the bank of Lochearn. Her husband was not at home, and as they were strangers, whose flagitious irruptions had formerly made them unwelcome guests, they were received with considerable apprehension, and not with the usual kindness

of Highland hospitality. She, however, placed
some bread and cheese before them, until better
entertainment could be prepared, and left the
room for that purpose. Before she returned,
they placed her brother's head, still dropping
with blood, on the table, and put a piece of
bread and cheese in its mouth, in derision of
such fare. She recognised the horrid spectacle,
and was so much affected that she ran out of
the house in a state of furious distraction. Her
disconsolate husband long sought her through
the woods and mountains ; and to heighten his
distress, she was in the condition of pregnancy.
The season of harvest was fortunately conducive
to her preservation, and though a wretched
maniac, heedless of her own deplorable situation, or the misery of her friends, she continued
to wander over hills and lonely glens, living on
such fruits and berries as grew spontaneously
among those wilds. After a long absence, some
of her own servants, employed in milking cattle
on the high pastures of the farm, beheld a half-
famished female form, lurking among the brushwood. Terror had painted her in their imagination as the spectre of their lady, and they told
their master the frightful tale. He conjectured
the truth, and means were concerted for recover-

ing the fugitive. She was taken, and happily, after her delivery, her senses returned, to the great joy of her family; but the son she bore was of fierce and ungovernable passions, and when he grew up, his appearance became savage, while the murder of his friend and superior officer, Lord Kilpont, indicated an inhuman disposition. *

The Macdonalds having exhibited such proofs of barbarity at Ardvorlich, carried the head of Drummondernoch along with them, and 'proceeded to Balquhidder, at no great distance, among their friends the Macgregors.

This action, however savage, was regarded as a just retaliation for the affront put on the Macdonalds; and the Macgregors, with their chief, having assembled on the following Sunday at the kirk of Balquhidder, all laid their hands on the head of Drummondernoch, previously set on the altar, and swore to defend the

* Lord Kilpont, son of the earl of Airth aud Monteith, had joined the Marquis of Montrose in August 1644, just before the battle of Tippermuir, with four hundred men. Three days thereafter he was basely murdered by James Stewart of Ardvorlich, for having refused a proposal of his to assassinate Montrose, Kilpont having signified his abhorrence of the deed, as disgraceful and devilish. Stewart, lest he might be discovered, stabbed him to the heart, and fled to the covenanters, who pardoned and promoted him; but Montrose was deeply affected at the loss of his noble friend.

Macdonalds from the consequences of this deed.

James the Sixth, at this time, being married by proxy to Anne of Denmark,—"his Majesty's dearest spouse,"—her arrival in Scotland was daily expected ; and the king, desirous to entertain his queen and her foreign suite in the most sumptuous manner, ordered Lord Drummond of Perth, who was styled Stewart of Strathearn, and principal forester of Glenartney, to provide venison upon the occasion ; it was while thus employed that his substitute was killed, as has just been stated.

Greatly enraged at this outrage, executed in seeming contempt of his feelings and authority, James and his council forthwith issued a denunciation of fire and sword against the clan Gregor, though it is believed that the order was granted on false information, furnished by their vindictive neighbours, who contemplated their overthrow, and who maliciously conjoined their name with the Macdonalds, who were the real authors of the murder, in consequence of the vow said to have been taken in the kirk of Balquhidder. But the decree was proclaimed with thoughtless and precipitate credulity, and declared that—"Ye cruel and mischievous pro-

ceedings of ye clan Grigor, so Long Continueing
in blood, Slaughters, heirships, manifest reifs,
and stouths, Committed upon his Hieness'
peaceable and good subjects Inhabiting ye
Counties eovest ye brays of ye Highlands, thir
mony years bygone, but specially heir after ye
cruel murder of umqill Jo. Drummond of Drum-
mondyrynch, be certain of ye said clan, be ye
council and determination of ye haill avowand
to defend ye authors yrof quoever wald perseu for
revenge of ye same, &c.   Likeas after ye murther committed, ye authors yrof Cutted aff ye
said umqll Jo. Drummond's head, and carried
the same to the Laird of M°Grigor, who, and his
haill surname of M°Gregors, purposely Conveined
upon the next Sunday yrafter, at the kirk of
Buchquhidder ; qr they caused ye said umqll
John's head be pnted to them, and yr avowing
ye sd murder, laid yr hands upon the pow, and
in Ethnic and barbarous manner, swear to defend ye authors of ye sd murder."   At the same
time, " A commission to endure for the space of
three years was granted to the Earls of Huntly,
Argyll, Athol, Montrose, Lord Drummond, the
commendator of Inchaffray, Campbell of Lochi-
nel, Campbell of Glenurach, Campbell of Cad-
del, Campbell of Ardkinglas, M°Intosh of Dun-

ashtane, Sir John Murray of Tullibardine, Buchanan of that Ilk, and Macfarlane of Ariquocher, to search for and apprehend Alister M<sup>c</sup>Gregor of Glenstrae, and all others of the clan Grigor or yr assistors, culpable of the said odious murther, qrever they may be apprehended. And if they refuse to be taken, or flees to strengths, and houses, to pursue and assege them with fire and sword."

This warrant, in the hands of such powerful chieftains, willing to put down and destroy the Macgregors, was followed up without delay; and Lord Drummond, impatient to take "sweet revenge," as he termed it, for the death of his cousin Drummondernoch the forester, appointed a day with Montrose to beset the valley of Balquhidder, and execute his purpose, even before he had time to ascertain who were the actual murderers of his relation. In this expedition Lord Drummond was joined by a party under Stewart of Ardvorlich, no less eager to avenge the fate of his brother-in-law. Having settled their mode of assault, the parties were punctual to their agreement, and stormed the habitations of the unsuspicious Macgregors, who, taken by surprise, were slain with such insatiable thirst for blood, that on one farm alone, thirty-seven

E

of the clan, who had not the means of defence, were butchered in cold blood.

It appears, that even after this foul and cowardly massacre at Balquhidder, which they were unwilling to attribute to James, the Macgregors were still firm in their allegiance, and in a subsequent trial of importance, stood forward in his support:—Affairs in Scotland had, about this time, assumed a complexion of distortion, the consequence of recent changes in the system of religion, and the government of the Church ; and the factions thereby produced, irreconcilable to each other, were at constant variance, and called up the hatred and hostility of the parties, whose differences nothing less than open war could appease.   Many flagrant acts of atrocity had taken place among the great families of the Highlands, and their subordinate branches, when the Popish lords, Angus, Huntly, and Errol, supported with money from abroad, assembled their followers, and bade defiance to the king.   James had delegated his authority to the Earl of Argyll, a youth without talent or experience ; but who commanded a numerous host of vassals.   Argyll, at first declining to oppose the insurgents, though solicited by the king, and implored by the clergy, was at length persuaded to invade their lands, in conjunction with the Lord Forbes, under the condition, however, of receiving the properties of all those whom they should conquer. Argyll craved the assistance of the chief of Macgregor and his followers, with that of other clans; and having collected an, army of 7000 men, marched into Badenoch and laid siege to the castle of Ruthven. In Glenlivit they were met by the rebellious lords with an inferior army; yet the incapacity of Argyll occasioned the discomfiture of his troops, and an almost total defeat, in, which the Macgregors were severely cut up, they having had the most arduous and important duty of the day assigned to them.

Among those who were outlawed for having joined the confederate lords, on this occasion, was Cameron of Locheil. Argyll had taken possession of his lands, and when application was made to the king to have them restored, it was refused, unless Cameron agreed to enter into indentures with Argyll to root out the clan Gregor, a proposal that he readily consented to, and which soon produced a battle with the disappointed Macgregors. It took place in the braes of Lochaber, where Macgregor had gone to chastise Locheil; but he, being joined by his

allies, the Macdonalds, presented a formidable
array.   Macgregor, however, with the assistance
of the Macphersons of the same country, attacked
his enemies, and totally routed them.

Wilfully forgetting their adherence to his
interest in the contest of Glenlivit, in which
many of their bravest friends had perished ;
and when the tranquillity of the northern
shires no longer required the aid of the Macgregors in his cause, the inveterate enmity
of James towards them seemed to return, with
all the pusillanimous ingratitude of which his
character bore such indubitable proofs.   In a
letter from him to the laird of Macintosh, still
extant, he thus expresses himself : — " Right
traist Freynd, we greet you heartilie well.
Having hard be report of the laite pruife given
be you, of your willing disposition to our
service, in prosequitcing of that wicked race of
McGregor, we haife thought meit hereby to
signifie unto you, that we accompt the same as
maist acceptable pleasure and service done
unto us, and will not omitt to regaird the same
as it deserves ; and because we ar to give you
out of our aein mouth sum furder directioun
thair anent,—it is our will, that upon the sight
hereof ye repair thither in all haist, and at yr

arriving we sall impairt or full mynd, and heir
wt all we haif thought expedient, that ye,
befoir yor arriving hither, sall caus execut to
the death Duncane M^cCan Caim" (a chieftain
of the Macdonalds, and a relation of the Macgregors), "latelie tane be you in yar last expedition agains the clan Gregor, and caus his
heid to be transportit hither, to the effect the
same may be affixt in sum public place, to the
terror of other malefactors, and so committ you
to God. From Halyrud hous, the penult day
of ——, in the year 1596." Signed, "James
R."

The black knight of Lochawe or Glenurchy,
wishing, as he pretended, to adjust some disputed marches betwixt his property and that
of the chief of Macgregor, appointed, what he
called, a friendly meeting at Killin, for that
purpose ; but, having hired eight assassins,
they were hid in a closet adjoining the room
where the meeting was held. Upon a signal
given they rushed out upon the too credulous
and unguarded Macgregor. He, however,
forced his way out of the house, and jumped
into a deep pool of the river close by, dragging
several of the assassins along with him, two
of whom were drowned. Having got to the

opposite bank, he was so weak with the
wounds he had received, and loss of blood, that
the remaining ruffians easily finished his life.
But not satisfied with this, the villains sent his
horse to his father, in token of his fate, and
afterwards murdered the old man in his hun-
dredth year.

From the coercive measures by which the
knights of Lochawe thus treated the Macgregors, and deprived them of their lands of
Glenurchy, a deadly feud originated; but owing
to the persecution which the latter, at the same
time, suffered, from the malignant and cruel
acts of the legislature, they never afterwards
were in a condition to recover, from the Campbells, any portion of their ancient inheritance,
so unjustly wrested from them.   About this
period, James, the chief of the clan Gregor,
was ensnared and taken prisoner by Sir Colin
Campbell.   In a manner shamefully inconsistent with the acknowledged laws of clan warfare,
even in more remote and savage times, the
prisoner was put to death in cold blood, at Ken-
more, in presence of " the earle of Athol, the justice clerk, and sundrie other nobill men ;" and
Sir Colin himself stood over the executioner
who beheaded Macgregor, to see that he did his

duty. This knight is said to have been "ane great justiciar, all his tyme, and to have caused execute to the death many notable lymmaris."

But this clan, though proscribed and harassed on all hands, still bore up against the torrent of opposition with unsubdued spirit, and a resolution that never forsook them ; and which, even in the times of their greatest adversity, would not submit to an insult or an act of injustice, with impunity.

Sir Humphrey Colquhoun, the laird of Luss, and his followers, about this time, seem, with others, to have been their determined enemies ; and if contemporary historians are to be relied on, were generally the aggressors in exciting quarrels, or committing depredations, and heirships, as they were called, on the clan Gregor ; but these were usually balanced by similar acts of retaliation on the lands and effects of Luss and his tenantry.

The contiguity of their possessions rendered such hostility more frequent and fearful, until at length their dissensions became so enormous as to call for the interference and mediation of their friends : and the chief of the Macgregors (Alexander of Glenstrae), not being averse to a reconciliation, went from his country of

Rannach to Lennox, in the spring of 1602, accompanied by two hundred of his friends and kinsmen, for the purpose, and with a full resolution of extinguishing the feud that had so long subsisted betwixt his brother, who lived in Balquhidder, and the chief of the Colquhouns.

This crafty individual, though aware of the purpose of Macgregor's approach, had no wish that any amicable arrangement should be effected ; and having laid his plans accordingly, he collected all his retainers and dependants, with many Buchanans, Grahams, and others of his neighbourhood, to the number of five hundred horsemen, and three hundred foot, intending, if the result of the meeting was not agreeable to his inclinations, to cut off the retreat of the clan Gregor, and overthrow them while in his own country.  Macgregor, though he had previous information of Colquhoun's insidious design, had yet the prudence to conceal his indignant feelings, and kept the appointment.  The annals of that period do not state the exact result of the conference, but the parties seem to have separated good friends.

Pacific measures, however, were incompatible

with the enmity which long had excited their mutual spoliation, and their meeting was no sooner dissolved than the laird of Luss followed the Macgregors, in order to set on them by surprise on their way home through the valley of Glenfruin, not suspecting that his insincerity was known to his antagonist, who was apprehensive of treachery, and consequently was upon his guard.

There was then no road along the right bank of Loch Lomond, as in the present day. The borders of that charming lake are so steep and woody, that, before the formation of roads throughout the Highland districts, it was hardly possible to pass that way. The road, therefore, from Dumbarton to Argyllshire, left the present line near the bridge of Fruin, and passed to the west along the valley of that name, in a circuitous direction, to the head of Loch Long, and again turned eastward to the head of Loch Lomond and Glenfalloch.

Near the middle of Glenfruin, about six miles from the confluence of its river with the lake, the Macgregors, when peaceably returning home, were fiercely beset by the Colquhouns. Macgregor immediately formed his clan into two divisions, one of which he himself commanded, giving the other in charge to his brother, who, having taken the circuit of a hill, assailed the laird of Luss and his followers in a manner they did not expect. The conflict was maintained on both sides with the utmost courage ; but the inherent bravery of the Macgregors, though opposed by the fearful odds of four to one, was yet victorious. Luss and his followers, unequal in valour, were beaten and dispersed, numbers of them lying dead and maimed in every direction. When the Macgregors had chased the remaining fugitives, even into the Lomond, where several of them met a death less honourable than that inflicted by the swords of their enemies, it was found that, besides many leading gentlemen and burgesses of the town of Dumbarton who had followed Luss, there were also left dead on the field two hundred Colquhouns, and that a multitude were at the same time made prisoners. Of the Macgregors it is remarkable that two only were slain. John Glass, the brother of their chief,* and another ; but many of them were dangerously wounded.

* This person was respectably connected, being married to a daughter of Sir John Murray, afterwards Earl of Tullibardine ; and he possessed fifteen farms in Balquhidder, besides a fortress situated at the south-eastern extremity of Loch Voil, called " The Castle of Macgregor's Isle." But although his father-in-

This battle, which nearly annihilated the name of Colquhoun, was unfortunately productive of another calamitous event.

The town of Dumbarton was, in those days, celebrated for a famous seminary of learning, where all the sons of the neighbouring gentry were sent to be educated, many of whom were Colquhouns. When these young men heard of a meeting where several of their friends were to be present, nearly eighty of them set off to Glenfruin. The Colquhouns became alarmed for the safety of the boys, and, to keep them from harm, locked them up in a barn ; but when the Macgregors won the day, they killed the guard to whom the charge of the barn was entrusted, and set fire to it, by which inhuman act all the boys were burnt to death. Another account of that horrible transaction states, that no sooner had the superior courage of the men of Rannoch prevailed, and the discomfiture and route of their enemies become general, than an attendant of Macgregor's, of the name of Flet-

law laid hold of these lands for behoof of his widow and children, and was the intimate friend of James VI., such considerations did not stay the vengeance of that monarch, nor prevent
their being included in the sweeping denunciation of the clan
which followed, it being represented that John Glass Macgregor
was the chief opponent of Luss.

cher, was ordered by him to take care of the boys until the battle was over, their former guard having been killed. Meantime the boys, impatient of their confinement, wished to be released, and became noisy; whereupon the wretch who stood watch over them, eager for the destruction of the whole race, put them to death. As they were the children of gentlemen, Macgregor was anxious to restore them in safety to their parents; and having returned to the barn for that purpose, he asked their guard where they were. The villain, brandishing his sword, said, " that can tell you." Macgregor, struck with sorrow and indignation at the atrocity of the deed, would instantly have cut down the murderer, but he fled, while Macgregor exclaimed that his clan was ruined.*

* This barn stood near the place where the Colquhouns made their first assault, and the site of it is still pointed out. Close by runs a rivulet, the Gaelic name of which signifies " the burn of the young ghosts ;" and in the former superstition of the country it was believed that if a Macgregor crossed the stream alone after sunset, he would be scared by some unhallowed spectre.

Every spring after this tragical event a ceremony, in commemoration of it, was performed by the young men attending the academy of Dumbarton. The boys of the two highest classes assembled on the morning of the anniversary at the gate of the seminary, whence they marched in military array, with the Praetor walking before and the Usher behind them, to a field at some distance, where they spent the day, having provisions

After the unhappy result of this journey, undertaken by the chief of the clan Gregor with the avowed intention of reconciliation, he and his people returned to their own country, deeply lamenting the loss of lives that had been occasioned by the obstinacy and foul conduct of Luss, whose treachery had forced them to take such measures for their own defence. The resolution which Luss had secretly formed of cutting off the Macgregors while they were in his own country, and seemingly in his power, and, as he believed, unsuspicious of his plan, confirms his guilt as the aggressor, so that to him seems due that blame and execration so unjustly bestowed on the Macgregors in their consequent proscription. Had Macgregor's design been hostile, he would not so quietly have taken his

along with them. In the evening the dux of the first class was stretched as a corpse on a board provided for the occasion, and covered with the clergyman's gown, which was always used for the purpose. He was then carried by a few of his companions, the rest following as at a funeral, their wooden guns reversed. When they arrived at the churchyard, the supposed dead body was laid on a particular grave-stone, when the whole attendant boys set up a cry of lamentation, after which they dispersed, leaving their companion as he lay. When they were gone, he got up and also left the churchyard. This ceremony was kept up until the year 1757, and confirms the circumstance of the murder of the Colquhoun boys at Glenfruin, which by many has only been considered as a fictitious story.

departure, after the termination of an unsuccessful conference ; nor would Luss have attempted
to surround and take him by surprise when he
was calmly marching back to his own dominions.

Of this combat, however, a partial statement,
representing the Macgregors as a set of cruel
murderers, who had deliberately butchered the
Colquhouns, was soon thereafter transmitted to
Edinburgh, where King James the Sixth then
resided. This account, sent by the laird of
Luss, was accompanied with two hundred and
twenty bloody shirts, many of which, it was believed, had been so stained by the way; they
were presented to the king, it is said, by sixty
widows of those slain in Glenfruin, who rode
upon white ponies, each carrying a long pole to
expose those murderous proofs, and give the
exhibition its due effect on the mind of his
majesty.

However melancholy those mourning dames
might appear when they set out on their journey,
they returned with different feelings ; for having
arrived at Drymen, they are reported to have
had recourse to some of their native beverage,
which so elevated their disconsolate spirits, that
they quarrelled ere they reached their homes,
to which many of them were obliged to be

carried ; and this seems to prove, that they were a parcel of hirelings, procured for the purpose of imposing on the credulity of the king.

Unfortunately for the clan Gregor, they had no friend at court to plead their cause, and give a faithful account of the unhappy affair, so that the former misguided malevolence of James towards them, which, owing to the pressure of more imperative concerns, had been dormant for some time, was easily rekindled, and he instantly denounced letters of rebellion and intercommuning against them.

We have before remarked of this monarch, that although mean and unaccomplished, he was vain and unprincipled ; and from religious weakness, credulous, and readily subjected to imposition. Destitute of inborn sentiment, of manly resolution, his opinions and decisions varied with every breath, and were altered according to the whim and selfish designs of all those who came in his way. Sincerity, indeed, does not seem to have formed any part of the character of his family; and some of them neither hesitated at the violation of veracity, nor blushed when their dissimulation was exposed.

With a king of such imbecility, the blessings

of justice and liberty were incompatible.  A
total disregard to every feeling of humanity,
alone could have dictated those dreadful cruelties he decreed against the clan Gregor ; and
the act of his council, dated in August 1603,
will remain a proof of his vindictive temper.
This paper ordered that the name of Macgregor
should for ever be abolished ; that all who bore
it should forthwith renounce it ; and that none
of their posterity should ever afterwards take
the name, under pain of death.  The declaration
was also accompanied by a private order to the
earl of Argyll, and the Campbells, to pursue,
slay, and if possible, to extirpate the race of
clan Gregor ; and it is a matter much to be
deplored, that in following up these instructions,
every feeling of sympathy and mercy, every
sense of shame and justice seems to have been
laid aside and disregarded ; and the young, the
old, the female as well as the male, were indiscriminately butchered by the miscreants thus
commissioned, until a dreadful catalogue of
horrors was presented to the nation, which
would have been disgraceful to the most wicked
and barbarous savages of antiquity.

But such was the determined and unexampled
bravery of the Macgregors, which was well

known to their implacable foes, that the latter never dared attack them, unless with numbers greatly superior, and even with that advantage, it was generally by stealth they came upon them; or by pacing after them in the dark, overpowering them by surprise. By those dastardly measures, the Macgregors were greatly reduced, and suffered the most terrible hardships. Their country was filled with troops ready to destroy them, so that all those who were able, were forced to fly to remote places, amidst rocks, and woods, and mountains, while those whom the frailty of age, the influence of disease, or the inability of childhood prevented from escaping, fell an innocent sacrifice to their ferocity.

Thus dispersed and harassed, but not dispirited, they could seldom collect a force in any respect equal to their enemies. On one occasion, the son of Campbell of Glenurchy, at the head of two hundred chosen men, came upon them at a place called Ben Duaig. Among the former were some of the clan Cameron, clan Nab, and clan Donald; and although Macgregor's men amounted only to sixty, he gave them battle. The young laird of Glenurchy, being in disguise, was not known, and

F

escaped unhurt ; but seven gentlemen of his name were killed ; and of the Macgregors, Duncan Abarach, one of their chieftains, and his son. *

After this skirmish, the Macgregors were unable to make any head.   Still hunted down and murdered, they were almost completely subdued, but not until, perhaps, an equal number of the clan Campbell had fallen by their swords.

Though now nearly overcome by the various snares, and modes of slaughter made use of against them, and by having their lands forfeited, and their goods confiscated, the king and his council still continued their sanguinary commands, and after the above stated conflict, a

* This was the son of the Macgregor formerly mentioned as having been assassinated at Killin.  He was named "Abarach," from his having been bred and educated in Lochaber ; and being a stout man of fine appearance, he was looked upon, among his countrymen, as a hero of promising parts.  Duncan Dow, the black knight of Glenurchy, dreading that this person, at that time young, vigorous, and brave, would make his old head answer for the murder of his father and grandfather, and likewise deprive him of lands he had unjustly acquired, endeavoured, long before the contest of Ben Duaig, to be reconciled to Macgregor.  By the influence of Locheil, Abarach was induced to keep quiet, and to accept from Sir Duncan, part of the Macgregor lands which he had wrested from them, so that, until a short time before the assault, just mentioned, they were on good terms.

new edict of revenge was given out, by which "all recepters and harbourers, and those who intercommuned with the clan Gregor, were to be fyned and punished." All these fines and forfeitures were given by his majesty to the Earl of Argyll, the commander of these murdering bands, "and converted to his use and benefit, as a recompense."

During all this persecution, no one was generous enough to undeceive the king and his ministry, or to point out the injustice with which the clan Gregor were treated. This may be accounted for by the peculiarity of their situation, as the lands they occupied were placed near the properties of several great chieftains, all of whom were desirous of the extermination of the race, that they might the more easily lay hold of such portions of the Macgregors' territory, as would best suit themselves: and this alienation of their country eventually took place, and occasioned the destruction of the clan.

Alexander Macgregor of Glenstrae, the chief of the clan Gregor, had, during their reverse of fortune, suffered many severe trials and privations. Often within the grasp of his enemies, his escape was almost miraculous ; and, although

he for some time inhabited the most inaccessible
recesses, and remained from day to day among
the dreary wildernesses of his country, in perfect
safety, yet having become wearied of his seclusion, he took the resolution of making the wrongs
and sufferings of his people known to the king.
It was, however, impossible for him to pass beyond the fastnesses of the Highlands, without
discovery by the emissaries of Argyll, the arch
foe of his clan.  He therefore sent that person
an offer, that if he would permit him to
travel into England, to state his grievances to
the king, he would give him thirty of the principal and most reputable persons of his name as
hostages, and in pledge for his return.  Argyll,
with that treachery for which he was so eminent,
readily consented, and Macgregor having sur-
rendered himself, with his thirty companions,
was, according to Argyll's promise, conducted to
Berwick, but was not allowed to proceed to
London, where James then was.  Argyll, indeed,
kept his word of permitting him to travel to
England ; but from Berwick he was brought
back to Edinburgh, where, without trial or delay,
the unfortunate chief was hanged, along with
his thirty hostages.  This perfidious breach of
faith in Argyll, sanctioned by the Privy Council,

and by which they expected at once to quell the Highland districts, and extinguish the name of the clan Macgregor, had no such effect, and only tended to render Argyll despicable in the eyes of all honest men.*

At this odious period of Scottish history, few of the Macgregors were permitted to die a natural death. As an inducement to murderers, a reward was given for every head of a Macgregor that was conveyed to Edinburgh, and presented to the Council ; and those carried off in a natural manner, were quietly and expeditiously interred, by their friends, as the very re-

* In the following lines, Montgomerie, the Ayrshire bard of his day, twits King James for employing himself in the punishment of an imaginary crime, in the alleged massacre of the Colquhouns, at the battle of Glenfruin, and neglecting to punish real enormities :—

"Schir, clenge your cuntrie of thir cruel crymes,
Adultries, witchcraftis, incests, sakeless bluid ;
Delay not, bot as David did, betymes
Your company of such men soon secluid.
Out with the wicked ; garde ye with the gude,
Of mercy and of judgment sey to sing.
Quhen ye suld styk, I wald ye understude ;
Quhen ye suld spair, I wish ye war benyng ;
Chuse godly counsell ; leirn to be a king.
Beir not thir burthens longer on your hak ;
Jump not with justice for no kind of thing ;
To just complaints gar gude attendance tak ;
Their bloody sarks cryis always in your eiris,
Prevent the plague that presentlie appeiris."

ceptacles of the dead were not held sacred. When the grave of a Macgregor was discovered, it was common for the villains employed in this trade of slaughter to profane those sepulchres, digging up, and mutilating the bodies, by cutting off the head to be sold to the Government, who seemed to delight in such merchandise.

A wretch named Duncan Campbell, baron, or laird of Drumcrasg, in Glenlochy of Perthshire, was an active collector and dealer in this horrid traffic, for which reason he was denominated, "*Donacha nan ceann,*"—Duncan of the heads. Of this worthy protege of Argyll's, it is told, that, being on his way to Edinburgh, with a select assortment of heads for the amusement of the humane rulers of the state, and, at the same time, with a view of receiving the reward for his diligence which the law enacted, they happened, by the roughness and irregularity of the road, or some other cause, to make a strange sort of noise. The villain, startled at this, seemed appalled by a momentary impulse of conscious infamy, and abandoned the horse that carried his prize. A countryman who observed his agitation, inquired into the cause, and was told that the panniers on the horse's back contained heads for the lords at Edinburgh, whither he

was carrying them, and that though they were
all children of the same family, they could not
yet agree. This answer did not satisfy the in-
quirer, who immediately became suspicious of
Campbell, and asked what kind of heads they
were ?  " Heads of the king's enemies, the Macgregors,"—was the reply.  " Then," said the
countryman, "thy cruel head shall keep them
company," and laying hold of the horse, he
gave Campbell a blow that brought him to the
ground. This was a chieftain of the Macgregors
in disguise. He whistled, and three stout fel-
lows sprung out of the surrounding wood. They
examined the panniers, and were struck with
horror. Campbell was instantly put to death,
and the heads of their kindred buried in secrecy. -
While this dreadful practice, so shocking to
humanity, continued, a person of some distinction among the clan Macgregor, who was
forced to shelter himself among the mountains,
died at a miserable cottage in the braes of Glenurchy. The kind peasantry who witnessed his
dissolution, anxious to prevent that decapitation
to which his remains would be subjected, if discovered by the bloodthirsty followers of the laird
of Glenurchy, who were prowling over the country for such purposes, had the body clandes-

tinely interred in a remote and unfrequented situation. A short time thereafter, a supernatural appearance is said to have presented itself to the foster-brother of this person, named Macildonich, who lived at a considerable distance, which complained in grievous terms of the place and manner in which he was buried, requesting of Macildonich to convey his body to Glenurchy churchyard, the burial place of his ancestors. This man immediately recognised the well-known voice, and complied with its desire. He raised the body of his deceased friend, carried it on his shoulders, and reinterred it in the proper place, at the distance of fifteen miles, in the course of one night, and that the new dug grave might escape the vigilance of his enemies, he also dug around it several others of the same appearance.*

* A gentleman of the clan has favoured us with a little poem, founded on this tradition; but whether it is a translation from the Gaelic language, or an original, we have not authority to state, though we believe it of the latter description :

" Oh Macildonich ! cried the shade,
    How sweet the slumber of thine eye,
While low in dust my corse is laid,
    Without a friend or kinsman's sigh.

Dark is my dwelling on the heath,
    No dear, no friendly ashes nigh ;
Cold, cold my lonely bed of death,—
    O bear me where my fathers lie.

Though several great proprietors of the Highlands exerted their energies against them, the principal enemy, and most insatiate foe of the clan Gregor, was Archibald, seventh Earl of Argyll. He and his family had benefited most materially by their inhumanity towards that devoted clan, and for every one they destroyed, they received an ample reward. In 1607, almost the last portion of their lands were bestowed on that nobleman, for " inbringing of the laird of Macgregor," in the honourable way we have stated : and in 1611, being still considered a " barbarous and thievish race," he was ordered to root them out. Not averse to such employment, he brought some of their

The moon, pale gleaming o'er the vale,
    Will guide thy steps by yonder tree ;
Beneath a rock is dug my cell—
    Oh, then—a long farewell to thee.

Then slowly o'er the wild it flew,
    Faint as the fading beam of night ;
His friend, well Macildonich knew,
    And quickly hied him o'er the height.

He bore the death cold corse away,
    Through many a lone and darksome glade;
And e'er the blushing dawn of day
    Beside his parents, Gregor laid.

He laid him by his kindred dust,
    And often dropt the swelling tear,—
The green turf marks his place of rest,
    The nettle gray, the dark yew near."

"principals," as he called them, "to justice ;" but
he neglected the true means of reformation : for
having dragged the parents to untimely death, he
left their children unprovided with food, and destitute of raiment, who naturally, as they grew to
manhood, resented their fathers', as well as their
own wrongs.

Unhappily for this race, and for their country,
the more they were oppressed, the more did
they contemn, and give opposition to the laws.
Their state of long and rigid proscription led
many of them to abandon every rule of equity,
and every sense of rectitude; and they attached
themselves to bands of marauding wanderers,
who regarded neither religion nor moral duty
in the prosecution of their spoliations.  To experience any feeling of compunction for a
crime, was incompatible with the course of life
which they led ; and the appropriation of every
thing that came within reach, to their own use,
was scarcely looked upon as an offence.  For
this condition of many of the clan Gregor,
we must blame the imbecility and credulity
of the legislature, who believed that no one
could steal a cow, hough (hamstring) cattle,
or set fire to a house, but a Macgregor ; and,
under this belief, were constantly letting loose

their acts of vengeance upon the unfortunate race. In January 1613, they were implicated for being at the fire-raisings, murders, slaughters, and depredations upon the lairds of Glenurchy, Luss,* and Aberuchil; and it was enacted, that they "suld at no tyme thairefter beare nor wear ony kynd of armoure bot ane pointless kniff to Cutt thair meate under payne of Deade;" while in another act, in June of the same year, 1613, all those who were formerly of the name were forbidden to meet in any part of the kingdom, "in gryiter numberis nor four persones, under the said pain of Deade."

* The laird of Luss, who fought the battle of Glenfruin, was, some time before this, killed in the castle of Banachra, situated at the opening of that valley, and the Macgregors were unjustly accused of committing the murder.   The following is believed to be the true account :—Colquhoun of Luss having been at a great party in Edinburgh, had grossly insulted the Countess of Mar.   About the same time, the laird of Macfarlane, whose lands lay about the north end of Loch Lomond, had, in a foray to the Leven, killed five gentlemen of the name of Buchanan, for which he fled, and concealed himself in Athol.   He there met Lady Mar, who, anxious to revenge the affront formerly given her by the laird of Luss, promised to obtain Macfarlane's pardon, if he would despatch Colquhoun.   Macfarlane accordingly set off, collected a few of his people, and went by water to Rossdow.   He was noticed by Colquhoun, who fled to Banachra, at a short distance, and concealed himself in a vault. Marfarlane followed, dragged him from his hiding place, and murdered him.   It is said his blood still stains the floor on which the deed was perpetrated.

For some years before the demise of James
the Sixth, the violent edicts that had been followed up so successfully against the Macgregors, found some relaxation, and the clan were
not molested ; but although the legislature had
ceased from oppression, the neighbouring clans
were not disposed to quietness, and the Macgregors were still treated as an outlawed and
vagabond race, often precluded from those
mercies that are the common privileges of mankind. The determined rancour of their inveterate opponent, the Earl of Argyll, had
brought upon them such general and destructive slaughter, that they eagerly looked for the
time when his sanguinary propensity would be
sated.

One of his clan, Campbell of Achnabreck,
was related to a family of the clan Gregor, and
from some conciliatory overtures which that
person had made to his chief in their behalf,
some gleams of hope broke through the dark
cloud that so long had hung over them :—
Achnabreck, along with his nephew, a young
chieftain of the Macgregors, of promising parts,
went by a special invitation from Argyll, to
pay him a visit at his castle of Inverary, and
was received with apparent attention and kind-

ness ; but after Macgregor had retired to his bed-chamber, he was treacherously laid hold of and carried out of the house. Next morning, Achnabreck's servant on opening the window of his master's apartment, started back ; and being questioned by his master as to the cause of his alarm, replied, that Macgregor was hanging on a tree facing the window. Filled with grief and horror at so base a breach of hospitality, Achnabreck instantly determined to be revenged ; but Argyll, and the person who instigated him to murder his guest, had fled to Edinburgh to avoid the uncle's vengeance, and took up their lodging in that house near the Tron Church, long afterwards occupied by the commissioners on the Scots forfeited estates. Thither Achnabreck followed them ; and rushing into their room with a drawn sword in his right, and a cocked pistol in his left hand, he accused Argyll of his infamous and dastardly violation of confidence, and told him briefly, that he must either instantly die himself, or be the executioner of his diabolical counsellor. Argyll, in self-defence, and with the meanness of a coward, plunged his dagger into the bosom of his friend and adviser, who was present.

Such perfidious treatment, so wantonly put

in practice, was not calculated to restrain the impetuous spirit of a valiant clan ; and being wholly excluded from every benefit of the laws of the land, they considered themselves free to exercise their own powers, in levying compulsatory imposts of black-mail, or other contributory fees, as best suited their peculiar circumstances: and, as the Government had marked them for its prey, they, in return, disregarded its enactments, and were heartily disposed to give opposition to all its friends and supporters. Under such impressions, it will not appear surprising that the Macgregors continued their irregularities, and were accused of various deeds of "heavy oppression," which had "broken forth over the counties of Perth, Stirling, Clackmannan, Monteith, Lennox, Angus and Mearns, the sheriffs of which, with the stewarts of Stratherne, Monteith, Bamffe, Invernesse, Elgin and Forres, along with the earls of Errole, Montrose, Athol, Perth, Tullibardin, Sea-fort, the lords Stormount, Ogilvie, the lairds of Glenurchy, Lawers, Grantullie, Weymes, Glenlyon, Glenfallach, Edinample and Grant, were ordered to hunt, mutilate, and slay them, for their rebellious practices." This curious act, 1633, says, "That by the great care of his highness umwhill dearest father of eternal memory, the clan Gregor was supprest and reduced to quietnesse ; yet that of late they are broke out. And for the timeous preventing the disorder that may fall out by the said name and clan of Macgregor, ratifie all acts against the wicked and rebellious clan, and ordain that every one of them, as they come to the age of sixteen years, shall thereafter give their appearance before the Lords of Privie Council, to find caution for their good behaviour and obedience in all time coming, and to take to them some other surname. And farther, for the better extinguishing and extirpating of the said wicked and lawless Limmers, ordaine that no minister nor preachers within the bounds of the Highlands, shall at any time hereafter baptise and christen any maie childe with the name of Gregour. Whatsoever person shall receave, supply, or intercommoun, with the saids rebels, or supply them with meate, drink, lodging, or weapons, or any other necessaries, shall be punished in their bodies, goods, and geare."

In putting this order in force, many people lost their lives, and others had narrow escapes from the hands of the clan. The laird of Lawers, mentioned in the order of Parliament just quoted, had, from the situation of his lands in Strathearn, favourable opportunities to entrap them, and his vigilance had rendered him successful in seizing three men, whom he gave up to their fate. A party of them, however, with a chieftain at their head, beset his house one night, with an intent to murder him, for the injury he had done their friends. For this purpose they dragged him from his bed ; but his wife interposed, and on her knees craved time to allow him to pray. They meant no injury to the lady, and yielded to her request; and having thus gained a moment's respite, he implored their mercy still farther, and requested leave to pray in a chapel near at hand. To this they also consented. On the way to the chapel he told them, that, if they would spare his life, he would give them 1000 merks on the afternoon of the following day. They agreed to his proposal, and having given him his liberty, returned to his house at the appointed time to receive his ransom. Lawers in the interim had obtained the sum, and was in the act of paying it, when the house was surrounded by military, whom he had collected. The Macgregors, after some resistance, were taken, and forwarded to Edinburgh, where they expiated their crime on the scaffold.

Another of their declared foes, the possessor
of Edinample, who had at this time devised
many plans to inveigle them, was not so fortunate in his escape, as his neighbour of Lawers.
The reward which the Lords of the Privy Council had offered for every Macgregor who was
brought in, was of itself a powerful inducement
to some puisne barons, as they were denominated, to lay every snare for them ; as the apprehension of a Macgregor produced more money
than the properties of many, and besides gave
them more importance in the estimation of the
legislature.　The laird or baron of Edinample,
being named in the commission before quoted,
which he regarded as very honourable, considered himself bound to harass the Macgregors,
and always kept some armed men near him for
that purpose.　Having heard that five of them
were in a public-house at the head of Lochearn,
a short distance from his place, he set out one
winter evening by moonlight, to lay hold of
them.　Not being endowed with much inherent
courage, he went cautiously into the house, as if
without any hostile design.　Appearing in no
better costume than the countrymen of his
vicinity, he was not at first recognised, but was
asked to sit down and partake of some whisky,

which the Macgregors were enjoying after a
long chase of a deer, they had killed, and which
lay on the floor.   He complied, and drank some
glasses.    Meanwhile, one of the Macgregors
having gone out, was surprised to see several
men in the other apartment, for there were
only two in the house, and some standing out-
side the door: and having learned from the
landlord who their guest was, and what was his
intention, the Macgregor, with a ready judgment,
speedily devised a stratagem to get quit of the
unwelcome visitors.   He said that Edinample
had sent him to desire that his lads would go
into the barn, and drink some whisky till he
should call for them ; and the coldness of the
night made this no disagreeable message.   The
whisky and a light were immediately procured,
with which they went to the barn, accompanied
by Macgregor.   He drank their healths, and
waited till all the men, seventeen in number, had
had a glass of whisky, then going out, he locked
the door, and carried away the key.   Returning
to his friends, with whom Edinample, ignorant
of the condition of his men, still continued to
drink and sit quietly, he collared him and
accused him of treachery.   His astonished
companions having heard what their clansman

said, were instantly for putting him to death; but from this they were dissuaded. He was, however, ordered to take the dead deer on his back, and accompany them along with it. He remonstrated against this, being, as he said, a gentleman; but it was in vain, the sight of an unsheathed dirk made him comply. They took the road towards Balquhidder, and having travelled several miles, during which Edinample frequently fell under his burden, from the roughness of the road, deeply covered with snow, they halted in the middle of a desolate heath. There they took from him his load, and stripping him of his clothes, left him in a state of complete nudity, to the mercy of the cold, and to get home as he best could.

The first Earl of Braidalbane, denominated John Glass, had a respectable tenant, Duncan Macgregor, of the family of Ardchoille (anciently the rallying rock and war-word of the clan Gregor), who was the son of Duncan Abarach Macgregor, who fell in the conflict of Ben Duaig with the Campbells, as formerly noticed; he held in lease several possessions in Glenlyon, with that of Coircharmaig in Glenlochy. Being an enterprising and valiant man, he was induced by the persuasion of Braidalbane, who

was the implacable enemy of all the neighbouring proprietors, to raise a " *Creach*,"—plunder of
goods or cattle,—from lands in Appin of Dul,
belonging to Sir Alexander Menzies of that ilk.
Menzies, for this wanton attack, demanded restitution of Braidalbane, which, being refused
with the earl's equivocal manners and habits of
dissimulation, the knight commenced an action
for spoliation against him.    The earl, from his
recent elevation to nobility, perceived the danger of his situation, had he acknowledged being
the instigator of the outrage on Menzies' property, and with his usual subtilty and disregard
of truth, he declared that his tenant Macgregor
had acted unlawfully and without his knowledge
in the foray, and that he would speedily deliver
him up to justice.    When we consider the subsequent conduct of this nobleman as to the part
he acted in the dastardly massacre of Glencoe,
and the duplicity he practised upon his coad-
jutors of the cabinet, the instance of his perfidy
now to be stated, will .perhaps not excite surprise.    Braidalbane, after the successful inroad
of Macgregor, invited him to his house at Ballach, now Taymouth, and expressed his obligation to him.    Some time thereafter, when he
was accused by Menzies, and likely to be dis-

graced, he again sent for Macgregor, to whom
he still owned his thanks, and made him sit
down to a refreshment ; but the earl had previously concealed a party of soldiers behind a
bed in the room, who, at a certain signal, sprung
upon Macgregor, made him a prisoner, and immediately carried him towards Edinburgh. Another of the clan, Gregor-Macgregor of Inverar-
drain, although he had formerly been at variance with Duncan, determined to rescue him ;
and for that purpose followed the party to
Falkland, which they reached the first night.
The prisoner, however, advised his friend to
desist and return home, as he would himself
effect his escape, which he soon after accomplished. He seized upon a sword belonging to
one of the soldiers, asked their commands for
Braidalbane, and walked off, none of them
daring to prevent him. This party was commanded by a son of the laird of Lawers, who
was so much affronted by the escape of his
prisoner that he never returned to his country.
Macgregor, on his way home, called upon the
earl, who at the time was in bed. He ran to
his chamber, and, throwing open the curtains
with his sword, upbraided the astonished earl
for his shameless conduct, and told him that his

life was in his hand, but that the only requital
he demanded for his ill-treatment was an immediate renewal of a lease of his possessions, a
request which the earl did not think it safe
to refuse.

A person of consequence among the clan,
about this era, possessed some land among the
hills of Braidalbane. It chanced that a man
from Ardkinglas, of the name of Sinclair, in
passing Macgregor's fold, while his dairymaid
was employed in milking the cows, asked some
milk to drink, which the woman refused. Thereupon he rudely compelled her to give him a
pailful, and having quenched his thirst, threw
away the vessel, and spilled the remainder.

The dairymaid having complained of the
treatment she had met with, Macgregor immediately sent a party after Sinclair to bring him
back, but he being refractory, a scuffle ensued,
in which he was killed. Campbell, of Inveraw,
hearing of the fate of Sinclair, who was his
vassal, resolved upon the destruction of Macgregor, who however was apprised of the design.
The law at this time having declared that no
more than four Macgregors should be seen together, this chieftain was obliged to leave his
house during the night, to avoid the implacable

resolution of Inveraw, and take refuge among the hills. One stormy night, however, which was tremendously awful, he did not deem it necessary to take his usual precaution, supposing that no human being would venture abroad ; but he was mistaken ; for at the moment he was consoling his family, and saying that they would not be in danger from their enemy on such a night, Inveraw and his party beset the house, murdered every soul within, and set it on fire.

The long continued and unjustifiable severities to which the clan had been subjected, rendered them wholly regardless of the laws ; and as they were seldom permitted to remain in the undisturbed possession of any land which they either accidentally might have retained, or which they rented, they were in a manner forced to form associations for mutual defence, as well as for purposes of spoliation. Their state of outlawry seemed to authorise this, and many of them having consequently become desperate, assimilated into bands, pursuing the loose and unprincipled occupation of banditti. Of this description a confederacy was entered upon in 1630, under solemn engagements and systematic rules, and conducted by a party of bold and enterprising Macgregors. They had

for some years conducted themselves with such
moderation among their own countrymen, that
the law, violent and unrelenting as it still continued, could take no hold of them ; and though
they persevered in the old system of exacting
black-mail, as a recompense for their services in
protecting the property and cattle of those who
paid such contributions, it was not regarded as
criminal, but was sanctioned by the government ; regular charters, which were considered
legal, being frequently entered into for that
purpose.

This sect of Macgregors, however, from their
vagabond lives, and ill-conducted schemes, had
wantonly, or of necessity, committed several
outrages over the country.  They were headed
by two brothers, Patrick and James Macgregor,
with the denominative term of Gileroy, and
ultimately became so notorious, that the elder
brother, and three of his companions, having
been taken in Athol by John Roy Stewart, a
singular character of his day, were sent to Edinburgh, and there executed.  This Roy Stewart
of Kincardine in Strathspey, though intimately
connected by marriage with the Macgregors,
seemed not to regard such ties ; and the younger
brother, James, equally despising Stewart for

his opposition, set fire to his house, and killed Stewart himself. Gileroy was soon after waylaid by the military, and, with seven of his followers, conducted to Edinburgh, and hanged on Leith Walk. This person was the subject of the beautiful Scottish melody of Gilderoy. *

Before this time, the earl of Moray was the friend and ally of Donald Macgregor, a chieftain of the family of Glengyle. He was the father of the afterwards celebrated Rob Roy, and during the minority of the chief, who was his nephew, he was styled, "Tutor of Macgregor." He assisted the earl with three hundred of his clan, in an expedition to the north, to quell an insurrection of the Macphersons,

---

\* " Gilderoy was a bonny boy,
    He had roses till his shoon ;
His stockings were of silken soy,
    Wi' garters hanging down.
It was, I ween, a comlie sight
    To see so trim a boy :
He was my joy, and heart's delight,
    My handsome Gilderoy.

The queen of Scots possessed nought
    That my love let me want ;
For cow and ewe he to me brought,
    And e'en whan they were skant :
All these did honestly possess
    He never did annoy,
Who never failed to pay their cess
    To my love Gilderoy.

who had risen against the earl, as proprietor of the lands they possessed. Having succeeded in putting down the insurgents, in returning through the forest of Gaig in Lochaber, belonging to the Earl of Huntly, Macgregor was challenged for shooting a deer, when he retorted by killing the forester, who was also a Macpherson, of the family of Cluny.

For his aid at this time, the Earl of Moray granted him a lease of a farm, which still remains in possession of the family.

From his situation as guardian of his chief, he took upon himself all the rights and privileges of his superior. As such, he was engaged by the heiress of Kilmaronock on the banks of the

> My Gilderoy, baith far and near,
>   Was fear'd in every town ;
> And bauldly bare away the geir,
>   Of mony a lowland loon :
> For man to man durst meet him nane,
>   He was so brave a boy ;
> At length, wi' numbers he was taen,
>   My winsome Gilderoy.
>
> Of Gilderoy sae fear'd they were
>   Wi' irons his limbs they strung ;
> To Edinborow led him thair,
>   And on a gallows hung.
> They hung him high aboon the rest,
>   He was sae bauld a boy ;
> Thair dyed the youth wham I lued best,
>   My handsome Gilderoy."

Leven, whose name was Cochrane, to protect
her lands from the depredation of thieves, for
which service he received sixteen bolls of meal
yearly. The lady, after having paid this tribute
of black-mail for several years, at length declined to continue it, supposing herself secure,
as the irruption of thieves had become less frequent in her neighbourhood. Macgregor, however, obstinately persisted in his demand, which
was as firmly opposed ; and seeing that force
was necessary, he brought down a body of men,
assisted by his son-in-law, Macdonald of Glencoe, who plundered and laid waste the lady's
property, and obliged her to feu it off to various
persons : hence the number of small lairds who
now hold these lands.

During the arduous and destructive campaigns
of Montrose in defence of his sovereign, the
Macgregors and other clans from the mountains, united their energies, and followed that
enterprising, though unfortunate nobleman, in
his undaunted career against the covenanters.

The tenets and frantic zeal of that sect were
perfectly obnoxious to the Highlanders ; and
in every battle where their opponents were
overthrown, they exulted no less over them as

enemies to the king, than as differing from themselves in principles of religious belief.

The Macgregors were much respected and beloved by Montrose, for the extraordinary courage they exhibited on many occasions, and he did not fail to represent their loyalty to the king, who afterwards rescinded the acts of parliament against them, and permitted the restoration of their name and other immunities, of which they had been deprived : and although no act of the legislature was given out as individually applicable to the clan Gregor, for sixty years thereafter, yet they were included with other refractory clans of the Highlands, in many intermediate decrees of parliament for the suppression of their outrages, and the general reformation of their country.

The exile of Charles the Second, and the subsequent usurpation of Cromwell, were incidents of extreme vexation to the Highlanders ; and the moment the commander of Cromwell's troops left Scotland, some inefficient gatherings of the clans began to take place. When accounts of their defection had reached the Lowlands, the Earl of Glencairn, with a degree of romantic chivalry which attended all his exploits, hastily set out to join them and take the command; and having procured the co-operation of several chiefs, among whom the chieftain of Glengyle, with 200 of his men, attended, he marched from the neighbourhood of Lochearn, and at the pass of Aberfoyle met, and beat with great loss, a large party of the Protector's army from the castle of Stirling.

Macgregor and his clan accompanied the small army of Glencairn, afterwards consisting of 5000 men, through various parts of the Highlands, until the latter was superseded by Lord Middleton, who took the command.

While this desultory army was in Ross-shire, a circumstance took place, which, though not immediately connected with our subject, may still be narrated, as exhibiting the rude manners of the times:— The first act of Middleton's authority was to order a review of the troops, which accordingly took place; and when it was over, Glencairn invited the general and superior officers to dine with him, at the laird of Kettle's house, four miles south of Dornoch, where he had his quarters. They were entertained with all the hospitality the country could afford; and after dinner, Glencairn addressing their new commander, said,—" My lord general, you see what a gallant army these worthy gentlemen here present and I have gathered together, at a time when it could hardly be expected that any number durst meet together; these men have come out to serve his majesty at the hazard of their lives, and of all that is dear to them : I hope, therefore, you will give them all the encouragement to do their duty, that lies in your power." On this, Sir George Monro started from his seat, and said to Glencairn,— "By G—, my lord, the men you speak of are nothing but a number of thieves and robbers ; and ere long, I will bring another sort of men to the field." The chief of Glengarry, conceiving himself implicated in this insulting remark, got up to chastise the impertinent baronet ; but Glencairn checking him, said,—"Glengarry, I am more concerned in this affront than you are." —And turning to Monro, replied,—"You, Sir, are a base liar ; for they are neither thieves nor robbers, but gallant gentlemen, and good soldiers." Middleton commanded silence. Next morning Glencairn and Monro met to decide the dispute in the field. They were on horseback, and having fired their pistols without effect, they drew their swords, when Monro having his bridle-hand wounded, begged to dismount. Glencairn agreed, and at the first bout,

Monro was cut on the brow, and gave up. The earl was then in the act of running him through the body, when his servant forced his sword aside, saying,—" My Lord, you have enough of him." Glencairn was put under arrest, and being completely disgusted with the bad treatment he had received, left the army which he had formed, in a secret manner, and took with him his own troop and some volunteers. Middleton's elevation was of short duration: he was deserted by the principal leaders, and being surprised among the hills of Lochaber, his army was wholly dispersed.

The executive government of the usurper, though rigorous in many instances against the Highlanders, yet sanctioned and enforced the exaction of black-mail among them. * But

* "At Stirling, in ane quarter sessioun, held by sum Justices of his highness' peace, upon the third day of February 165⅔, the Laird of Touch being Chyrsman.

"Upon reading of ane petition given in be Captain MᶜGregor, mackand mention, That several heritors and inhabitants of the paroches of Campsie, Dennie, Baldernock, Strablane, Killearn, Gargunnock an uthers, wtin the Schirrefdome of Stirling, did agree with him to oversee and preserve thair houses, goods and geir frae oppression, and accordinglie did pay him ; and now that sum persones delay to mack payment according to agreement and use of payment, thairfoir it is ordered, that all heritors and inhabitants of the paroches afairsaid, make payment to the said Captaine M'Gregor, of their proportiones for his said service, till the first of February last past, without delay. All there can be no doubt, that this practice led to more general and oppressive extortions, being often made a pretence for the indiscriminate spoliation of those who had come under no such stipulation.

It will appear singular, that the clan Macgregor, though thus persecuted, and run down with such incessant cruelty and unfeeling wantonness, were generally accounted loyal, and seemed attached to every succeeding monarch who reigned over the kingdom.

But the ungracious requital they experienced, showed a degree of barbarity and wickedness in those sovereigns, which cannot be too much regretted. They did not appear to consider the Macgregors as human beings, or mortals endowed with rational souls.

constables in the severall paroches are hereby commandit to see this order put in execution, as they will answer the contrair. It is also hereby declared, that all qo have been ingadgit in payment, sall be liberat, after such time that they goe to Captaine Hew M<sup>c</sup>Gregor, and declare to him that they are not to expect any service frae him, or he to expect any payment frae them. Just copie.

Extracted be JAMES STIRLING,
Cl. of the peace, for Archibald Edmonstone, bailzie of Duntreath, to be published at the kirk of Strablane."

*From the* Rev. W. M'G. STIRLING's *History of Stirlingshire*, 1817, *p.* 623.

The first act of lenity passed by government in their favour, as we have remarked, was not until 1663, they having, for the space of two centuries before, been regarded as a proscribed and outlawed race. During this period, multitudes of the clan were compelled to renounce their name and their country. They migrated into distant regions where they were unknown, being only then in safety ; for the edicts of the legislature held them up to such universal reproach, that with the name of Macgregor was coupled some horrible idea, frightful, not only to old women and children, but to men who had the popular character of courage in the field, and wisdom in the state.

That they were, however, misled, and instigated to such inhumanity by the neighbouring heads of clans, is not to be disputed. Jealous of the race, they trembled at their bravery and increasing power : while the extensive territories they at one time held in their possession, called forth their envy, and a rapacity which left no means untried to ruin the clan : their influence, with a profligate council, too readily effecting their purpose.

After the removal of the proscription, under which the Macgregors were kept down for

H

ages, the government was sensible of the injustice of their treatment; and the general amelioration of the condition of the Highland districts, though it has not been successful, (1819), became an object of public interest.

# MEMOIR

OF

# ROB ROY MACGREGOR,

AND SOME

## BRANCHES OF HIS FAMILY.

---

*" The eagle he was lord above,*
*But Rob was lord below."*

WORDSWORTH.

WHILE the clan Gregor laboured, as we have attempted to describe, amidst hardships and calamities nearly unparalleled in the history of the British nation, a champion arose among them, whose disposition led him to avenge, though he could not effectually redress their wrongs ; and who supported, with undismayed resolution, the native hardihood and valour of his race :—This was the celebrated ROBERT MACGREGOR, or ROB ROY. He was denominated Roy,—a Celtic or Gaelic phrase, significant of his ruddy complexion and colour of hair, and bestowed upon him as a distinctive appellation among his kindred ;—in accordance with a

practice long adopted, and still followed in the
Highlands; where names are bestowed, from
the most trifling fortuitous incidents, for bodily
appearance, and often in derision, which always
adhere not only to those who receive them,
but to their posterity.

Rob Roy was the second son of Donald Macgregor, of the family of Glengyle, a lieutenant-
colonel in the king's service, by a daughter of
Campbell of Duneaves or Taineagh, consequently of no discreditable birth.

The family of Glengyle owed their origin to
the fifth son of the laird of Macgregor, about
1430. He was named Dugald Ciar,—of the
mouse colour. Having been received into the
family of a person of the name of Macintyre,
who resided at Invercarnaig in Balquhidder, he
afterwards became his heir. Ciar had two sons;
but Gregor Dow, the younger, appears to have
been the founder of the Glengyle branch of the
clan. He was first a cottar under a subordinate
tribe, named M'Cruiter, who held some lands
from the laird of Buchanan; but these tenants
having lost their means, and Gregor growing
richer, he eventually expelled them. Being of
good repute, and in favour with the young laird of
Buchanan, he got a lease of Glengyle, which was

afterwards renewed to his great grandson, when the lands fell into the hands of the family of Montrose. Gregor's residence was then at Inverlochlarig, among the braes of Balquhidder, and as the oral genealogical accounts denote, he was the "Fear Tighe," or head of the house. Gregor Dow was married to a Macgregor, a relation of his own, by whom he had Callum, or Malcom.

This Callum, while a young man, was implicated for an outrage on the property, and an attempt to carry off the person, of an heiress in Strathtay: and having failed to appear at Perth to answer for his conduct, he was outlawed. Under this sentence he continued for several years, wandering about the most unfrequented parts of the Highlands; but chiefly among the recesses of his own country. The young lady whose abduction he had tried, was distantly related to the Earl of Argyll, who made several exertions to seize Callum. Near the head of Balquhidder, at that period, stood a small public house, which Callum occasionally frequented for refreshment, and to hear what news was stirring; but to avoid detection, his visits were in the dark. Argyll, with his wonted antipathy for the clan Gregor, having heard that Callum often resorted to this house, went to it one night with a party of men, expecting to surprise Macgregor; but he was disappointed. He stepped in, however, and got some whisky, with its usual accompaniment of bread and cheese. While thus employed, Callum arrived at the house: but took his usual precaution of looking through a small window to see who was within. He was surprised to see Argyll, and listening to his conversation, heard him say, that he "wished he had as firm a hold of Callum Macgregor, as he had of a piece of cheese he was then cutting." Callum's servant, who also heard the wish, cocked his gun to shoot Argyll; but his master would not allow him. A few days thereafter, Callum wrote to Argyll, mentioning the narrow escape he had had, when Argyll, in gratitude, instantly applied to the Privy Council for Callum's pardon, which he obtained, and Macgregor was restored to his liberty.

Callum was first married to a daughter of the laird of Macfarlane, whom he repudiated, and afterwards married a lady of the house of Keappoch in Lochaber, by whom he had two sons, John and Donald. This Donald, as before noticed, married the daughter of Campbell of

Taineagh, who had two daughters and two
sons—John, and our hero, Rob Roy.

During the early years of Rob Roy Macgregor, he was not observed to possess any remarkable feature of that characteristic sagacity
and intrepidity which afterwards distinguished
him among his countrymen. The education he
received, though not liberal, was deemed sufficient for a man who was only intended to follow the quiet avocations of a rural life ; but he
was endowed with strong natural parts, and
readily acquired the essential, though rude, accomplishments of the age. The use of the
broad-sword was among the first arts learned
by young men, being considered an indispensable qualification for all classes ; and Rob Roy
could soon wield it with a dexterity which few
or none could equal. In this he was favoured
by a robust and muscular frame and uncommon
length of arm, advantages which made him daring and resolute. His knowledge of human
nature was acute and varied ; and his manners
were complacent when unruffled by passion ;
but, roused by opposition, he was fierce and
determined.

At an early period he studied the ancient
history, and recited the poetry of his country ;

and while he contemplated the sullen grandeur of his native wilds, corresponding ideas impressed his soul, and he would spend whole days in the admiration of a sublime portraiture of nature. The rugged mountains whose summits were often hid in the clouds that floated around them ; the dark valley encircled by wooded eminences ; the bold promontory opposed to the foaming ocean, and sometimes adorned by the castle of a chieftain ; the still bosom of the lake that reflected the surrounding landscape ; the impetuous mountain cataract ; the dreary silence of the cavern—were objects that greatly influenced his youthful feelings, and disposed his mind to the cultivation of generous and manly sentiments. These impressions, received when his imagination glowed with the fervour of youth, were never afterwards eradicated. They continued to bias his temper, and to give his disposition a cast of romantic chivalry, which he exemplified in many of his future actions.

His parents were of the Presbyterian church, in which faith he was also reared ; but he was not free from those superstitious notions so prevalent in his country ; and although few men possessed more strength of mind in resisting

the operation of false and gloomy tenets, he
was sometimes led away from the principles he
had adopted to a belief in supernatural ap-
pearances.

Though possessed of qualities that would
have fitted him for a military life, the occupa-
tions assigned to Rob Roy were of a more
homely description. It was customary at that
time, as it is at present, for gentlemen of property, as well as their tenantry, to deal in the
trade of grazing and selling cattle, and to
this employment did Rob Roy dedicate himself. He took a track of land in Balquhidder
for that purpose, and for some years pursued a
prosperous course. But his cattle were often
stolen, in common with those of his neighbours,
by hordes of banditti from the shires of Inverness, Ross, and Sutherland, who infested the
country, so that to protect himself from the depredations of these marauders, he was constrained to maintain a party of men ; and to
this cause may be attributed the warlike habits
which he afterwards acquired.

In the latter days of his father, Rob Roy
assisted him in all his concerns, especially in
that of collecting his fees of protection ; and
after the old man's demise, he pursued a similar

course of life, and received black-mail from
many proprietors of his vicinity ; an engagement which he fulfilled with more determination
and effect than had formerly been experienced.
It was in a pursuit after some thieves that he
gave the first proofs of his activity and courage.
A considerable party of Macras, from the western
coast of Ross, had committed an outrage on the
property of Finlarig, and carried off fifteen head
of cattle. An express informed Rob Roy of
the circumstance, and being the first call of the
kind he had received, he lost no time in collecting his followers to the number of twelve, and
setting off to overtake the men of Ross and
their spoil. They travelled two days and a
night before they obtained any other information as to their track than at times seeing the
impression of the cattles' feet on the ground.
On the second night, being somewhat fatigued,
they lay down on the heather to rest till morning in a dreary glen situated near the confines
of Badenoch. It was deep and dark, and appeared encompassed by mountains whose tops
were not visible to the eye. No sound disturbed
the silence of night, except the hoarse croaking
of the raven as she sought her nest among the
crags. A river that ran along the valley was

hid by thick coppice wood that skirted its margin, through which a half-formed path conducted
the traveller.

Rob Roy and his men had not long stretched
themselves on the heath, when one of them discovered a fire at some distance. This he communicated to his companions, and they went on
to reconnoitre, when they found it was a band
of tinkers, who had pitched a tent close by, and
were carousing. Their mirth, however, was
turned into terror when they beheld Rob Roy
and his party, as they little expected such intrusion in so secluded a place. But they soon recognised Macgregor, whose appearance was so
striking, that, to have seen him once, was sufficient to impress his features on the memory,
and fix his image in the recollection of the most
indifferent observer.

The tinkers informed him that they had seen
the Macras, who were at no great distance, and
two of the fraternity agreed to conduct his
party to the spot, for which they set out, after
having partaken of such fare as the wallets of
the gang could afford.

The freebooters had halted, for the security
of their spoil, in a narrow part of the glen, confined by semicircular rocks. There the Macgre-

gors overtook them just as they were setting
out, and as the morning began to dawn on the
lofty pinnacles of the mountains. Rob Roy,
with a voice which resounded among the craggy
acclivities, charged them to stop on their peril ;
but as they disregarded the order, he instantly
rushed upon them, and before they had time to
rally, six of their number were wounded and
lay prostrate on the ground. Eleven who remained made a stout resistance, and it was not
until two were killed and five more wounded
that they gave up the contest. Four of Rob
Roy's lads were sorely wounded and one killed,
and he himself received a cut on his left arm
from the captain of the banditti. The booty,
being thus recovered, was driven back, and restored to the rightful owner.

Rob Roy received great praise for this
exploit, achieved under such disadvantageous
circumstances, and those who had not formerly
afforded him their countenance, were now anxious to contribute a donation of black-mail.

In raising this tax, Rob Roy was sanctioned,
if not by Act of Parliament, at least by custom
and local institution ; an instance of which has
formerly been given. He was for some time
employed in assisting the police of the different

districts in collecting imposts that were paid for
maintaining the " Black Watch," a corps of pro-
vincial militia, whose duty it was to protect the
lives and properties of the people from distant
plunderers. This corps, wholly composed of
Highlanders, was supported by levies thus
laid on, which were extorted in a manner no
less compulsatory than the more private contri-
bution of black-mail, à modification of the
same tax. These independent companies of
the Black Watch, from the celebrity they
acquired, afterwards became regular troops, and
were the origin of the gallant 42d regiment of
foot, for a long time known by the name of the
Highland Watch.

Rob Roy, whose private engagements of protection were thus in a great degree authorised,
freely claimed these dues of black-mail as his
just right, and sometimes extorted them by
strong measures, which gave rise to reports of
his being unjust and cruel.

This tributory impost had long been suffered
to prevail in the Highlands, and though it often
became oppressive, the custom of many ages
had confirmed the practice, so that it was considered neither unjust nor dishonourable to
enforce it ; and from its effects being in general

beneficial in securing the forbearance and protection of those to whom it was paid, it was
commonly submitted to as an indispensable
usage.   It consisted of money, meal, or cattle,
according to agreement.

The respectability of his connections, and his
birth as a gentleman, entitled our hero to be
treated as such, and he was received into the
first families, and admitted to the best company
in his country.

He formed a matrimonal engagement with
Mary, a daughter of Macgregor of Comar, who
was a woman of an agreeable temper and
domestic habits ; active and economical in the
management of her family ; and though steady
and resolute, yet far from being the inhuman
virago she is represented in the late novel
of " Rob Roy " ; nor does it appear, excepting
on one occasion, afterwards to be mentioned,
that she took any part in the desultory concerns
of her husband.

Rob Roy was not, as has been said, possessed
of any patrimonial estate.   His father usually
lived in Glengyle as a tenant, and took upon
himself latterly the tutorship of his nephew,
who was tacksman of these lands ; but Rob
Roy afterwards became proprietor of the estate

of Craigcrostan in the following manner:—
When Macgregor of Macgregor was driven
from his possessions in Glenurchy by the
Campbells, he bought the lands of Inversnait
and Craigcrostan, then of small value, although
of considerable boundaries, extending from the
head of Loch Lomond twelve miles along its
eastern border, and stretching far into the
interior of the country, and partly round the
base of the stupendous mountain of Ben
Lomond.   On the demise of the chief in 1693,*
he left his property to a natural brother, Archibald, who was laird of Kilmannan.   This person was succeeded by his son Hugh, who
courted a daughter of the laird of Leny; but
Rob Roy, from what cause is not known, raised
suspicions against him in the mind of the
young lady, who, in consequence, rejected her
lover.   He then paid his addresses to a daughter of Colquhoun of Luss, and their marriage-

* This Gregor Macgregor died at the age of thirty-two, and
was buried on the island of Inchcallich (witch's isle), in Loch
Lomond.   He gave instructions some time before his death,
that no woman should, at any after period, be interred in his
grave.   Many years having elapsed, the body of a woman was
by accident placed in it, as the people who attended her funeral
were not aware of Macgregor's request.   Some of his clan
heard of the circumstance, and holding the promise of their
fathers as sacred and binding on them, they removed the corpse
of the woman from the place, and interred it elsewhere.

day was fixed, when Rob Roy again interfered, and Miss Colquhoun also refused to fulfil her engagement. Mortified at such treatment, the young chieftain went to Falkirk, where he married a woman of mean extraction, which so displeased his friends, that they no longer regarded him as their connection. But Rob Roy, now vexed to see him discarded, altered his behaviour, and ever after paid him much attention. The young man, owing to this treatment, was so thoroughly disgusted with his clan, that he gave up his estate to Rob Roy, and leaving his country, was never more heard of ; nor was it ever known whether Rob Roy gave value for the property, or if it was gifted to him : He afterwards, however, took the title of Craigcrostan, and was sometimes denominated *baron* of Inversnait, a term long applied to puisne lairds, all over Scotland.

The peculiar constitution of clanship among the Macgregors, formed a bond of union which no privation could tear asunder, nor contention overcome; and the modifications of that system which Rob Roy adopted among those who followed him, brought their compact to a plan of such solidity, as rendered them the terror of surrounding countries.

In many of those desultory forays from the mountains, which took place in his day, and spread dismay and misery among the inhabitants of the Lowland borders, Rob Roy was not the commander. Several other tribes who assumed his name, were often guilty of rigorous extortion, and committed irregularities which he would have considered disgraceful ; and some of his boldest conflicts were manifested in chastening the impudence of those marauders.

Many of those evils which arose from feudal manners, and hereditary antipathies, still remained in the Highlands with unabated virulence, and at this time were greatly aggravated by the madness of church politics, that defied all rational restriction ; led to the commission of barbarities shocking to nature; and rendered the parties no less despicable as men, than unworthy as Christians.

The great families of Montrose and Argyll, long at variance on political topics, were now at personal animosity ; and jealous of the growing importance of each other, were anxious to conciliate the friendship of Rob Roy, whose independent mind, and daring spirit, made him either a valuable auxiliary, or a formidable enemy.

I

When Macgregor was fairly settled, and tacitly confirmed as laird of Craigcrostan, he was still a young man, and he was naturally elated with an acquisition that gave him some consequence in his country. Montrose, his near neighbour, foreseeing the necessity of gaining his confidence, made a proposition to enter into copartnery with him in the trade of cattle dealing, a plan in which he readily acquiesced. Being considered a good judge of cattle, and a successful drover, Montrose had every reliance on his abilities. He accordingly advanced Rob Roy 1000 merks (about £50 sterling), he being also expected to lay out a similar sum, while the profits were to be divided: but this was not the only pecuniary transaction which took place betwixt them, for Montrose, at different times, gave him money on the security of his estate.

About this time, Highland cattle were in great request in England, and to that country Rob Roy was in the habit of making frequent journeys for carrying on this traffic. During these excursions to the south, from his obliging disposition, lively conversation, and strict regard to his word, which no consideration could induce him to violate, he gained the esteem of all who knew, or did business with him.

On the other hand, the Earl of Argyll, whose family had been the scourge of the clan Gregor, not only relaxed from all severities against that people, but was now willing to form an alliance with Rob Roy, whose character for resolute bravery had become notorious, hoping, from his local situation, that he would be a source of constant annoyance to Montrose.

Other motives, certainly more commendable, though not so probable, have been assigned as the cause of Argyll's attention to Rob Roy. Argyll, it is said, felt conscious of the cruelties and injustice his ancestors had exercised over the clan, and was inclined to befriend Rob Roy, their descendant, who seemed determined to support the former consequence of his pro- genitors. To this he was also incited, from the belief, that out of respect for him, Rob Roy had assumed the name of Campbell, that of Mac- gregor being under proscription ; but Rob Roy, though he did this in compliment to his mother, and in compliance with the law, was yet acknow- ledged in the country, and by his clan, under no other name than that of Macgregor. His signa- ture, however, afterwards appears to a writ dated in 1703, as " Robert Campbell of Inversnait."

Though Rob Roy, in common with his clan,

was compelled to resign his family name, the
wrongs which his ancestors had sustained still
rankled in his bosom, and he spurned at the
overtures of Argyll : but an incident afterwards
took place, that effected an important change in
his sentiments and conduct towards Montrose,
and laid the foundation of a lasting friendship
betwixt him and Argyll, which materially
influenced his future destiny.

In his transactions with the Marquis of Montrose, Rob Roy was the active manager. He
had carried them on with various success for
some time; but a Macdonald, an inferior partner,
being on one occasion entrusted with a large
sum of money, fled from the country, and eluded
pursuit. This greatly shattered Rob Roy's
trading concerns, and he was neither able to
pay Montrose his money, nor to support his
own credit. The copartnery being dissolved
from this circumstance, Rob Roy was required
to make over his property in satisfaction of the
claims of Montrose against him ; but this he
rejected, as contrary to his principles and purpose. The threats and entreaties from Montrose's factor, Graham of Killearn, were equally
unavailing, and a law-suit was at length instituted against Rob Roy, in which he was com-

pelled to give up his lands in wadset (mortgage) to Montrose, under the condition that they should again revert to himself, when he could restore the money. Some time thereafter, Rob Roy's finances having improved, he offered to return the sum for which his estate was held ; but it was pretended, that besides interest, and various other expenses, the amount had greatly increased, and that it would take time to make out this statement. In this equivocal manner he was amused, and ultimately deprived of his property.

The circumstances of the Revolution which had just taken place, produced great commotions in the Highlands, where the natives were well affected to the expelled house of Stewart ; and many of the chieftains were arraying their people to be in readiness for acting in their cause.

Argyll at first attached himself to the Prince of Orange, but not having been restored to his property and jurisdictions, since the attainder and judicial murder of his father, he was faltering in his sentiments, and like the majority of his countrymen, was desirous of having his followers in readiness to proceed as occasion might require. And aware, that in the unsettled state of the times, Rob Roy would be a valuable auxiliary, he renewed his entreaties to him, and from his late disagreement with Montrose, readily obtained promise of his assistance.

The suspicions of Montrose were awake, and he kept a watchful eye over the conduct and transactions of Argyll, of whose intimacy with Macgregor he had been informed, and eager for the destruction of a family who appeared to rival him in greatness, wrote a letter to Rob Roy, in which he promised that if he would go to Edinburgh, and give such information as would convict Argyll of treasonable practices, he would not only withdraw the mortgage upon his property, but in addition, give him a sum of money. Rob Roy, however, despising the offer, took no other notice of the letter, than to forward it to Argyll, who soon took occasion to confront Montrose with a charge of malevolence. But Rob Roy was the sufferer, for Montrose immediately procured an adjudication of his estate, and it was evicted for a sum very inadequate to its value.

The resentment of Macgregor was now kindled into fury, not so much for the loss of his property, as for the forcible expulsion of his family, during his absence, under circumstances of the utmost indignity and barbarity, by Graham of Killearn. This man, with the wantonness and cruelty of a savage, treated Mrs Macgregor in a manner too shocking to be related,* an outrage which her husband never forgave, and which certainly justified the measures of retaliation he afterwards adopted.

The civil discord which had prevailed in the nation, during the atrocious reign of Charles the Second, became still more dreadful on the accession of his brother James, whose bigotry permitted the most odious crimes, and authorised such oppression and cruelty as the mind shudders to contemplate. At such scenes of horror, Rob Roy had often been present, not as a perpetrator, but a silent spectator, whose soul burned with indignation at their wickedness, regretting, that although his arm was powerful, it was not sufficiently vigorous to crush the whole band of inhuman wretches who implicitly executed the bloody commands of the king. After he had been expelled from his estate, he went to Carlisle, in order to recover a sum of money due to him. Returning by Moffat, he observed an officer and a party of military engaged in hanging, on a tree, four peasants,

* See Macgregor Stirling's History of Stirlingshire, p. 715.

whom they called fanatics. While this execution was going on, a young woman who was
bound to the same tree, bewailed the fate of her
father and brother, two of those who suffered.
The deadly work being completed, four of the
soldiers seized the young woman, unloosed her
from the tree, and having tied her hands and
feet, were carrying her towards the river, to
plunge her in the flood, regardless of her tears
and entreaties for mercy. Our hero interposed,
his heart being wrung with sympathy, and
amazed at such unmanly cruelty, commanded
the perpetrators to stop, demanding an explana-
tion, "why they treated a helpless female in so
barbarous a manner." The officer, with an arro-
gant tone, "desired him to be gone, otherwise
he would be used in the same manner, for
daring to interrupt the king's instructions."
The miscreants, basely exulting in their barbarity, were about to toss the girl into the
stream over a steep bank. Rob Roy thus de-
rided, became frantic with rage, and with herculean strength, sprung upon the soldiers, and
in an instant, eight of them were struggling in
the water.

The officer and the remaining ten men were
so much confounded, that they stood motionless.

In this pause Rob Roy cut the cords that bound
the girl, and drawing his claymore, attacked the
officer, who speedily fell. The soldiers beset
him on all sides, but having killed two of them,
the rest fled to the town, and left him master
of the field, to the unspeakable joy of the young
woman, and the great delight of the peasantry
who stood around.

Leaving the field of action, our hero immediately bent his course towards home, pursuing
his journey with all expedition, lest he might be
overtaken by the military, for his interference
with them on this occasion ; but when he found
himself, as has been stated, thus forcibly deprived of his property, and in a manner which
he considered both unjust and oppressive on the
part of Montrose and his factor, he seemed to feel
it as a duty he owed to himself and his family, to
take ample revenge on the authors of his misfortunes ; and for that purpose he retained a party of
men, who were no less resolute than himself, and
keen to enter on exploits that promised them
redress.

His first act of hostility against Montrose
was at a term, when he knew the tenantry
of that nobleman were to pay their rents,
notice having been given them of the time.

Two days previously Rob Roy and his lads called upon them, and obliged them to give him the money, for which, however, he granted them acknowledgements "that it was on account of Montrose."

In this compulsatory manner he levied the rents from the tenants for several years, and Montrose, conscious, perhaps, that he had taken undue advantage of Rob Roy, seems to have overlooked the matter until a subsequent occasion, when the factor was collecting his rents at Chapellaroch in Stirlingshire.

Rob Roy had given out some days before, by proclamation at the church door, that he had gone to Ireland, and the factor consequently concluded that he would meet with no interruption in his duty. Towards evening, however, Rob Roy placed his men in a wood in the neighbourhood, and went himself with his piper playing before him, to the inn of Chapellaroch, where Killearn was attended, as a matter of compliment, by several gentlemen of the vicinity. Alarmed at the sound of the pipes, they all started up to discover whence it proceeded; and Killearn, in great consternation, beheld Rob Roy approaching the door.

He had finished his collection, but the bags

containing the money were hastily thrown for concealment on a loft in the room. Rob Roy entered with the usual salutation, and the factor, though he trembled for his money, at first had no suspicion of his final purpose, as he laid down his sword, and partook of the entertainment. It was no sooner over, than he desired his piper to strike up a tune. This was a signal to his men, who, in a few minutes, surrounded the house, and six of them entered the room with drawn swords, when Rob Roy laying hold of his own, as if about to go away, asked the factor, "How he had come on with his collection." "I have got nothing," said Killearn, "I have not yet begun to collect." "No, no, chamberlain," replied Rob Roy, "your falsehood will not do with me, I must count fairly with you by the book." Resistance being useless, the book was exhibited, and according to it, the money was given up, for which Rob Roy granted a receipt.

But from the infamous treatment his family received from Killearn, together with the part he had acted in the infringement of the contract that deprived him of his property, Rob Roy was resolved to punish him, and he had him immediately conveyed and placed in an island near the east end of Loch Ketturin, now rendered conspicuous, as the supposed residence of the fair ELLEN, the LADY of the LAKE.

> "———————— the shore around ;
> 'Twas all so close with copse-wood bound,
> Nor track nor pathway might declare
> That human foot frequented there,—
> Here for retreat, in dangerous hour,
> Some chief had framed a rustic bower."

In this island was Killearn confined for a considerable time ; and when set at liberty, he was admonished by Rob Roy no more to collect the rents of that country, which he meant in future to gather himself ; declaring that, as the lands originally belonged to the Macgregors, who lost them by unfair attainder, and other surreptitious means, such alienation was an unnatural and illegal deprivation of the right of succeeding generations. From this conviction, he continued to be the constant enemy of the Grahams, the Murrays, and the Drummonds, who then claimed, and still inherit those extensive domains.

The steady adherence of the Highlanders to the expatriated house of Stewart, was so well known, and so much dreaded by every prince who succeeded them on the British throne, that their motions were constantly watched with a jealous eye, and they were constrained to hold

their communings, which related to the affairs
of the exiles, in the most secret and clandestine
manner.

Some time subsequent to the unsuccessful
attempt of the Highland clans under Dundee,
at Killicrankie, a great meeting of chieftains
took place in Bräidalbane, under pretence of
hunting the deer, but in reality for the purpose
of ascertaining the sentiments of each other respecting the Stewart cause. Opinions were
unanimous; and a bond of faith and mutual
support, previously written, was signed. By the
negligence of a chieftain, to whom this bond
was entrusted, it fell into the hands of Captain
Campbell of Glenlyon, then at Fort-William.
He, from his connection with many whose
names were appended, did not immediately
disclose the contents; but the deserved odium,
which was attached to him from his having
a command in the party who perpetrated the
infamous massacre of Glencoe, made him justly
despised and execrated even by his nearest
friends, and when it was known that a man of
such inhuman feelings held the bond, those who
signed it were seriously alarmed, and various
plans were suggested for recovering it. Rob
Roy, who was at this meeting of the clans, had

also affixed his name ; but on his own account
he was indifferent, as he regarded neither the
king nor his government. He was, however,
urged by several chiefs to exert himself, and if
possible to recover the bond. With this view
he went to Fort-William in disguise, not with
his usual number of attendants, and getting
access to Captain Campbell, who was a near
relation of his own, discovered that, out of
revenge for the contemptuous manner in which
the chieftains now treated the captain, he had
put the bond into the possession of the governor
of the garrison, who was resolved to forward it
to the Privy Council ; and further learning
by accident the day on which it was to be
sent, he took his leave, and went home. The
despatch which contained the bond was made
up by Governor Hill, and sent from Fort-
William, escorted by an ensign's command,
which in those countries always accompanied the
messages of government. On the third day's
march, Rob Roy, and fifty of his men, met this
party in Glendochart, and ordering them to
halt, demanded their despatches. The officer
refused ; but was told that he must either give
up their lives and the despatches together, or the
despatches alone. The ferocious looks and

appearance of his antagonist bespoke no irresolution. The packet was given up ; and Rob Roy
having taken out the bond he wanted, begged
the officer would excuse the delay he had occasioned, and wishing him a good journey, left the
military to proceed unmolested. By this bold
exploit many chieftains saved their heads, and
the forfeiture of a number of estates was prevented.

We have formerly noticed, that several mighty
chiefs of the Highlands had augmented their
territories by the suppression of inferior lairds,
who did not hold their lands by subordinate
charters. In order to reduce these unprotected
barons, and annex their properties to the estate
of the more powerful families, a knighted elevè
of the house of Argyll was commissioned, and
among some others, he seized upon a small
estate in Glendochart. This iniquitous practice
was insisted upon after the junction of the kingdoms under the sixth James, that it might be
known upon what grounds landlords held their
estates ; but our hero considering it as repugnant
to justice, was determined to redress the grievance. He therefore sent his men to Glenurchy, to waylay the obnoxious knight, at a
defile which wound along the craggy cliffs of

Ben-Cruachan. After waiting for some time, they readily effected their purpose, secured the baronet, and conveyed him towards Tyndrum, where Rob Roy met them. He reproached the knight with his injustice, and made him sign a letter, restoring the lands to the rightful owner: which, when he had done, he took him to St Fillan's pool, near that place, and ducking him heartily, told him, that from the established virtues of that pool, a dip in it might improve the knight's honour, so that he would not again rob a poor man of his lands.*

* This baronet had rendered himself despicable by many similar acts of irregularity, prior to this period, one or two of which we shall state for the reader's amusement :—Having heard that Maclean of Kingaerloch, though he could show a long line of ancestry, could produce no charter or legal feoffment by which he held of a superior, the knight set out by sea, with a party of armed vassals, to fasten on this property, and turn out the owner ; but his ungracious employment always created suspicion, and made him be regarded as a dangerous scourge, and Maclean was aware of him, and observed his approach.    He hastily collected some armed men, placed them in a concealed situation, and walked alone to the shore to receive the knight.    On their way towards the house, the baronet asked Maclean if he had a charter for his lands ; to which he replied that he had ;—and coming immediately on his armed band, who then brandished their swords,—"There," said Maclean, "is my charter."    The knight asked no more questions, and they parted as friends.

But he was more successful with another estate, the proprietor of which was a more fit object for his designs, being a man of imbecile judgment.    His name was Macdougal : he had

Contracts of *wadset*, as they were called, were then a common practice in the Highlands, and as we have observed, many small proprietors were swallowed up by superiors, from unfair advantage which was taken under the supposed obligations of those agreements. Many flagitious means were adopted to evade and disannul the privileges of the needy proprietor ; and from the extraordinary authority which a superior claimed over his vassals

been married for several years, but having no children to heir his property, the baronet advised him to turn off his wife, adding that he would provide him with another. This was accordingly done, the knight got him a near relation of his own, and immediately brought an action against him for bigamy, seized his lands as a forfeiture, and added them to the estate of his patron.

A near relation of the knight's, Campbell of Calder, was going by boat to visit his property of the island of Islay. In passing through a narrow channel on the west coast of Argyllshire, he was fired at from the shore and killed. Suspicion of this murder fell upon Campbell of Tirifour : but no proof of his criminality could for some time be obtained. The prying genius of the baronet, however, found a track in which, by the old rule of a Scots proverb, he made the discovery. He knew that this Campbell of Tirifour had a wife, whose pride and vanity were her leading passions ; and according to her own estimation, fitted her for a more elevated rank. In the absence of her husband, the knight frequently waited upon her, with the view of extracting some confessions regarding his guilt ; but the lady was no less cautious, than the baronet was cunning, until one day he assumed more than ordinary seriousness in his manner. He told her that he had long respected her abilities and appearance, and regretted to see her in a situation so far

K

during the feudal ages, it was scarcely possible for the inferior to resist his rapacity, or to defend his lawful heritage against such powerful odds.

The lands of Glengyle were under a redeemable bond of this description, when Rob Roy's nephew succeeded to them. A neighbouring chieftain had lent a sum of money on them, which if not repaid in ten years, the lands were to be the forfeiture, though the sum was not

beneath her deserts ; and that having thus professed himself her admirer, no means appeared by which he could promise himself the happiness of raising her to importance, unless it were getting quit of her husband, by declaring and proving him to be the assassin of Calder. The lady heard and believed the promises of the knight, to confirm which he gave her a written assurance, that upon her giving such information as would convict her husband of the imputed murder, he would himself marry her. Satisfied with this paper, she exhibited the required proof of her husband's guilt, and his life as well as his property was the expiation. Turned out of her house, and become despicable from having brought her husband to the gallows, she at last applied to the knight that he might fulfil his promise of making her his wife. He received her politely, and told her, that from his being bred for the church, he was ready to perform his promise, and would marry her to any man she pleased. Mortified at the disappointment, shocked at her own conduct, and the duplicity of the knight, despair took possession of her mind, and her end was miserable.

The animosity which the Campbells bore to the more ancient clans, was always a source of contention, particularly with the Macdonalds, their most powerful rivals. A tribe of this clan, under the distinguishing name of MacIans (sons of John), occupied the extensive wilds of Ardnamurchan,—(point of the

half their value. Rob Roy, knowing that every
advantage would be taken of the contract, gave
his nephew the money for the purpose of retir-
ing the bond. The period of redemption had
only a few months to run ; and under pretence
that the bond could not then be found, the
money was refused. Rob Roy in the meantime
having been otherwise engaged, the matter lay
over, and the bond was allowed to expire. The
holder of it sent a party to take possession of

great ocean)—and were regarded by the Campbells as fit objects
of spoliation. From the success that had attended some of
the knight's exploits in that way, he marched at the head of an
armed force, with an avowed intention to wrest from that
people their ancient jurisdiction. But suspicious of his purpose,
and not deficient in the native intrepidity of their race, they
met him and his followers at Strontian, the south-eastern
boundary of their country, determined on opposition. Both
parties halted on the opposite banks of the river ; but the Campbells seeing the resolution of their opponents, their pretended
demands of feu-duty were easily accommodated, and mutual
forbearance took place. As both clans were preparing to
depart, one of the Campbells made a signal insulting to the
Macdonalds, and degrading to their proud spirit. This was
instantly resented. One of the Macdonalds levelled his piece,
and killed the fellow on the spot ; but no other hostility was
then offered on either side. The head of the dead man was cut
off, and forwarded by an express to the Privy Council at Edinburgh, with a false and aggravated account, stating the lawless
condition of the MacIans, and craving letters of fire and sword
against them. These, from the temper of the king's administra-
tors, were readily granted, and speedily put in force by the baronet and his sanguinary band, whereby the Macdonalds were expelled, and their country wrested from them.

the lands in his name, got himself infefted on
them in the common form ; and young Macgregor was ordered to remove himself, his dependants, and cattle, in eight days.    Rob Roy
could not suffer such treatment ; and having assembled his *gillies*, set out to obtain restitution.
The chieftain whom he sought was then in
Argyllshire, whither our hero proceeded ; but
he met him travelling in Strathfillan, took him
prisoner, and carried him to a small inn not far
distant.    He told the chieftain that he would
not allow him to depart until he gave up the
bond of Glengyle, and desired that he would instantly send for it to his castle.    The chieftain,
aware of Rob Roy's disposition, and apprehensive of personal injury, agreed to give it up
when he got home ; but our hero put no trust in
his promise, and he was forced to comply.    Two
trusty men, along with two of Rob Roy's, were
despatched, and at the end of two days returned
with the bond.    When it was delivered, the
chieftain demanded his money ; but Rob Roy
would pay none, telling him that the sum was
even too small a fine for the outrage he had attempted, and that he might be thankful if he
escaped in a sound skin.

The arbitrary and uncertain tenures by which

proprietors in the Highlands held their lands and supported their consequence for many ages had, even at this late period of their history, scarcely experienced any amendment ; and frivolous and unjust pretences were often considered sufficient to deprive a man of his right. Against such acts of violence, though overlooked by the indifference of government, Rob Roy Macgregor manfully and openly drew his sword. He was the strenuous opponent of every deed of cruelty or breach of faith, especially if committed upon those under the pressure of misfortune ; the orphan, the widow, the poor were those for whom he stood boldly forward, and proclaimed himself the champion ; and to supply their wants with the means of the rich was his greatest delight ; an appeal to his generosity never being disregarded. Lest his own resources might not be adequate to those charitable ends, he entered into agreement with different proprietors for their mutual defence ; and a contract founded upon this reciprocal basis was entered into betwixt him and Buchanan, of Arnprior ; and with the Campbells of Lochnell, Glenfallach, Lochdochart, and Glenlyon, about the same time.

On the estate of Perth, a clansman of Rob

Roy's occupied a farm on a regular lease ; but the factor, Drummond of Blairdrummond, took occasion to break it, and the tenant was ordered to remove. Rob Roy, hearing the story, went to Drummond Castle to claim redress of this grievance. On his arrival there, early in the morning, the first person he met was Blairdrummond in front of the house, whom he knocked down, without speaking a word, and walked on to the gate. Perth, who saw this from a window, immediately appeared, and, to soften his asperity, gave him a cordial welcome. He told Perth that he wanted no show of hospitality, he insisted only to get back the tack of which his namesake had been deprived, otherwise he would let loose his legions on his property. Perth was obliged to comply, the lease was restored, and Rob Roy sat down quietly and breakfasted with the earl.

Graham of Killearn, who was the chamberlain or factor on the estate of Montrose, was second cousin to that nobleman, and left no means untried to recover the rents of his lord, in doing which he often displayed great want of humanity and fellow-feeling. Being in the constant practice of distressing those tenants who were in arrear, he was consequently despised in

the country. He had once sequestrated the
goods and cattle of a poor widow, for arrears of
rent, and when Rob Roy heard of the matter,
he went to her and gave her the 300 merks she
owed, at the same time desiring her when she
paid it to get a receipt. On the legal day the
officers of the law appeared at the widow's
house to take away her effects, when she paid
their demand ; but Rob Roy met them after
they left her, made them surrender the money
they had extorted, and gave them a good drub-
bing, with an advice never to act in the same
manner.

Under similar circumstances he relieved a
needy tenant on the same estate, who was deficient in the rent of three years. When the
man afterwards offered to repay the loan, our
hero would not receive it, as he said he had got
it back from Killearn.

Feuds and violent conflicts of clans still continued prevalent, with all the animosity which
marked the rude character of the times ; and a
contest having arisen betwixt the houses of
Perth and Athol, Rob Roy was requested to
take part with the former. Though Perth
was no favourite with him, he readily agreed to
give his assistance, as a return for a good office,

and as he would undertake anything to distress
Athol. Having assembled sixty of his clan, he
marched to Drummond Castle with seven pipers
playing. The Atholmen were already on the
banks of the Earn, and the Macgregors and
Drummonds proceeded to attack them; but
they no sooner recognised the Macgregors,
whom they regarded as demons, than they fled
from the field, and after the loss of several men,
were pursued to the precincts of their own
country.

The practice of carrying off the cattle of
other clans was still common in those countries;
and the followers of Rob Roy were often guilty
of this practice, when necessity or the unfriendly
disposition of other tribes occasioned dispute.
Montrose being considered his worst enemy,
the estate of that nobleman was often plundered,
and the cattle driven even from the parks that
surrounded his house. A meal store which he
had at a place called Moulin, usually supplied the wants of Rob Roy's family in that
article; and when any poor persons in his
neighbourhood were in need of it, he went to
the store-keeper, ordered the quantity he required, gave a receipt for it, and made the

tenants carry it with their own horses to his house, or wherever else it was wanted.

The cause of provocation which Rob Roy had sustained from Montrose and his dependants, constantly kept alive that spirit of opposition with which he regarded them ; but, though he had them often in his power, he never intended to take any serious personal revenge, preferring occasional retaliation on their property.

The harassing state in which that nobleman was kept by the depredatory incursions of our hero induced him to apply to the Privy Council for redress ; yet dreading the enmity of Rob Roy, his name was intentionally kept out, and the Act was expressed in general terms— " to repress sorners, robbers, and broken men, to raise hue and cry after them, to recover the goods stolen by them, and to seize their persons."

This decree, though despised by Rob Roy, made him more watchful of his foes; but, though generally favoured by fortunate incidents, he could not always expect to escape with impunity. Having by many coercive means pressed hard on Montrose, that nobleman, under authority of the act of council, called out

a number of his people, and sent them, headed
by a confidential Graham, and accompanied by
some military, to lay hold of Rob Roy; but he
chancing to be absent with his band, they
assailed his house during the night, and having
learned the course he had taken, followed, and
arrived by day-break next morning, at Crin-
larach, a public house in Strathfillan, where
our hero and his men had taken up their quarters
for the night—he in the house, and they in an
adjoining barn.   The Grahams immediately
broke open the door.   Rob Roy was instantly
accoutred to meet them, and levelled them man
by man, as they approached, until his own lads,
roused by the noise, attacked the Grahams in
the rear with such determination, that they re-
treated to some distance, leaving behind them
several of their party sorely wounded.   Having
fortified his men with a glass of whisky, they
then ascended the hill towards the head of
Loch Lomond.   The Grahams, expecting still
to obtain some advantages over them, followed
at a short distance, till the Macgregors shot
some of the military, and drowned one soldier
in a mill-dam, when the Grahams thought
proper to withdraw.

   After this inglorious attempt to overcome

Rob Roy, though with five times the number of men, Montrose ceased for a while to give him any obstruction, until he, grown, if possible, more adventurous than ever, made a descent into the plains, and swept away cattle, and almost every moveable article, from the country round Balfron, and in Monteith; an outrage commonly called *the herriship of Kippen*. On this occasion, he was pursued by some country people who were sufferers, assisted by a party of military from Cardross Castle; and they would have overtaken him, but one of his men, Alister Roy Macgregor, fired on the pursuers from behind a dyke, and killed the foremost, which so intimidated the rest, that they not only dreaded proceeding farther, but made the best of their way home.*

This appears to have been the greatest misdemeanour of which he stood accused, as it seriously attracted the notice of government: and the western volunteers were marched into the Highlands to curb his insolence, and that of his marauding clan, as they were denominated. These volunteers went to Drymen; but finding

---

* An humorous Gaelic song, composed on the occasion, is still chanted in that country, detailing the swiftness of the retreat.

their entertainment very bad, and the people
much disaffected, they lay upon their arms all
night, dreading the approach of the Macgregors,
who were within a few miles of them, to the
number, as they heard, of five hundred ; but
they were not molested, being allowed to depart in peace. Several parties of horse, however,
were afterwards dispersed over the country to
apprehend Rob Roy, and a reward of £1000
being offered for his head, he was obliged for
some months to take shelter in the woods, and
in his cave at the base of Ben Lomond, on the
banks of the lake.

This celebrated recess had formerly sheltered
the gallant Bruce from enemies who sought his
destruction ; and our hero, with the highest
veneration for the memory of a patriot king,
believed that he could not consecrate to himself
a more appropriate retreat. The entrance is
near the water's edge, among huge fragments of
rock, broken from the lofty mountain crags that
seem to overhang the lake, which are fantastically
diversified by the interspersion of brushwood,
heath, and wild plants, nurtured to extreme
growth in the desert luxuriance of solitude.
The access to this subterraneous abode is extremely difficult and hazardous, from the preci-

pitous ruggedness of the surrounding heights, which almost exclude a passage to human feet.

In this seclusion Rob Roy was perfectly secure, and had he been attacked in it, could have defended himself from almost any number of men ; but he frequently left it, and took excursions to distant parts of the country to see his friends and enjoy their fellowship.

While under this concealment he was only attended by two men. One day when travelling in a sequestered place along the side of Lochearn, they were unexpectedly met by seven horsemen, who demanded their names and what they were. To this an evasive answer was given, but from our hero's great stature and warlike appearance, they had no doubt of his being the person they sought. There was no time for parley, and they sprung up the hill followed by the troopers. Rob Roy rapidly gained the higher ground, where neither the horses nor fire of the riders could touch him ; but his companions were not so lucky, as they were overtaken, and, in defending themselves, were killed. Being exasperated at this, he fired upon the troopers in return, and killed three of them and four of their horses, when the remainder galloped away.

Having continued to wander from place to place, somewhat forlorn, though not broken in spirit, he became solicitous about the safety of his family, and went to see them privately. Some days before his arrival, a message from the Duke of Athol was sent to his house, requesting a visit from him at Blair Castle. But Rob Roy, though he believed that Athol had then no deadly enmity towards him, did not incline to trust himself in such hands, without some written assurance of his personal safety. He therefore wrote to Athol, wishing to have his commands, and candidly stated his want of confidence in his Grace. Athol, who had previously corresponded with the court regarding the most effectual plan of securing our hero, immediately replied to his letter, and gave him the most solemn promises of protection, saying that he only wanted to have some conversation with him on certain political points. This letter was followed by an embassy, who gave even more positive assurances that no evil was intended, and delivered to him a protection from the government. Our hero consented to go, fixing a day for being at Blair, and accordingly set out on horseback, attended by a servant. On his arrival, Athol ran to embrace him, pro-

testing he knew not how to express the joy he
felt at the sight of so brave a gentleman ; but
as his duchess would not suffer any person to
enter the castle armed, he requested him to lay
aside his sword and dirk, which he did, and they
walked into the garden, where they met the
lady, who expressed her surprise at seeing Rob
Roy unarmed.    This remark having given the
lie to her husband, Rob Roy now felt he had
done wrong in parting with his arms, and he
gave Athol a look that perfectly declared his
feelings :—" I understand you, Macgregor," said
he ; "but you have committed so much mischief,
that you must be detained, and sent to Edinburgh."    " I am betrayed then ! " said Rob Roy;
" has a man of your quality such a mean rascally
soul, as to forfeit his word, his faith, his honour,
for a pitiful reward ? " and clenching his fist in
his face, continued—" Villain you shall repent
this."    He would have knocked him down, but
the garden door instantly opened, when    an
officer with sixty men entered, and made Rob
Roy a prisoner.

Our hero being thus perfidiously ensnared, was
removed for the night to a paltry inn of the
village, while Athol immediately despatched a
messenger on horseback to Edinburgh, to inform

the court and his friends of his having succeeded
in apprehending Rob Roy, and desired a party
of military from the commander-in-chief to receive and carry him to the capital.

Athol, however disgraceful the circumstance
was to himself as a man, was vain of effecting
the seizure of our hero, which no other had been
able to accomplish ; and not satisfied with the
account of his prowess which he sent to Edinburgh, he also transmitted to the Secretary of
State in London, an elaborate detail of his wonderful exertions in laying hold of " the desperate
outlaw and undaunted robber," as he termed
him : and so publicly did he announce himself
the champion who had conquered Rob Roy,
that in a few days it was known all over Scotland. The issue, however, which soon overturned this bravado, placed Athol low in the
eyes of all men.

The party of military sent from Edinburgh to
receive our hero proceeded to Kinross. He
was to be delivered to them by a band of undis-
ciplined mercenaries that Athol had demanded
from the governor of Perth, who set out for
Dunkeld for that purpose. They were met by
Athol, but he desired them to return, being resolved to dismiss the soldiery and escort the

prisoner by his own vassals, that the whole merit and profit might accrue to himself: and until they could be got ready, Rob Roy was detained at Logierait, under a strong guard. But although in confinement, our hero was not idle. He conciliated the good offices of his attendants, by profuse libations of his country's beverage, and as they considered him a gentleman, he was allowed more than ordinary freedom.

Having written a letter to his wife, his servant, who had previously received his instructions, was ordered to get his horse in readiness to go off with it : and the animal being brought from the stable, Rob Roy, under pretence of delivering a private message to the servant, was allowed to walk to the door along with a sentinel, while the others, nearly inebriated, had no suspicion of his design. Appearing to engage in serious conversation with the servant, he walked a few steps from the door, then getting close to his horse, he quickly leaped into the saddle, and was out of sight in a moment.

The mortification of Athol and his party on this escape of our hero was very great, as they expected that he would have given some information prejudicial to Argyll, whose politics

L

were in opposition to those of the adminis-
tration.

Rob Roy's family at this time lived at the
farm of Portnellan, near the head of Loch Ketturin, and his enemy, the factor of Montrose,
hearing of his return from Athol, and of his
being at home, assembled a multitude of the
tenantry, in order to take him by surprise.
With this intent they set out, with Killearn
at their head, and surrounded our hero's house
one morning before he was out of bed ; but
he speedily appeared, sword in hand, and they
fled with the utmost precipitation.

From this place he afterwards removed to
Balquhidder, where a farm, to which he and his
family claimed some right, had been taken by
his connections the Maclarens.  The Macgregors
put them out by force, and the Maclarens, who
were also related to the Stewarts of Appin,
applied to them; whereupon Appin assembled a
strong body of his clan, to put his friends in possession.  The parties came in sight of each other
near the Kirkton of Balquhidder.  After a pause,
which men naturally make before they assail their
friends and kinsmen, Rob Roy stepped forward,
and challenged any of his opponents to fight
with the broadsword.  This was accepted by

Stewart of Invernahyle. When they had fought for some time, a parley was demanded, and terms of accommodation being agreed to, they separated without bloodshed.

About this time, the government, either ashamed of their frequent opposition, or despairing of being able to get hold of Rob Roy, withdrew the horsemen who pursued him, and he could proceed without restraint in his usual courses ; but he had still to guard against his inveterate enemy, Athol, who had so basely treated him, and whose machinations were even more alarming than the denunciations of the law.

Rob Roy, however, considering himself justly entitled to retaliate on the duke, frequently ravaged the district of Athol, carried away cattle, and put every man to the sword who attempted resistance : yet, for all his caution, he had again nearly fallen into his hands.

The duke having sent a party of horse, they unexpectedly came upon and seized him in his own house of Monuchaltuarach in Balquhidder, and placed him on horseback, to be conveyed to Stirling Castle ; but on going down a steep defile, he leaped off, and ran up a wooded hill, where the horsemen could not

follow.   On another occasion, Athol sent twenty
men from Glenalmond, to lay hold of him.   He
saw them approaching : but did not shun them,
though alone, and his uncommon size, the large-
ness of his limbs, the fierceness of his countenance, and the posture of defence, in which
he placed himself, intimidated them so much,
that they durst not go near him.   He told them,
that " he knew what they wanted : but if they
did not depart, none of them should return."
He desired them to " tell their master, that if
he sent any more of his pigmy race to disturb him, he would hang them up to feed the
eagles ;" and having sounded his horn, for he
often carried one, Athol's men became alarmed,
and speedily took their leave.

Although Rob Roy, from his great personal
prowess, and the dauntless energy of his mind,
which, in the most trying and difficult emer-
gencies, never forsook him, was the dread of
every country where his name was known, the
urbanity and kindness of his manners to his
inferiors, gained him the good will and services
of his whole clan, who were always ready to submit to any privation, or to undergo any hard-
ship to protect him from the multitude of
enemies who watched to destroy him ; and one

or two, among many instances of their attachment, may here be mentioned :—A debt to a
pretty large amount, which he had long owed to
a person in the Lowlands, could never be recovered, because no one would undertake to
execute diligence against him. At length a
messenger at Edinburgh appeared, who pledged
himself, that with six men, he would go through
the whole Highlands, and apprehend Rob Roy,
or any man of his name. The fellow was stout
and resolute, he was offered a handsome sum,
if he would bring Rob Roy to the jail of Stirling, and he was allowed men of his own choice.
He accordingly equipped himself and his men
with swords, cudgels, and every thing fitted for
the expedition, and having arrived at the only
public-house then in Balquhidder, inquired the
way to his house. The party was at once known
to be composed of strangers, and the landlord
learning their business, sent notice of it to his
good friend Rob Roy, and also advised them not
to go farther, lest they should have reason to
repent of their folly; but the advice was disregarded, and they went forward. The party
waited at some distance from the house, and the
messenger himself went to reconnoitre.

Having announced himself as a stranger who

had lost his way, he was politely shewn by our
hero into a large room, where—

"—— all around, the walls to grace,
Hung trophies of the fight or chace ;
A target there, a bugle here,
A battle-axe, a hunting spear,
And broad-swords, bows, and arrows store,
With the tusked trophies of the boar,"

which astonished him so much, that he felt as if
he had got into a cavern of the infernal regions;
but when the room door was shut, and he saw
hanging behind it a stuffed figure of a man, intentionally placed there, his terror increased to
such a degree, that he screamed out, and asked
if it was a dead man ? To this Rob Roy
coolly answered, that it was a rascal of a messenger who had come to the house the night
before ; that he had killed him, and had not got
time to have him buried. Fear now wholly
overcame the messenger, and he could scarcely
articulate a benediction for his soul, when he
fainted and fell upon the floor. Four men carried
him out of the house, and, in order to complete
the joke, and at the same time to restore the
man to life, they took him to the river just by
and tossed him in, allowing him to get out the
best way he could. His companions, in the
meantime, seeing all that happened, and sup-

posing he had been killed, took to their heels :
but the whole glen being now alarmed, met the
fugitives in every direction, and gave every one
of them such a complete ducking, that they had
reason all their lives to remember the lake and
river of Balquhidder.

These people were no sooner out of the hands
of the Macgregors, than they made a speedy
retreat to Stirling, not taking time on the road
to dry their clothes, lest a repetition of their
treatment should take place ; and upon their
arrival there, they represented the usage they
had received, with such exaggerated accounts of
the assassinations and cruelties of the Macgregors, magnifying their own wonderful escape
and prowess in having killed several of the clan,
that the story being reported to the commander
of the castle, he ordered a company of soldiers
to march into the Highlands, to lay hold of Rob
Roy. A party of Macgregors, who were returning with some booty which they had acquired
along the banks of the Forth observing the
military on their way to Callander, and suspecting their intention, hastened to acquaint Rob
Roy. In a few hours the whole country was
warned of the approaching danger, and guards
were placed at different stations to give notice

of the movements of the soldiers, while all the
men within several miles were prepared to repel
the invasion, in case it was to lay waste the
country, which had often been the intention
before ; but the military appearing to have no
other orders than to seize Rob Roy, he considered it more prudent to take refuge in the
hills, than openly to give them battle.

After a fruitless search for many days, the
soldiers, unaccustomed to the fatigue of climb-
ing the mountains, and scrambling over rocks,
and through woods, took shelter at night in
an empty house, which they furnished with
heath for beds ; but the Macgregors, unwilling
that they should leave their country without
some lasting remembrance of them, set fire to
it, and speedily dislodged them.    In the
confusion, one man was killed by the acci-
dental discharge of a musket, many of them
were hurt, and a number lost their fire-
arms.  The military party being thus thrown
into confusion, broken down by fatigue, and
almost famished for want of provisions, withdrew from the country of the Macgregors, happy
that they had escaped so well.

The tribute of black-mail, already noticed,
extended under Rob Roy's system, principally

to inferior proprietors, and to the tenantry: the
more powerful chieftains, though they at times
considered him as a useful auxiliary, and
though their property was often subjected to
spoliation, would seldom consent to that compulsatory regulation, as being too degrading to
the consequence they were anxious to maintain.
Rob Roy did certainly, as occasion required,
exact what he conceived to be his due in this
way, with some severity ; but he often received
the tax as a voluntary oblation.  Of this last
description was an annual payment made to
him, for many years, by Campbell of Abruchil ;
but this proprietor having at length omitted to
pay him, he went to his castle with an armed
party to demand the arrears.  Leaving his men
at some distance, he knocked at the gate, and
desired a conversation with the laird ; but he
was told that several great men were at dinner
with him, and that no stranger could be admitted.  " Then tell him," said he, " that Rob
Roy Macgregor is at his door, and must see him,
if the king should be dining with him."  The
porter returned, and told him that his master
said, he knew nothing of such a fellow, and desired him to depart.  Rob Roy immediately
applied to his mouth a large horn that hung by

his side, from which there issued a sound that
appalled the castle guard, rung through every
corner of the building, and so astonished Abruchil and his guests, that they quickly left the
dining-table.   In an instant Rob Roy's men
were by his side, when he ordered them to drive
away all the cattle they found on the land : but
the laird came hastily to the gate, apologised for
the rudeness of the porter to his good friend,
took him into the castle, paid him his demand,
and they parted apparently good friends.

About this time, a party of Macras again
made their appearance in our hero's neighbourhood, and stole from the lands of Stirling of
Craigbarnet, a flock of sheep to the number of
two hundred.   Such acts of depredation were
not then styled theft, but "liftings," and Rob
Roy in his compacts of black-mail, was not
bound to restore any stolen cattle if under
seven.   The above number, however, being considerable, the laird of Craigbarnet immediately
sent an account of his loss to Rob Roy, who
without delay took measures for discovering the
thieves ; but it was several weeks before he
could trace them to the hills of Kintail in Ross-
shire, whence the spoil was brought back to
Craigbarnet, with the loss of only one sheep.

Among other coercive measures, which from time to time were adopted to suppress the practices of the Macgregors, was that of planting a garrison in their country at Inversnaid, upon the spot whence Rob Roy formerly took one of his titles, and this was done by the advice, and under the direction of Montrose.

The immoderate length to which the rigorous decrees of government had been carried, not only by its immediate instrument, the military, but also by the other clans who surrounded the Macgregors, still drove them to such desperation that they held the laws in contempt, and as they were wholly excluded from their benefit, so nothing appeared too hazardous nor too flagrant for them to perform. This fortress, though its erection was strenuously opposed by him, had been garrisoned some time before any sally from it had given annoyance to Macgregor; and though the number of soldiers which it generally contained was no great obstruction in his estimation, yet they were a sort of check upon those small parties which he sometimes sent forth. He therefore determined to intimidate the garrison, or to make the military abandon it. He had previously arranged his plan, and secured the connivance of a woman of his own

clan, who served in the fort. Having supplied
her with a quantity of Highland whisky, of which
the English soldiery were very fond, she contrived, on an appointed night, to intoxicate the
sentinel ; and while he lay overcome by the
potent dose, she opened the gate, when Rob
Roy and his men, who were on the watch,
rushed in loaded with combustibles, and set the
garrison on fire in different places, so that it was
with difficulty that the inmates escaped with
their lives. Though Rob Roy was suspected as
the incendiary, there was no immediate proof,
and the damage was quietly repaired.

The various assaults which Rob Roy had
made upon the Duke of Athol, and his numerous
vassals, were not dictated by a wish for spoil,
but intended as a chastisement for the treachery
of that nobleman, who did not respect his
bravery, although he had often seen and dreaded
its effects. Having shewn no inclination to
desist from those practices, Athol resolved to
correct him in person, as all former attempts to
subdue him had failed, and with this bold intention he set forward to Balquhidder. A large
portion of that country then belonged to Athol
in feu : and when he arrived there, he summoned the attendance of his vassals, who very

unwillingly accompanied him to Rob Roy's house, as many of them were Macgregors, but dared not refuse their laird. Rob Roy's mother having died in his house at this time, preparations were going forward for the funeral, which was to take place on the day that Athol appeared at his door ; and at such a time, he could have dispensed with such unwelcome and unlooked for guests. He suspected that the purpose of their visit was to lay hold of him, and escape seemed impossible; but with his wonted strength of mind and quickness of thought, he buckled on his sword, and went out to meet the duke. He saluted him very graciously and said, " that he was much obliged to his Grace for having come unasked, to his mother's funeral, which was a piece of friendship he did not expect." Athol told him that " he did not come for that purpose, but to desire his company to Perth." He, however, declined the honour, as he could not leave his mother's funeral ; but after doing that last duty to his parent, he would go, he said, if his lordship insisted upon it. Athol replied that the funeral could take place without him, and would not delay. A long remonstrance ensued ; but the duke was inexorable, and Rob, apparently complying, went away amidst the cries and tears of his sisters and kindred. But their distress roused his soul to a pitch of irresistible desperation, and breaking from the party, several of whom he threw down, he drew his sword. Athol, when he saw him retreat, drew a holster pistol and fired at him. Rob Roy fell at the same instant, not by the ball, which never touched him, but by slipping his foot. One of his sisters, the lady of Glenfallach, a stout woman, seeing her brother fall, and believing he was killed, made a furious spring at Athol, seized him by the throat, and brought him from his horse to the ground. In a few minutes that nobleman would have been choked, as the by-standers were unable to unfix the lady's grasp, but Rob Roy went to his relief, when the duke was in the agonies of suffocation.

Several of our hero's friends, who observed the suspicious haste of Athol and his party towards his house, dreading some evil design, speedily armed, and running to his assistance, arrived just as Athol's eyeballs were beginning to revert into their sockets. Rob Roy then declared that had the duke been so polite as allow him to wait his mother's burial, he would have then gone along with him; but that this having been refused, he would now remain in spite of all his efforts;

and the lady's embrace having much astonished
the duke, he was in no condition to enforce his
orders, so that he and his men departed as
quickly as they could.   Had they stayed till the
clan assembled to the exequies of the old
woman, it is doubtful if either the chief or his
companions would have ever returned to taste
the *brose* indigenous to their country.

Rob Roy, who was in a great degree sanctioned to raise black-mail, openly demanded his
dues, and always took strong measures to enforce the payment when it was resisted, and his
attack on Garden Castle was of that description :—The owner was absent when he went
to claim his right, which had long been with-
held on pretence of not being lawful.   He however took possession of the fortress ; and when
the owner returned, refused him admittance,
until he would pay the reward of protection,
which he imperiously refused to do.   Rob Roy
thereupon ascended the turrets, with a child from
the nursery in his arms, and threatened to throw
it over the walls, which speedily brought the laird,
at the intercession of his lady, to an agreement,
when our hero restored the keys of the castle,
and took his leave.

In passing the place of Achtertyre near Stirling, Rob Roy observed a young horse, grazing in a park, with points that much pleased him, for he was a perfect jockey, and he went to the house to inquire if the animal was for sale. The proprietor was not within, but Macgregor was recognised by the servant, and ushered into a parlour where the landlady was sitting. He politely told her that he wished to purchase the pony he saw in the park, if the price could be agreed on ; but she appeared offended, and said that "the horse would not be sold, having been broke for her use." Her husband having come in, sent for her to another room, and asked her "if she knew the stranger, and what he wanted?" "Wants!" said she, "he wants to buy my pony, the impudent fellow!" "My good lady," replied her husband, "if he should want yourself, he must not be refused, for he is Rob Roy," and the landlord immediately went to him and agreed upon the price of the horse, which was instantly paid.

The lease of farms which Rob Roy had long occupied in Balquhidder having expired, he was induced, from that and various other considerations, to leave that country and settle on the lands of Brackley in Glenurchy, the proprietor of which, a relation of his own, and at that time

possessing indisputable claims to the chieftainship of clan Gregor, had deserted his estate in
consequence of some disgrace brought upon him
by the behaviour of his wife. Some time thereafter, however, he removed from that place to a
mountain farm belonging to the family of Argyll,
who continued to foster him with considerable
attention.

In this retreat he continued for several years,
still accompanied by his faithful adherents, who
paid frequent visits to the lands of Montrose
and Athol, from which they abundantly supplied
all their wants. But when Montrose understood
that Rob Roy had an asylum so immediately
under the protection of Argyll, he accused him,
in presence of the Privy Council, of harbouring
an outlaw, who ought to be given up to the
offended laws. Argyll did not deny the charge,
and excused himself by saying, " My lord, I only
supply Rob Roy with wood and water, the common privileges of the deer ; but you supply him
with beef and meal ; and withal, he is your factor, for he not long since took up your rents
at Chapellaroch." These facts could not be
denied ; and it is believed that after this period
Montrose relinquished all opposition to Rob
Roy, who also became less severe in his retalia-

M

tion on the estate and effects of that nobleman ;
indeed, he often declared that had Montrose
treated him with discretion and lenity, he never
would have disturbed him ; but that as matters
had turned out so prejudicial to his family,
though he ceased to annoy, he could not forgive
the injuries he had sustained.

Exulting at times in the recollection of some
of his achievements, our hero used to relate the
following incident as one of the most agreeable
occurrences of his life :—While he continued in
Argyllshire he frequently traversed that interesting country, exploring its most unfrequented
valleys and hidden recesses.   One evening in
autumn, as the declining sun had nearly sunk
beneath the Atlantic wave, and the parting tinge
played upon the towering pinnacles of the lofty
Ben-Cruachan, he was travelling alone through
the sequestered passes of Glenetive.   An unusual stillness reigned over the face of Nature,
and nothing seemed to ruffle the tranquillity
except the gentle murmuring of the tide, as it
played over the pebbled shore of the lake, which
increased the solemn placidity of the hour, and
touched the mind with a full conviction of the
inimitable grandeur of the scene that was now
presented to the contemplation of Rob Roy.

He felt, with enthusiastic delight, the sublimity of the objects before him, and sat down on the point of an elevated rock, that his soul might enjoy the perfect magnificence he beheld.

This arm of the sea stretches far to the north, surrounded by majestic mountains that rise, as it were, from the bosom of the water in immense cones, and form one of the most delightful views to be met with in the Highlands.

Our hero was particularly struck with the beauty of the scene, and continued to gaze on the prospect till the dim outline could scarcely be traced betwixt him and the horizon, and the sombre shades of the mountains, dying away from the sight, were no longer reflected from the surface of the water.

From this musing mood he was aroused by the sound of voices at a distance, and the shrieks of a female, which now and then broke on the silence of the night. It was now dark; and listening, he readily distinguished the direction whence it came, and immediately determined to follow it; but all was silent. He had not, however, proceeded far when he again heard, and hastened towards it, although this was attended with much difficulty and danger, for he had to scramble through hazle wood, over steep and rugged rocks, and to ford streams which held an impetuous course through deep ravines, forming eddying pools and foaming cataracts. But nothing was too arduous with him in the cause of humanity or justice, and he doubted not that the cries he heard were those of some helpless woman who required his aid.

After much exertion he came at length to an open field amidst the wood; but as the voices had ceased for some time, he was uncertain how to proceed, and lay down on the grass. The moon had by this time risen high over the mountains, and showed in bright illumination the tops of the trees around this grassy spot; but it could not penetrate the deep foliage of the woods, within which all was dark and impenetrable to the eye. Rob Roy had not long reclined when he observed two men emerge from the wood, but so distant that he could neither discern their features nor distinctly hear their conversation, although from their gesticulation he could perceive that they were much interested in it. He lay quiet among the long grass that grew around him, eagerly listening. As they approached he heard one of them say, " But what will her father think of our ingratitude ?" " Oh ! " said the

other, " I care not what he thinks, since his
daughter is under my control." " Yet you do
not mean to treat her ill," replied the former.
" She is too amiable to be harshly used."
" Peace!" said the other; "though you have
assisted, you are not to dictate to me." " My
right to insist on honourable means, Sir Knight,
is not inferior to yours, and I will maintain it,"
was the reply.    " Well, well," returned the
knight, "this is neither a time nor a place for
dispute; let us leave this desert and secure our
prize in a more hospitable region.  My trusty
spy has returned and assures me that, having
despaired of success, the laird of * * * * * has
given up all search after us, and we may safely
get away from these horrible wilds." Not so
safely, perhaps, thought our hero, who was now
satisfied that the cries he had heard were those
of a distressed female; and the unknown knight
and his companion having again darted into the
wood, Rob Roy immediately followed them,
determined to know more of this affair.

Though the thickness of the trees rendered
the passage rather difficult, Macgregor was
better acquainted with such places than those
he pursued, and he at first readily traced them,

but at such a distance as to prevent his being
seen.

Having followed them for some time, they
suddenly disappeared ; but supposing that they
were hid from him by the obscurity of the wood,
which now became more deep and impenetrable,
he proceeded.  Unable to discover them, he
went first one way, then another, stopped, listened, gazed; but all was silent.  Vexed that
he had not made up to them, he stood still, lean-
ing against an oak tree, to reason with himself on
the possibility of their being elves of the wood ;
an absurd notion of the times, of which he was
not wholly divested; as such supernatural beings
were supposed to inhabit gelid cavities of the
rocks, and gloomy retirements of the forests,
often alluring men to their destruction.  But he
was not long in suspense; the screams of a female
again dissipated his reflections, and he started
forward, to ascertain whence they came.

After some search, he reached a decayed
mansion, placed on a rocky eminence, partly
surrounded by a rapid stream, and wholly encompassed by stately trees.  The building, on
which the pale light of the moon shone partially
through the wood, appeared semi-castellated,
but unroofed and in ruin, with only one turret

retaining any of its original shape. The walls were in a state of rapid decay, and the whole seemed to have been long deserted by human inhabitants, and only now occupied by owls and ravens, who croaked around the falling battlements. Rob Roy surveyed this fortress, which, at a remote period, had been the residence of a feudal baron, with emotions of reverence for its antiquity, and regret for its hastening desolation.

While thus deploring the fate of the mansion, a mournful cry issued from the castle. He looked around, but could perceive no window nor opening in the walls, save those too high for access; and went on till he came to what had been the great gate, which was so obstructed with large fragments of the broken walls, as to prevent his approach. The voice, however, at times being still heard, he was convinced that it came from the ruins, and he went forward to discover some opening by which he could enter. Having walked partly round the rock on which the castle stood, he came to a thick bush of copsewood, growing close to the base of the rock, where the sounds were most loud. He examined the bush, and found that it concealed a vaulted passage, which appeared

to lead to the interior ; and he had no doubt that
it would also unravel the mystery of the sudden disappearance of the men he had followed,
as well as develop the meaning of their conversation which he had overheard.

With a full resolution to explore every part
of the pile, he unsheathed his dirk, and entered the vault with cautious steps.  He went
on a considerable way through this confined
and dreary entrance, till at last it seemed to
terminate in a large space, where he now heard
men in angry conversation.  The place was
dark and dismal ; but he was led by a faint
ray of light to a door, from which proceeded
many piteous sighs, that appeared to be those
of a person in distress.

He entered the apartment, and by the light
of a wood fire that blazed in a corner, he beheld a female figure lying on a parcel of dried
grass.—" Alas !" said the lady, as she turned
round to look at our hero,—" what am I now
doomed to suffer ?  Do you come, ruffian, to
finish my life with your dagger ?"  " No,
madam," said he, " I come to save your life,
if it is in jeopardy.  I heard your cries, and
came to relieve you.  Who are you, and what
brought you to this miserable place ?"—

"Say'st thou so, stranger!—Heaven bless thee!"—and raising herself upon her elbow to examine the person who thus accosted her, she shuddered at his appearance, and continued— "Ah, you deceive me!"—"No, young lady," replied he, "I have no deceit in me—I am Rob Roy Macgregor, and will rescue you ; but you must be brief—Who are you ?"—"I am," said she. "the daughter of the chief of * * * * * ; I have been decoyed, and forcibly carried away from my friends, by a base and cruel knight of ¡England."—"Well," said Rob Roy, "trust in me ; but stir not from this, till I return. I go to wait upon the knight." And sheathing his dirk, he left her.

The dispute he heard on his entrance still continued, and had now become more vociferous. He stole gently to the door whence the noise issued, and heard the two men in violent discourse.—"You treat me ill," said one. "No, Sir James," returned the other ; "I went to * * * * castle as your friend, and you have betrayed me into a scandalous act of discourtesy to a kind host, and inhumanity to his amiable daughter. Dare not to treat her indecorously, or we separate for ever." "So, Percy!" replied Sir James, "you will give up your friend, be-

cause he wishes to conquer the antipathies of a
Highland girl." "Your conquest would be disgraceful," said Percy, "as your attempts have
been mean and cowardly."

Our hero judging this a favourable moment,
stepped boldly into the hall, where those who
disputed, and other three men, were pacing
along the floor. They were all armed, but were
so much astonished at his unexpected appearance, and stern deportment, that they shrunk
back the instant he entered, believing him to be
a spectre who inhabited the doleful caverns of
the mansion : but they soon discovered that he
was formed of more substantial materials than
the fleeting vision of an aerial spirit, when he
thus addressed them—" What brawl is here, at
such an hour ? Who are you that disturb the
silence of this place ? Know you, that here
you have no right to revel, unless you are
demons of the midnight hour, who glory in its
darkness."

The singularity of this speech, so much in
character with the countenance and costume of
Rob Roy, and in unison with the melancholy
desolation of the place, produced a silence of
some seconds. At last Sir James, having recovered some degree of resolution, said, in a tre-

mulous voice, "Pray Sir, who are you, and what
brought you here? We have no money about
us. We are only benighted travellers, that do
nobody any harm." "None, perhaps, but the
chief of * * * * *," returned Rob Roy. "I am
no robber, Sir," continued he, "but you and your
companions must go back with me to the castle
of * * * * *, from which you came so hurriedly
away, that the chief did not bestow upon you
the usual Highland benison."

Sir James from this believed that Rob Roy
had been sent in pursuit of him, but seeing him
alone, he became more courageous, put his hand
to his sword, and said, "that he would comply
with no such order." They drew and fought;
but in a moment, Sir James lay wounded on
the floor. Percy stepped back, amazed at the
sudden discomfiture of the knight, who was
powerful and intrepid; but two of the other
men with great fury rushed upon Rob Roy, who
speedily killed them both.

Percy entreated that the life of Sir James
might not be taken. "No, generous young
man, it shall not," said Rob Roy, "I disdain a
cowardly action : but, if he survives, he shall
expiate his guilt in a more humiliating manner,
than to die by my sword. As for you, I have

heard your sentiments, and they shall not be unrequited."

Meantime, Sir James grew pale as death, for his wounds bled profusely; but Percy and the remaining servant having bound them up, he revived, and seemed heartily to repent the part he had acted.

Our hero having gone to the young lady, found her trembling with apprehension, and dreadfully alarmed at the noise she had heard. He, however, cheered her drooping spirits by saying, "Be not afraid, young lady, Sir James has paid for his basencss, and you shall immediately be escorted to your friends." The pleasing tidings were no sooner communicated, than instantly her lovely countenance beamed with joy, and a flood of tears gushed from her eyes, while she expressed her fervent thanks to her deliverer.

The morning was now far advanced, and Rob Roy having proposed to Percy to remain by the wounded knight, till he could procure a boat and men to transport them to the Castle of * * * * *, left the party for a little. Having soon obtained a boat, he returned to the ruin, and the party took leave of the gloomy recess which had concealed them for several days.

Sir James, unable to walk, was carried to the shore, and placed in the bow along with his servant, while the young lady, with Percy, and Rob Roy, who managed the helm, took their seats in the stern of the boat.

Sir James and Percy were young men of family from England, and both were visitors at the Castle of * * * * *, under particular recommendations to the chief. Both also had become enamoured of his daughter ; but their passions were not equally pure. One evening when walking along the shore, not far from her father's castle, the lady was persuaded to go along with them into a boat to enjoy the sea breeze. The servants of Sir James, previously instructed, managed the boat, and left the shore at a considerable distance. Night came on, and she, becoming alarmed, remonstrated against their remaining longer on the water, urged the distress which her absence must occasion, and entreated their instant return; whereupon Sir James declared his passion, and his intention of carrying her to his own country to make her happy. Percy, till now ignorant of his friend's design, argued against the impropriety of his conduct, but in vain : and it being impossible for him to employ any other means at that time, he was constrained to

silence, hoping that some fortunate incident
would occur, when he might rescue the young
lady.   From this consideration, and the love
which he himself had for her, he was induced
to continue along with her, to protect her from
insult : and Sir James, not aware of his feelings
or intention, frequently urged his assistance to
overcome the scruples of the lady, at which
proposal he constantly spurned.

Without any knowledge of the country, they
had wandered for some days from shore to
shore, until accident led them to the concealment, where our hero as accidentally discovered
them.

In returning to the Castle of * * * * *, the
voyage was protracted by numerous conflicting
tides, which render the navigation of the western
seas intricate and hazardous.   The young lady's
mind had suffered such agitation, that her spirits
were much depressed, and her frame greatly
enervated ; and she was terrified at the foaming
spray that dashed against the bounding prow
of the vessel; but Rob Roy soothed her fears
with assurances of safety.

As they proceeded, Sir James often requested
to be put on shore, as he dreaded to encounter
the vengeance of the injured chieftain ; but

though this was refused, our hero promised to intercede for him, and soften the anger of the insulted * * * * *.

The boat at last approached the destined harbour. It was descried from the lofty turrets of Castle * * * * *, long ere it reached the shore, and the whole inhabitants were assembled on the beach, anxious for its arrival. The joy of the chief of * * * * *, cannot be described, when he embraced his daughter, who nearly fainted in his arms. " There, * * * * *! " said Macgregor, " I restore your child at the peril of my own life. Let not your clan again say, that Rob Roy Macgregor is incapable of generosity to them, though they have often wronged him." " Noble, brave Macgregor! " replied the chief, shaking him by the hand, " you have done me a service never to be forgotten. Ere long you shall be a free man. My interest is great, and it shall be exerted to recall the decree that hangs over you." Approaching the boat, he observed Sir James and Percy, and instantly drew his sword, and ran towards them, exclaiming " Villains! "—but Rob Roy interposed, and said, " Stop, * * * * *! your hospitality has been abused, and your anger is just; but I have pledged my honour that the life of Sir

James shall be safe, and it must be so.  As for
Percy, he is your friend, and has been the
means of preserving your daughter's honour.
Treat him as such.  Take neither the life of Sir
James, nor further punish him, but do with him
else what you see fit."  The vassals of the chief,
who stood by, were with difficulty restrained
from plunging their dirks to the heart of Sir
James, who was conveyed to the dungeon keep
of the castle.

The return of the chief's daughter was celebrated by many days of festivity and mirth,
during which Rob Roy was distinguished by
every mark of attention and respect from * * *
and his clan ; and having received their hearty
acknowledgments, he set sail, and arrived in
safety at his own home.  Soon after, Percy was
married to the chief of * * * *'s daughter ; and
after a few weeks of salutary confinement, Sir
James was allowed to depart, and set off immediately for his own country.

Though our hero, during his residence in
Argyllshire, was in some degree secure from his
enemies, he was nevertheless in a situation that
precluded him from other advantages which he
considered of importance to his family : and the
chief of * * * * having kept his promise, Rob

Roy received a letter from him, containing a remission of the outlawry that had been proclaimed against him, so that he was now at liberty to go where he pleased, without any personal danger. He consequently relinquished his possessions in Argyll, and returned to Balquhidder, the soil of his nativity; but he continued occasionally to revisit that country, as he had many friends, and several relations there, who shewed him all manner of kindness and attention.

On one of these occasions, about the year 1713, while at the house of a powerful chieftain of that country, nearly related to himself, he was introduced to two French gentlemen who had arrived on the west coast, as emissaries from the house of Stewart : and being well acquainted with the state of the Highland districts, and those among them who were favourable to that family, he was requested to accompany them among the northern clans, that measures might be concerted for the restoration of the Stewarts.

Considering that family as his legitimate sovereigns, he did not hesitate to conduct their friends to Lochaber, and provide them with guides to escort them through the most unfrequented and devious paths to the Isle of Skye, where they had despatches for the chiefs of

N

Macdonald and Macleod. Rob Roy's intercourse, however, with those foreigners, was made
known to the officers of state at Edinburgh, and
he was summoned to appear before them.   He
accordingly went there, and waited upon the
commander in chief for Scotland, who acquainted
him of the accusation brought against him ; but
he denied that he was guilty of any breach of
loyalty to his king, and defied his lordship to
produce evidence to that effect.   The examina-
tion of our hero was postponed till the following
day, and this officer took his word of honour
that he would attend at the appointed hour.

Meantime Rob Roy understood that Macdonald of Dalness was the evidence to be adduced against him.   This Dalness was a hireling
of government, employed to give information of
disaffected persons in the Highlands ; but Macgregor devised a stratagem to get rid of him,
being unwilling so soon again to come under the
cognizance of the law.

One of the officers of the town guard, being a
particular friend of Rob Roy's, he immediately
waited upon him, and after the usual salutation,
asked him if he would give him a sergeant
and twelve men for a couple of hours that
evening ; at the same time assuring him that he

would not employ them in any act of violence, as he merely wished to frighten a man who had done him an injury. His friend, the officer, knowing how rigidly he adhered to his word, agreed to let him have the soldiers.

Having secured the aid of the townguards-men, he went by himself to Dalness' lodgings in the evening, to avoid discovery, and having seen the landlady, said to her in the dialect of her "guid toon :"—"Guidwife, I'm a Highlan'man, a near frien' o' your lodger's, and gif he's no i' the house, ye maun tell him whan. he comes hame, to tak' tent an' keep out o' the gate, for the toun guard's stacherin' about seeken for him to wind him a pirn, and transport him ower the sea, or maybe to hang him. The mis-lear'd chiels will hae nae mercy on him, gin he be grippet. Now mind, an' dinna forget to tell him o' his danger." The woman was amazed, and trembled at the idea "o' sodgers rypen her house," and said—"But wha'll I say was speerin' for the laird ?" "Just tell him," —replied Rob Roy, "it was a Highlan' cousin o' his ain, a black-a-vic'd man, an' he'll ken by that ;" and took his leave. At the time men-tioned, the guard appeared at his lodging, and Dalness, conscious in all likelihood that his conduct was not correct towards the government he seemed to serve, instantly escaped by a back door, and made the best of his way to the wilds of his own property; when our hero, satisfied that Dalness had taken flight, dismissed the soldiers as he had promised.

On the following day, he was punctual to his appointment with the commander in chief. The witness Dalness was not to be found, and no other evidence being produced, Macgregor boldly demanded his passport, which being granted, he took his departure, not, however, without throwing out some reflections on the credulity of government, for the unnecessary trouble given to honest men like him, while the informers were themselves more guilty. Dalness, however, was the sufferer, for he was disgraced, and his allowance from government withdrawn, while Rob Roy returned home in triumph, exulting in the success of his scheme.

For a considerable period after the Reformation, the establishment of Presbyterian clergy was very difficult and precarious, particularly in the Highland districts, where the Romish persuasion long struggled for predominance.

The caprice or mistaken zeal of the parishioners often resisted their settlement, and after they were fairly admitted to their charge, their stipends were ill paid, it being customary for the lairds to fix the payment of them on their tenantry, who were also made liable for any augmentation of stipend the incumbent might afterwards obtain. Soon after our hero's return from Argyll, a Mr Ferguson was appointed minister of the parish of Balquhidder ; but his introduction was opposed by the whole body of the people, and he would not be admitted until he promised not to apply for an increase of salary. Finding, however, that he could not live on so small a sum, he was necessitated to take the usual legal steps for procuring an addition ; but Rob Roy put a speedy termination to the business. He got hold of the minister, forced him into a public-house near his own church, made him drink profusely of whisky, told him he was not a man of his word, and caused him sign a paper renouncing every future claim of augmentation ; but he gave at the same time his own obligation, binding himself to send the minister every year half a score of sheep and a fat cow, which, during his life, was regularly done.

Though Rob Roy was conscious how little the personal virtues of the Stewart family entitled them to support, he yet considered their right to the crown as hereditary, and consequently indefeasible ; and from this conviction he resolved that his exertions should be directed to their cause. When the clans, therefore, began to arm in favour of that house in 1715, he also prepared the clan Gregor for the contest, in concert with his nephew, Gregor Macgregor of Glengyle.

A large body of Macgregors were about this time collected, and became very formidable. They marched into Monteith and Lennox, and disarmed all those whom they considered of opposite principles.

Having secured all the boats on Loch Lomond, they took possession of an island in it, whence they sent parties over the neighbouring countries to levy contributions, and extort such penalties as they judged proper. But more serious apprehensions were entertained of their disposition for mischief. Their depredations were so much dreaded at Dumbarton that the inhabitants, alarmed on account of their approach, removed their most valuable effects, while reports were circulated that Rob Roy's men intended to descend in the night, murder the military, and set fire to the town.

The ferment which this occasioned was exces-
sive, and the friends of government determined to
act on the offensive, and by speedy measures to
overawe the children of the misty Ben-Lomond.
Several armed boats from the men-of-war in the
Clyde made their way into Loch Lomond, and
considerable numbers of militia, lairds and their
tenants, assembled and united in a mass.  This
multitude secured the boats belonging to the
Macgregors, who, being dislodged from the
islands of the lake, joined a camp of Highlanders from other quarters in Strathfillan ; but
not till after many struggles with the king's
troops, different detachments of which they
defeated.

The progress of the Earl of Mar, with his army
of disaffected Highlanders, greatly alarmed the
government, and immediate orders were transmitted to Edinburgh, to secure such suspected
persons as were thought inimical to the king,
among others, Rob Roy Macgregor being
specially named.  He, however, conducted himself with some caution on this occasion, and
waited to observe the complexion of matters
before he should proceed farther, as his friend
Argyll had espoused the part of King George,
a circumstance which greatly distressed him.  In

a state of considerable indecision he proceeded
to the Lowlands, and hovered about both armies
prior to the battle of Sheriffmuir, without making any declaration or offer to join either ; and
during that event remained entirely inactive.
This unexpected conduct arose from two motives equally powerful,—a wish not to offend his
patron, the Duke of Argyll, should he join the
Earl of Mar, and that he might not act contrary to his conscience by joining Argyll against
his expatriated king.

His enemies, at all times anxious to place the
motives of Rob Roy's conduct in the worst
point of view, had propagated a report that the
Duke of Argyll, knowing that his principles led
him to espouse the cause of the opposite party,
had bribed him with the small sum of eighty
guineas not to join the Earl of Mar ; but it is probable that to an independent mind like his, acting on the basis of conscious rectitude, the offer
of a bribe would have been regarded as a marked
insult ; and the duke was too well acquainted
with his temper to try such an experiment.
The motives, therefore, assigned for his inaction
at Sheriffmuir appear to be those which he himself afterwards declared, and which seem to
be the most consistent with the situation in

which he stood. It has likewise been remarked by different authors, that had he joined either party in this contest, it would have terminated decisively.

There cannot, generally speaking, be a more genuine chronicle of events than local ballads, which depict particular incidents of the times in which they were written ; and there is, perhaps, not a more correct account of the affair in question than the first stanzas of two songs on that subject.

> " There's some say that we wan,
>     Some say that they wan,
> Some say that nane wan at a', man !
>     But one thing I'm sure,
>     That at Sheriffmuir,
> A battle there was which I saw, man ;
>     And we ran, and they ran, and they ran,
>         and we ran, and we ran, and they ran awa', man. "

> " —— was you at the Sheriffmuir,
>     And did the battle see, man ?
> Pray tell whilk of the parties won ?
> For weel I wat I saw them run,
> Both south and north, when they begun
>     To pell and mell, and snill and fell,
>     With muskets snell, and pistols knell,
>     And some to hell--did flee, man.

> " But Scotland has not much to say,
>     For such a sight as this is,
> Where baith did fight, baith run away,
>     The devil take the miss is.

That every officer was not slain,
That run that day, and was not ta'en,
Either flying from or to Dumblain ;
      When Whig and Tory, in their fury,
      Strove for glory, to our sorrow
      The sad story—Hush is."

If the small force our hero had with him could have turned the fortunes of either side on that day, it is but a sorry account of the opposing armies ; but those historians who say so, allow him more merit than was usually conceded to him, on that or any other occasion.

Though the undecided issue of this trial eventually brought about the dispersion of the Highland army, the Macgregors continued together; but unwilling to return home without some substantial display of conquest, they marched to Falkland, and garrisoned the ancient palace of that place, where without much ceremony they exacted rigorous fines from the king's friends. Rob Roy considered this a venial offence, by no means so odious as if he had fought either against Argyll or Mar; and at that place he and his men remained till Argyll arrived at Perth, when they retired to their own country with the spoils they had acquired ; but they continued in arms for several years thereafter, in the pursuit of their usual

compulsory habits, to the no small disturbance
of their neighbours.

Those daring practices seem to have been
the reason why, in the subsequent indemnity,
or free pardon, the Macgregors were excluded
from mercy in these words :—"Excepting all
persons of the name and clan of Macgregor
mentioned in an act of parliament made in
Scotland in the first of the late King Charles I.
intituled, anent the clan Macgregor, whatever
name he or they may have, or do assume, or
commonly pass under ; " and consequently our
hero's name appeared attainted, as "Robert
Campbell, *alias* Macgregor, *commonly* called
Robert Roy."

The severities which followed this unquiet
period were peculiarly afflicting to Rob Roy.
Reduced in his finances, and unable to pursue
his usual occupation, his comforts were few, and
he was forced to leave his farm and retire to a
wild and distant part of the Highlands. But
there, although he lived in obscurity, in a mean
and solitary cottage, half hid with copsewood,
and situated under the brow of a rugged and
barren mountain, he was not permitted to live
in peace.

While he occupied this sequestered abode,

he was sitting early one morning by the side
of the path which formed the chief road of the
district, when an officer with thirty men suddenly appeared, making towards him. He was
surprised at seeing military in such a place,
and though he suspected their errand, did not
consider it safe to make his escape. He therefore remained where he was till they came up
to him, when the officer saluted him with—
" Good morning."—" Good morning to you, Sir,
you are early on the road," replied Rob Roy.
" Yes we are," said the officer, " we have marched
all night, and are fatigued in this unhallowed
country of yours."—" The country is indeed
rough for gentlemen to travel in by night,"
replied our hero; "your business must be
pressing."

From the tenor of their conversation the
officer found he was sagacious and intelligent;
and having asked him several questions, said—
" Pray can you inform me where a noted
brigand, a fellow called Rob Roy Macgregor or
Campbell, is to be found hereabouts? I would
give fifty guineas to lay hold of him." " I know
him well," returned Rob Roy, "and for the
money you offer, I shall produce him to you:
But if you take my advice, do not go nearer his

house, which is only a short way off, otherwise
it is a chance if any of you will ever return, for
his lads are numerous, and always so placed in
ambush round his dwelling, that you will all be
shot without seeing a man. He must be in-
veigled by stratagem, and if you follow my
directions, I shall give you him by the hand in
a short time, without firing a shot."—" But how
is that to be accomplished ?" said the officer.
"Only in one way," replied our hero, "you
passed a public house not far distant, return to
it, and wait for me. I shall go to the fellow's
house, and tell him such a story as will bring
him alone to the inn : but great caution must
be used, for he is one of the most fierce and
cunning men in the world, whom in his rage I
would not face with all your men by my side."

The soldiers listened, and seemed happy
when they were ordered to wheel about for the
inn, where they soon arrived, while Rob Roy
proceeded to his own house.

He directed his men to assemble all the
people within reach, and place them on the side
of the hill in battle array ; and having buckled
on his dirk, which he concealed under his plaid,
he walked on to fulfil his engagement. He now
told the officer that he had seen Rob Roy, who

promised to be with him immediately; but
that it would be necessary to conceal his
soldiers and their firelocks ; for if Rob Roy
should see any of them, he would not come near
the house. The muskets were accordingly de-
posited in a press bed, while the men were put
in an out-house.

Our hero endeavoured to amuse the officer by
his conversation, to give his people time to collect ; but growing impatient, Rob Roy assured
him he should not be disappointed ; and the
moment he observed his men at their station,
he said to him,—" Now, Sir, give me the sum
you promised."—" I cannot do that, till you
make good your promise," rejoined the officer.
" It will then be too late," was the reply,—" for
Rob Roy will see that he is betrayed, and I
would never after be able to hold up my head
in the country ; the people would set fire to my
house, and take away my cattle: and if I do
not, as I said, give you Rob Roy by the hand,
you and your men are surely able enough to
take back the money from me." The officer
acquiesced in the justice of his remarks, and
paid down the money, which having counted
and put into his pocket, he shook hands with
the officer, saying, " Now, Sir, I keep my

word, you have Rob Roy by the hand, detain
him if you can ; " and bidding him good day,
was instantly out of the house. The officer was
so much astonished, that he stood motionless
for some time, so that before he got out to order
his men to arms, Rob Roy was far beyond their
reach.

Whether Rob Roy had ever paid respect to
religious duties, or what might have been the
extent of his creed during the more prosperous
part of his life, is not certain, though he was by
birth a protestant. Whether affected by remorse
for his past irregular life, or because he had
seriously come to the persuasion that he might
obtain forgiveness for all his errors through the
interposition of catholic priests, from their
declared power of absolving from all species of
sin, has not been transmitted to us, but he
had taken the resolution of becoming a Roman
Catholic, and he accordingly left the lonely
residence we have described, and returning to
Perthshire, went to a Mr Alexander Drummond,
an old priest of that faith, who resided at Drummond Castle. What the nature of Rob's confessions were, or the penance which his offences
required, has been concealed ; but if we may
judge from the account he himself gave of his

interview with this ecclesiastic,—"that the old man frequently groaned, crossed himself, and exacted a heavy remuneration,"—his crimes must have been of a sable dye, and of difficult expiation :— "It was a convenient religion, however," he used to say, "which for a little money could put asleep the conscience, and clear the soul from sin."

But whatever amendment this apostacy from the tenets of his fathers might have effected in our hero's principles of morality, which, it is believed, were previously loose and unsettled, certain it is, that the restless and active temper of his mind did not long allow him to remain a quiet votary of his new faith ; and a desperate foray into the northern Highlands having been projected by his nephew, he was requested to take the command. Tired of inactive life, to which he had never been accustomed, and willing to do anything to retrieve his decayed circumstances, he readily consented, and set out at the head of twenty men. It has been affirmed upon good authority, that these Macgregors, with other Highlanders, joined some Spaniards who landed on the north-west coast in 1719, and were with them at the battle of Glenshiel ; and that Rob Roy and his party plundered a Spanish

ship, after it had been in possession of the
English, which so enriched him, that he again
returned to the braes of Balquhidder, and began
farming.

While engaged in the cattle trade, Rob Roy
had purchased a cow from a widow on Tay side,
and on the following Sunday chanced to be at
Logierait, as the clergyman was preaching to
his congregation in the churchyard.  He stepped
in to hear the discourse, the subject of which
was a caution against fraud and roguery.  The
preacher expatiated largely on their intricate
ramification ; and in the course of his remarks,
threw out many hints, evidently meant for our
hero, who was observed by the minister, and was
well known to all his hearers.

When the sermon was over, Rob Roy waited
upon the clergyman, and told him that " he
understood his discourse, but wished to know
what he meant, and would be glad if he could
point out any instance of his fraud or roguery.
For observe, reverend Sir," continued he, " that if
you cannot do this, and have abused me before
your parishioners, and me innocent, I shall make
you recant your words in your own pulpit."
" Macgregor," said the minister, " I will own
that I alluded to you.  Did you not buy a cow

O

from a widow in this parish, at little more than half its value ? She is a poor woman, and cannot afford this." " I was ignorant of her being so poor," answered Rob Roy; " she appeared glad to get the price." " True," replied the minister, " for her family are starving." " If that be the case," returned our hero, " she is welcome to keep the money I paid, and she shall also get back her cow," which she actually did next day; and on the following Sunday, the minister mentioned this act of charity from the pulpit, as worthy the imitation of the " hard-hearted gentry of his parish," as he termed them.

In his trade of dealing in cattle, Rob Roy often had occasion to travel to different parts of the Lowlands, and his last visit to Edinburgh was to recover a debt due him by a person who was reputed opulent, but who had taken refuge in the sanctuary of the Abbey. There he went and saw his debtor, but the sacredness of the place did not protect him ; for although he was a strong man, Rob Roy laid hold of him, dragged him across the line of safety, and having some officers of the law in waiting, gave over his charge to them, by which means he got his money.

The numerous exploits of Rob Roy had rendered him so remarkable, that his name became
familiar everywhere ; and he was frequently the
subject of conversation among the nobility at
court. He was there spoken of as the acknowledged protegè of Argyll, who often endeavoured to palliate his errors ; but that nobleman
was frequently rallied, particularly by the king,
for his partiality to Macgregor. On several
occasions his majesty had expressed a desire to
see the hardy mountaineer : and Argyll, willing
to gratify him, sent for Rob Roy, but concealed
his being in London, lest the officers of state,
aware of the king's hatred, might take measures to detain him. Argyll, however, took care
that the king should see him without knowing
who he was, and for this purpose made Rob
Roy walk for some time in front of St James'.
His majesty observed, and remarked that he
had never seen a finer looking man in a Highland dress, and Argyll having soon after waited
on the king, his majesty told him of his having noticed a handsome Scots Highlander,
when Argyll replied, that it was Rob Roy
Macgregor. His majesty said he was disappointed that he did not know it sooner, and
appeared not to relish the information, con-

sidering it as too serious a jest to be played
upon his authority, and one which seemed to
make him, among others, a dupe to our hero's
impudence.

Montrose did not yet hold the lands he had
wrested from Rob Roy by the strict formality
of law, but by that coercion which the same
authority put into his hands; nor had any
arrangement of their accounts hitherto taken
place. While Rob Roy was in London, Argyll
judged it a proper opportunity to bring about
a reconciliation. He therefore made such a proposal to Montrose, who at first objected to it,
as he dreaded personal injury from Macgregor;
but Argyll pledging himself for our hero, a
meeting took place. It was a singular one,
for they had not seen each other for years;
but mutual promises of forbearance were ex-
changed, and Rob Roy having got an account
of the money he owed Montrose, also received
an assurance that he should have possession
of his estate, as soon as the sum for which it
had been adjudged was repaid; but this arrangement never took place, and it was not until
twenty years after our hero's death, that the
family of Montrose were regularly vested in the
property of Craigcrostan.

Though Rob Roy was now considerably advanced in life, he yet bore an imposing and youthful appearance. On his way from London at this time, he was accidentally introduced into the company of some officers who were recruiting at Carlisle. Struck with his robust and manly stature, they considered him a fit person for the king's service, and wished to enlist him ; but he would accept no less than treble the sum they offered, to which they agreed. He then remained in the town a few days, paying no regard to them, and when he was ready to continue his journey came away, the military being unable to prevent him ; and the enlisting money paid his expenses home.

While in England, Lennox, the proprietor of Woodhead, in the vicinity of Campsie, having refused to pay his dues of black-mail, Roy Roy's wife equipped herself, went on horseback attended by twelve men, and so intimidated the gentleman that he paid the stipulated sum, saying that he could not refuse a lady, and would not attempt to oppose her.

The achievements of Rob Roy, so universally known, were everywhere extolled as the matchless deeds of unconquered Caledonia ; and though his prowess could not be said at all times to have been displayed upon occasions strictly meritorious, yet the general tenor of his conduct was admired in his own country, as it accorded with an ancient *Gaelic* saying already noticed, which marked the well-known character of the Highlander, that *he would not turn his back on a friend nor an enemy.* He neither boasted of his strength nor his courage, and did not look on his past exploits with the pride of a victor, but with the honest exultation of having supported the valour of his clan, and opposed the devouring tide of oppression. Steady in these principles, he never wantonly engaged in a quarrel ; and from a consciousness of his own powers, he was unwilling to adopt personal contention ; yet he was often challenged to single combat, and actually fought twenty-two battles of this description.

Macneill of Barra, who was considered an excellent swordsman, and possessed at the same time a chivalrous and romantic spirit, that would have done honour to the age of the crusades, having often heard of Rob Roy's renown as unequalled in the use of the broad-sword, was determined to ascertain the truth of the report. He arrived at Buchanan, and learned that Rob Roy had gone to a market at Killearn,

Thither he proceeded, and, when near the place, met several gentlemen on horseback returning from the market. Barra accosted them, and asked "if they knew whether Rob Roy Macgregor was at the market?" and was answered, "He is here; what do you want with him?" "I want to see him," was the reply. The gentlemen who were along with our hero immediately stopped, from motives of curiosity, while he went up to Barra, and said he was Rob Roy. "Macgregor," said Barra, "I never saw you before; but I have heard of you. I am the laird of Barra, and have come here to prove myself a better swordsman than you." The gentlemen, who looked on, were surprised at such an errand, and many of them burst into laughter. "Laird of Barra," replied Rob Roy, "I have no doubt of your being what you assert; but I have no wish to prove it, as I never fought any man without cause." "Then you are afraid," said Barra. "Your valour is in words." Our hero, irritated at the expression, said, "Dismount then, Sir, and you shall have more than words;" and giving his horse to one of his friends, drew his claymore, and continued, "as you are a stranger, you shall not go without your errand." They immediately set to, but Rob Roy soon gave his antagonist cause to repent his timerity, nearly cutting off his sword arm, which confined him in the village of Killearn for three months.

Rob Roy was never known to have refused a challenge, excepting upon one occasion, from a countryman named Donald Bain, because, he said, he never fought duels but with gentlemen.

The power which Macgregor possessed in his arms was very uncommon, and gave him a decided superiority over most men in the use of the broad-sword. It was scarcely possible to wrench anything out of his hands, and he had been known to seize a deer by the horns and hold him fast. His arms were long, almost to deformity, as when he stood erect he could touch the garters under his knee with his fingers ; and some of his neighbours might indeed say that he had long arms, but they often gave him cause for stretching them.

Being now far advanced in years, he began to feel his vigour decline apace, but his spirit remained unbroken. Having met with the laird of Boquhan on some merry occasion, they sat up a whole night drinking in a paltry inn at Arnprior, in Perthshire ; but towards morning they quarrelled, the influence of the indigenous beve- rage of their country having overpowered their reason. Boquhan had no sword with him, but he found an old rapier in .a corner, and they fought. Macgregor, from age and considerable inebriety, was then unfit for the combat, and, dropping his sword, they made up the differ- ence, and continued drinking together during the following day. On a future trial with Stewart of Ardsheal, he was also worsted, when he threw down his sword, and vowed that he would never take it up again, for by this time his sight was greatly impaired, his strength had suffered from the decrepitude of old age, and he felt the gradual decay of his faculties. Some characteristic lineaments, however, continued to illumine his spirit, even to the latest hour.

When nearly exhausted, worn out by the laborious vicissitudes of a restless life, and con- fined to bed in a state of approaching dissolu- tion, a person with whom in former times he had had a disagreement, called upon him, and wished to see him. " Raise me up," said he to his attendants ; "dress me in my best clothes ; tie on my arms; place me in the great chair. That fellow shall never see me on a death-bed." With this they complied, and he received his visitor with cold civility. When the stranger had taken his leave, Rob Roy exclaimed, " It is all over now; put me to bed. Call in the piper. Let him play '*Cha teill mi tuille*' * as long as I breathe." He was faithfully obeyed, and calmly met his death, which took place at the farm of Inverlochlarigbeg, among the braes of Balquhidder, in 1735. His relics repose in the churchyard of that parish, with no other escutcheon to mark his grave than a simple stone, on which some kindred spirit has carved a sword, the appropriate emblem of the man:—

" Clan Alpine's omen and her aid." †

In surveying the character of Rob Roy Macgregor, many excellent traits appear, from which we cannot withhold our admiration, while other incidents of his life, perhaps, may deserve reprehension ; but if it be considered that he lived during a period when the northern parts of the kingdom were torn by civil discord and distracted politics, and when the government had neither wisdom nor energy to remedy those evils that arose from feudal manners and

* I will never return.

† The funeral of Rob Roy was attended by all ranks of people within several miles of his residence ; and so much was he beloved, that universal regret seemed to pervade the whole company. An old man whom we have seen, although then young, attended the solemn occasion, and was present some time before when Rob Roy fought Ardsheal.

the discordant interests of chieftainship, we cannot be surprised at the liberties he took, and
the deeds he performed.

Rob Roy was among the last remains of the
genuine Highlanders of the old stock, who
wished to support the ancient privileges and
independence of the race. His clan had suffered great cruelties, which were attributed,
with much truth, to their envious neighbours :
and when we consider the measures directed
against Rob Roy as an individual, we cease to
wonder at the opposition he gave to the families
of Montrose and Athol. Although in his partial warfare he may not always have acted in
conformity to nice principles of justice, yet it
may be said that the greater number of his
errors were venial, and such as in his time
must have appeared no more than the fair
and justifiable retaliation for injuries which he
himself, or others connected with him, had sustained.

Of his being a free-booter, and heading a
band of desperate banditti, there is no proof.
He was never known wantonly to have made
an unprovoked attack, or to have broken a
promise he had given. He was generous and
humane to all who suffered from disease or

poverty ; and he cannot be denied the meed of respect for his bravery, which never was exerted against the unfortunate.

Rob Roy left several children; but our limits will only admit a short notice of those who became obnoxious to the state, and whose destiny was considered peculiarly severe. Though they had, in the life of their father, too forcible an example of misguided abilities, and pursued a course of outrageous practices, yet we must deplore their fate as melancholy instances of that feeble and apparently partial justice which marked the party principles of those times, and led the elder to die in want in a foreign land, and the younger to close his life on the scaffold.

For some time prior to the death of their father, the elder sons had not only pursued the same compulsory levying of black-mail, but were also accused of serious and terrible acts of violence on the properties of the lieges. The more perfectly to secure their rapine, and conduct their schemes of mischief, they associated themselves with a band of daring outlaws, and took possession of an old peninsulated castle at the eastern extremity of the lake of Balquhidder, as a place of resort. But though the sons of Rob

Roy were to be sharers of the booty collected by these banditti, they did not always accompany them on their excursions for depredation. They had a leader, Walter Buchanan of Machar, who had wholly abandoned himself to a dissolute life, and commanded the gang, chiefly composed of lawless ruffians from distant parts.

These plunderers were a source of great terror to the neighbourhood, and frequently to travellers who fell in their way, although they committed no personal cruelties on those who quietly submitted. The ruins they occupied were not far from the road, and had often, by the hospitality of those men, sheltered the traveller, when benighted or overtaken by the violent storms that suddenly visit those mountainous regions ; and on such an occasion did the unfortunate Lady Grange and her escort find refuge there, when on her way to be confined in the distant isle of St Kilda.*

By the death of their father, which happened soon after they had betaken themselves to those disorderly courses, they were deprived of that sage and prudent counsel which used to keep them free from many difficulties in which

* See the subsequent notices of that lady.

they were afterwards involved; but an incident occurred that speedily subjected them to the scrutiny of the law. A James Maclaren, the nephew of Rob Roy's wife, who appears to have been a person devoid of feeling, considering his aunt as a destitute and unprotected widow, purposed to turn her out of the farm she possessed, by offering a greater rent, but her youngest son Robert, then a boy little more than twelve years of age, feeling the injury intended to be done to his mother, and perhaps instigated to revenge by his relations, fired at Maclaren while he was holding his plough, and killed him. The boy immediately fled, and was conducted to the continent, where he remained till the commotions of 1745 and 6 brought him back to Scotland. Two of his brothers, James and Ronald, were tried at Perth as accessories to the murder of Maclaren; but though acquitted by the jury, the court, by a stretch of arbitrary power, obliged them to find bail for £200 each, to keep the peace for seven years, which they did. They afterwards sustained trials for theft and reset of theft, but no proof could be produced, so that the proceedings against them could only originate in malice and oppression.

After the return of young Robert in 1746, he joined the regiment of the last Duke of Argyll, then General John Campbell, to serve King George, and remained in the country unmolested for many years ; but from the rancorous spirit with which the Macgregors were still regarded, he was arraigned for the forcible abduction of a young widow, who had become his wife ; and although she had always declared that she was happy with him, and that they had lived in peace together, he was taken at a market in his own country by a party of soldiers from Inversnaid, carried to Edinburgh, and there condemned, and executed in February 1754, three years after the death of his wife.

His brother, James Macgregor, who occasionally took the name of James Drummond, was implicated for the part he was supposed to have taken in the enterprise, and it drew down upon him also the strong arm of the law : he was taken up and put in confinement in the castle of Edinburgh. Previous to this affair, James evinced the military ardour of his clan, and along with his cousin, Macgregor of Glengyle, in 1745, took the fort of Inversnaid, and made eighty-nine prisoners, with only twelve men.

He then joined Prince Charles Stewart as
major, at the head of six companies of Macgregors, in the fruitless contest which that
young man had instituted for the recovery of
the British throne.   He had his thigh bone
broken in the battle of Prestonpans ; and
though, from this accident, he could not accompany the prince on his ill-concerted march into
England, he again joined him in the concluding battle of Culloden, and with many more of
his partisans came under the consequent act of
attainder, which spared neither rich nor poor,
young nor old, and covered the country with a
dreadful visitation of fire and sword, in base
violation of those claims of humanity that are .
the sacred rights of the conquered.

While James Macgregor was a prisoner in
Edinburgh Castle, he received an indictment to
stand his trial ; and from a memorial in his own
hand-writing, addressed to Prince Charles Stewart (faithfully copied in a subsequent page), we
learn that his doom was almost certain.

The address of his daughter in effecting his
escape was admirable.   Having previously concerted her plan, she, on the evening of 16th
November 1752, went to his prison, in the dress
and character of a cobbler, carrying in her hand

a pair of mended shoes. Her father immediately put on the disguise, and having held
some angry conversation with the supposed
cobbler, for making an overcharge, so as to deceive the sentinel, he hastily passed him undis-
covered, and got clear of the outer gate. A
cloudy evening favoured his retreat, and taking
the nearest way of leaving the city, by the West
Port, he was beyond the reach of detection before his escape was known ; but the moment it
was observed, the alarm was given, and all the
gates of the city were shut.

After the first sensations which impelled his
flight had subsided, he felt an almost irresistible
inclination to direct his steps to his own country; but as he supposed that he might there be
pursued, he relinquished the wish to see his
family, tender and pressing as it was, and took
his way towards England. On his route he
avoided passing through any town during the
day, and assumed different disguises as circumstances required.

After a fatiguing journey, at the close of the
fourth day, he was benighted on a lonely moor
in Cumberland. Ignorant of the country, he
did not know how to proceed, but kept a straight
course, though the darkness of the night and

P

the rugged surface of the ground much retarded his progress, until having travelled some miles, he quitted the moor, and entered a wood, when its deep shade, added to the blackness of the night, rendered it impossible for him to go farther. He therefore sat down at the root of a tree, determined to remain till morning, but was not long there till he was roused by the sound of voices at no great distance, hallooing in wild tones. He sprang to his feet, cocked a pistol, for his friends had supplied him with a pair of them and a dirk before he left his confinement, and stood for some time in this posture, in anxious expectation and considerable apprehension, fully resolved to die rather than again be taken, conceiving it more honourable to fall in defence of his liberty than by the hands of an executioner. The voices became more faint, but he still heard them talking violently, and a ray of light gleaming among the trees pointed out the direction whence the sound came.

Wishing to ascertain who those nightly revellers were, he stole cautiously to the place, and saw an old woman holding a light to three men who were placing panniers on a horse's back, with which one of them rode off, while the others went into a hut close by. Macgregor at first took them for banditti, but in one of the men whom he saw, he thought he recognised the figure and countenance of old Billy Marshall, the tinker, whom he had often seen in the Highlands. Encouraged by this idea, he ventured forward to the hut and knocked at the door, convinced that if Billy was actually there, he would not only be safe, but effectually sheltered and assisted in his escape. He was not mistaken, for Billy came to the door; and though Macgregor was still in the poor disguise his daughter had provided for him, he knew and welcomed him to the hut. He had heard of Macgregor's mishap, but rejoiced that he had now given his enemies the slip, and apologised for the poverty of his present habitation, which he said was only temporary, until some ill-will which he had got in Galloway for setting fire to a stack-yard would blow over. In this hovel, secure in the honour of his host, was Macgregor sumptuously entertained for two days. Early in the morning of the third, he and Billy set out on horseback, and before the tinker took leave of him, he saw him embark in a fisherman's boat near Whitehaven, with a fair wind, for the Isle of Man. Thence he went to Ireland, but no traces of him are to be had until his arrival in France, when we again hear of him by the following application to Prince Charles Stewart, formerly referred to.

" PARIS, 20*th Sept.* 1753.

"SIR,—The violence of your Royal Highness Enemies has at last got the better of the resolution I had taken after the unhappy battle of Culloden, never to leave the Country, but stay at home, and be as useful to your cause as I possibly could. Even after they had got me into their hands I continued firm in this resolution, they having no new Treason as they name it to prove. Your Royal Highness friends ordered my Escaping from prison to shun certain Death. This the Advocate made no ceremony to own he had orders from Court to bring about at whatever rate or by whatever means. And the method he took of indicting me upon obsolete Acts of Parliament, and making up a jurie of the most envenomed Hanoverian Scots made my fate certain, if I had not saved myself by escaping. I was even unwilling to come abroad to be troublesome either to your Royal Highness or your friends, but necessity now obliges me to beg your directions how or to whom to apply, I having try'd every way I could think of or was advised, without as yet having any hopes of success. This is not the only reason now of giving your Royal Highness this trouble, the route I took to get home by the Isle of Man and the coast of Ireland put it in my way to learn what must be of the greatest consequence to the Cause upon a proper occasion, but is put out of my power to be communicated save to your Royal Highness, the King your Father, and my Chief Balhadies, who wishes he had a method of informing your Royal Highness of what must be of so much use to your cause. I have in vain hitherto endeavoured to find out the means of laying myself at your

Royal Highness feet, which necessitates my now writing his, and that your Royal Highness may be in no mistake about me, I am James Drummond Macgregor, Rob Roy Macgregor's son who joyned no corps with his men t the battle of Prestonpans, and had his Thighbone broke n the Action, which incapacitated me from following you into England, but upon your return joined the Army with Six Companeys of Macgregors which the Duke of Perth engaged me to add to his Regiment untill my Chief Balhadies arrived from France, where I continued to serve as Major to the unhappy Culloden. I ever am with the greatest Respect Sir Your Royal Highness most humble and faithful Servant.

" JAS DRUMMOND MACGREGOR."

About the same time he also addressed a memoire, "A Monseigneur le Marquis de Saint Contin, &c. Ministre et Secretaire D'Etat." A copy of this, in his own handwriting, and recently in the author's possession, appears to have been sent to his chief, as it is addressed, " To Macgregor of Macgregor at Baivre."

Every one, even slightly conversant with the juridical history of Scotland during the last century, will be acquainted with the trial of James Stewart—a foul transaction, which throws an indelible stain on the memory of those venal men who composed his jury. The story is briefly this :—The Stewarts and Campbells had been on opposite sides in the recent contest of 1745 and 6 for the crown. A Campbell of Glen-

ure was appointed factor over the estate of
Ardsheal, which had been confiscated after
that period ; and being supposed partial, he
removed some old tenants from the lands
to give place to others of his own choos-
ing. This was resented by an assassin named
Allan Breck Stewart, who waylaid Campbell,
and shot him, in May 1752, and immediately
fled to France. James Stewart was supposed
to be accessory. He was taken up without
legal warrant, carried to Inverary, and though
no proof was adduced, condemned to death and
to be hung in chains, by the Duke of Argyll,
as Lord Justice-General, and a jury, of whom
eleven were Campbells, and under the Duke's
authority. It would seem as if government,
afterwards blushing for the cruelty of the deed,
were desirous of bringing the actual murderer,
Allan Stewart, to justice ; and as it was known
that he had taken refuge in France, the proposal was made to James Macgregor, when he
was discovered likewise to be in that country,
that if he would seize this Allan Breck, and
bring him to Britain, he should himself receive
a pardon, and be allowed to return to his
country and family. But as Macgregor's original letters, lately in the author's custody, will

best declare his history after this period, the
following are faithful transcriptions of them.
They are addressed to the chief of the clan
Gregor, who was himself a voluntary exile in
the French dominions for the part he had taken
in the cause of the Stewart family :—

"DUNKIRK, *April 6th*, 1754.

" DEAR CHIEF,—No doubt you'd be surprised to hear
of my being openly in London and that I did not acquaint you of my intention before I parted with you, I
was not sure at that time whether I could go there or
not, and besides there was a particular reason why I
did not think you ought to know, or to be known to the
project I intended then to put in execution as much on
your own account, as mine, if not more so, otherwise you
might imagine me to be the most ungrateful person on
Earth, considering the parently usage I had the honour
to receive from you, and when I have the pleasure of
seeing you, you will be fully satisfied on that head, I fell
upon ways and means to procure a license from under
George's own sign-manual, and after I appeared before
the secretaries of state and delivered my case to be laid
before the ministry, and had also delivered the enclosed
case for my brother who suffered conform to his sentence,
and the way and manner I represented my own case, as
well as my brothers to the ministry, who seemed favourable, until the Duke of Argyll interposed, and also Grant
advocate for Scotland, the duke has represented your
clan in general the most disaffected in Scotland, and
after a very odious manner he represented also that the
whole clan was Popish.   It is certain my brother's dying
openly Roman catholic, hurt me much, and gave the
ministry a very bad impression.   I was at the time much
indisposed of a fever otherwise would have had a better

chance to save my brother and myself. Squire Carrol made me a party on your account and told that he thought it a favour done himself to serve any of your clan. After I had recovered my illness about fourteen days ago, I was sent for by the under Secretary who gave to understand by the earl of Holderness' orders, that with great difficulty, his lordship had now procured for me handsome bread in the government's service, and that I was to go off soon to Edin$^r$ where a sham trial was to pass upon me, to satisfy the public. He then acquainted me with the employ I was to have, which I thought proper not to accept of, and I desired that he would acquaint the earl of Holderness, that I was born in character of a gentleman, that I never intended to accept of that which would be a disgrace to my family, as well as a scourge to my country ; nor did I think when his lordship would consider with more mature deliberation upon the offer made me but that he would forgive my refusing it ; but if his lordship thought me a proper subject to serve in any station in which other gentlemen of honour served, that I was very well satisfied, and no otherwise. The same secretary sent for me next day, when he gave me to understand that it was the ministry's orders to me to retire out of his majesty's dominions within three days, upon which there was a messenger set over me for fear I would retire to Scotland. The messenger was ordered to see me landed on this side upon their own charges. I could not have time to wait on my friends as the messenger attended me so close, only saw Gregor Drummond who knew my whole transaction with them, our friends who spoke much against me sometime (fearing what brought me thither), began now to speak in the most favourable manner, they then knowing the treatment I had received from the ministry, and tho' the offer made me was very advantageous, as to the purse, as I stood to my resolution it was approved by every body, even of some of the other side.

This job was very expensive upon me, yet had I had the luck to save my poor brother I would not grudge any thing. Before I went to London I received from Major Buchanan £103 and he still owes me £30, which is to be paid against Martinmas next. All that I have saved of the whole I carried with me is about £40 and £16 I have sent my wife. I thought it my duty to let you know of this that you'd be so good and write next step you may think I ought to take. I am advised if I could carry on a small trade in this place and had some credit with the little money I have, that by taking care, I might make good bread, but would do nothing till I would hear from you. I would be glad to know if you had an answer to the letter you drew the draught of sent from me to a certain great man, and also what method you think most proper to procure a gratification. I thought better to remain here as I am not yet well recovered, rather than go up to Paris, not knowing but you would approve of my settling here, which seems to me very feasible, yet as you are my head, I leave you to dispose of me as you shall seem fit and proper, and therefore shall wait your orders, if you please to desire by yours, an ample account of the project which procured the licence, and an account of that worthy employ offered me, you shall in full by my next. I beg pardon for this long letter, and that I have the honour of manifesting my gratitude, is the sincere wish—Dear Chief, Your own to command,

"JAS DRUMMOND."

"DUNKIRK, *May 1st, 1754.*

"DEAR CHIEF,—I had the honour of your's some time ago, and would have made a return ere now, but that these eight days past I have been taken ill of an ague which continues. I make no doubt our friends the Stewarts will endeavour as much as possible to make a handle of my being in London, but I leave you to judge, if it was not reasonable for me to make an attempt tho'

never so hazardous if I could expect to be of service or
relief to my Brother, or procure my own liberty to support my distressed wife and numerous family. The way
and manner I procured the license to return to Great
Britain, was this. Captain Duncan Campbell,* who is
nephew to Glengyle, and my near relation, wrote me in
June last about Allan Breck Stewart, and begged therein,
if there was any possibility of getting him delivered in
any part of England, that if I could be of use in this
matter, that I might expect my own pardon, I returned
him answer after I was at Paris, that I would use my interest to endeavour to bring Stewart the Murderer to
justice ; but that as I could not trust any with the secret,
that I could not act alone, so well as if I had a Trustee
to support me, after receipt of this, both Captain Duncan
and the present Glenure† wrote in a most pressing manner (which letters I still retain,) and desired therein to
acquaint them upon receipt of these letters, and if I desired that a Trustee, and money should be sent me to
support the carrying on of the project, I wrote for this
person to support me,  After this gentleman came to
Paris I waited upon him, he showed me proper recom-
mendation he had for the earl of Albemarle, upon whom
he waited and disclosed the matter to his lordship, and
told his lordship, at the same time, nothing could be done
without me, nor could the murderer be brought to England unless his lordship would procure a Licence to me
for that purpose, his lordship frankly consented to send
express to London for the licence, which being come, at
the same time came David Stewart Brother to Glenbuckie,
who with little Duncan M'Gregor, whom you recom-
mended to Lord Ogilvy, put Allan Breck the murderer
so much upon his guard, that the very night I intended to

* This was the person from whom the Earl of Perth escaped in
1745.
† Son of him who was shot by Allan Stewart.

have carried him off, made his escape from me, after stealing
out of my Cloakbag several things of cloathes, linens, and
4 snuff boxes, one of which was G. Drummonds, all this
scene was acted in presence of your Shoemaker's wife
and daughter. After the murderer made his escape, my
friend went to Lord Albemarle, and acquainted him of
what happened, his lordship sent for me, and I told his
lordship the way and manner he made his escape, his
lordship told me had I been lucky enough to have
succeeded, that were I guilty of never so much
Treason, that I might shuredly expect my pardon,
I acquainted his lordship that I was not guilty of
Treason, for that I was not only freed by the act of
indemnity, but that in the year 1747, I had received
a pass from Andrew Fletcher, Lord Justice Clerk then
for Scotland, and as his, your lordship, meaning Albemarle, commanded in Scotland at that time, your lordship gave consent to my having said pass, which I then
produced, and his lordship remembered the affair very
well. He then inquired into my case, which I laid open
before his lordship, and the distress that my wife and
family was in, this other Gentleman told his lordship
that I had 14 children, great many of whom were
very young, this other Gentleman moved that now as
there was a licence procured for me to return into Great
Britain, that as I used my utmost endeavours to bring
the murderer to justice, that I might be allowed by his
lordship to go to London to represent both my own and
my brother's case, and begged his lordship's recommen-
dation for that purpose. To which his lordship answered,
that he was afraid that though he would incline to do me
service, and have it done for me, that all those of the Clan
M'Gregor were too zealous Jacobites ; but that if he
thought I could be trusted that he did not know, but
something might be done for me, and my numerous family.
Upon which his lordship wrote a letter to the Earl of

Holderness in my favours, and allowed I should go to
London, to know what could be done for me, upon which
I parted and went to Ipres, to wait on Major Buchanan,
and from thence to London, how soon I waited on the
Earl of Holderness, his lordship desired me to put my
case in writing, and that he would lay it before the ministry ; but at the same time that I behoved to lodge in a
messenger's house, where I would be entertained at the
King's expence, that lodging there was not meant as
any restraint upon me, but for some other reason ; neither
should any restraint be put upon me, but have my liberty
conform to my licence, Eight days after I was called to
the Earl of Holderness's house, where I was examined in
a most civil manner, but was so much sifted with questions, and cross questions, that I was like to be put into
confusion ; but upon mustering up all my spirits, having
nothing else for it, I endeavoured that they could not read
through Stones, and at the same time, made such compliance answers as I thought suited best those subjects.
I understood some time after, that Secretary Murray, to
my knowledge, was both a liar, villain, and a very great
coward, and that at the time he was mostly employed by
the young Pretender, as I then called him, which I
thought made an impression upon both the Chancellor
and Holderness, none else being present, I was dismissed,
and a few days after I contracted a fever and gravel,
which continued till the middle of March, and what happened after that, I have acquainted you therewith in my
last. This is the whole affair from the beginning, and
considering Glenure's being so nearly related to me and
my wife, and that the Stewarts had shown themselves on
all occasions the cut throats of our people, no mortal
needs be surprised, if I should endeavour to bring my
friends murderer to justice, besides that very family of
Barcaldine is the greatest support your Clan has in Scotland, I mean the parts I lived in formerly, and there-

abouts, now I leave you to Judge, whether I acted right or not in keeping my design secret from you, my reason you may judge, but when I parted with you I was not sure of going to England, now if you find my conduct amiss you may chastise me without control, as you may think proper, for as I am your own, it is no other person's business what you do with any of your Clan. I understand Stewart the murderer has openly declared, that if ever I returned to France, that he would murder me, I think when a proof of this is to be had, he ought to be put into close custody, of this I leave you to judge. As I never expect to get home any more, I now take my own name, And I hope you will believe me to be for ever —Dr Chief yours to command

"JAS. MACGREGOR."

"DUNKIRK, 8*th* *June* 1754.

"DEAR CHIEF,—According to your desire I gave you as genuine a confession of what I had done, as if I was before my father confessor, and if my behaviour is faulty, no doubt you are the only man that has a right to chastise me. I am afraid you disprove of what I have done, as I had not the honour of hearing from you, but I hope, when you consider, of both my past conduct and behaviour to my prince, and what baits and encouragement I had offered me from the contrary party which I had refused, that you will imagine I am not to be suspected, as I can prove that my fidelity was as much put to the trial as any whatever, and at the same time make appear that I never violated that trust that was reposed in me. And now in my greatest misery, and in a foreign country without friends, that I will be upbraided and supposed of mistrust, I think my fate very hard especially when it is evidently known how much I have served my prince and what I suffered in his service, besides the loss of all my effects, which was to me no small article : And now if by my going to England has lost me your countenance it is hard. Pray dear Sir, would you have me to presume to tell you a lie, or was I not to let you know everything, as I valued myself on your being my head, and my only support, and now if I am not to expect that friendship to whom can I apply, no doubt if I have lost your's, the world will say, (though unjustly,) that I have been guilty of some villanous thing, otherwise my Chief would never desert me, but let the case be as it will, I pray God an occasion worthy would offer which might show the deserts of man, and it is very possible, for all the misfortunes I have laboured under, that I would shew, by my friends and followers, that a chief would have very good reason to have some value for me, Sir, forgive me to tell you that I have done a great deal of honour, once in my time, to you, and your clan, and I hope in God to do more or I die. If you be so good as favour me with a letter on receipt of this, that I may not labour under the doubts of your displeasure, otherwise I will not presume to give you further trouble till once time will satisfy you of the verity of what I have wrote you, and I ever am with grateful submission and due respect—Dr Chief—Your's to kill or cure                    "JAS MACGREGOR."

"PARIS, *Sept.* 25*th*, 1754.

"DR CHIEF,—I came here last night and thought it my duty to let you know that I was oblidged to leave Dunkirk for my safety, for Lochgarry last week (as I was informed) had lodged an information against me to the Grand Baillie letting him know I was sent on purpose from England to be a spy. I was advised by some friends to withdraw for fear I should be laid up upon suspicion as I had no friends there to report my innocence, and as the officers of the place had received orders to take me up, I was oblidged to come off in a hurry, that it confused me entirely, as I was oblidged to come off with little Cash in my pocket, and though I had (had) full time I had

not a great deal more, as I was put to so much charges
by my illness and keeping company with the English
gentlemen I was with at St Omers, who would have made
my fortune, had not Lochgarry come and given him the
worst character of me which could be given.   By all appearance I am borne to suffer Crosses, and it seems y'r
not at an End for such is my wretched Case at present
that I do not know earthly where to go or what to do, as I
have no Subsistance to keep Soul and Body together.   All
that I have carried here is about 13 livres, and has taken
a Room at my old quarters in Hotel St Pierre, Rue de
Cordier.   I send you the bearer begging of you to let me
know if you are to be in Town soon, that I may have (the)
pleasure of seeing you, for I have none to make Application to but you alone, and all I want is if it was possible
you could contrive where I could be employed, so as to
keep me in Life without going to entire Beggary.   This
probably is a difficult point, yet unless it's attended with
some difficulty you might think nothing of it, as your
long head can bring about matters of much more Difficulty and Consequence than this.   If you'd disclose this
matter to your friend Mr Buttler it's possible he might
have some Employ wherein I could be of use, as I pre-
tend to know as much of breeding and riding of Horses as
any in France, besides that I am a good Hunter either
on horseback or by fowling.   You may judge my Reduction as I propose the meanest things to serve a turn till
better cast up.   I am sorry that I am oblidged to give you
so much trouble, but I hope you are very well assured
that I am grateful for what you have done for me and I
leave you to judge of my present wretched case.   I am
and shall forever continue Dear Chief—Your own to command                                    " JAS MACGREGOR."

" *P.S.*—If you'd send your pipes by the Bearer, and all
he other little trinkims belonging to it, I would put them

in order, and play some Melancholy tunes, which I may now with Safety, and in real truth. Forgive my not going directly to your house, for if I could shun seeing of yourself I could not choose to be seen by my Friends in my wretchedness nor by any of my Acquaintance."

On the cover is the following note: "Letter from James Macgregor, on his arrival at Paris the week before he died, October, 1754."

The above letters, while they exhibit a spirit of Highland independence, and evince the devotion with which a chieftain was regarded, must at the same time claim our admiration for the man, who, suffering under all the horrors of exile, want, and separation from his family, was bold enough to scorn an appointment, in itself lucrative, but which was to be a scourge to his country, and was derogatory to his character as a gentleman; and we must deplore the severity of those decrees that excluded such men from mercy, though, by a temporary misguidance of principle, they became amenable to the offended laws of their country.

James Macgregor died at Paris, eight days after he wrote the last letter above transcribed; and in him his clan lost one of its ablest and most enthusiastic supporters.

The only other branch of that name which we can at present notice, was Gregor Macgregor of Glengyle, known by the appellation of *Ghlune Dhu*, from a black mark on one of his knees. He was the nephew of Rob Roy ; and became no less eminent, as he followed the steps of his uncle, whom he wished to emulate, having often been his companion upon expeditions of danger. Gregor, like his uncle, had changed his name, and assumed that of James Graham, from the same proscriptive edict against his clan. During his juvenile years he had closely attended the precepts of his uncle, and looked up to him as his protector ; until his strength was matured, however, he did not head any foray of his clan. But his uncle having been wounded in an attack upon a party of military, who opposed his carrying off some cattle from the vicinity of Dumbarton, Gregor was deputed to take the command along with his cousin James.

They made an irruption to Drymen, and summoned the attendance of the surrounding lairds and tenants to the church of that place, to pay them their *black-mail*. They all complied but one person, whose cattle they drove away ; which work gave their lads some trouble, owing to the ferocity of a bull, which, however,

Q

they contrived to tame before he reached the Trossachs.

The next of Gregor's exploits was that of taking the fort of Inversnaid in 1745, accompanied by his cousin James and twelve men. In the fort they only found nine soldiers, the rest of the garrison having been out working at roads ; but they also secured the whole of them in name of Prince Charles Stewart, and marched them, eighty-nine in number, as prisoners, to the Castle of Doune.

Two friends of Gregor's being suspected of treason about this time, were taken into custody by a military party of forty men. Gregor, with his twelve men, pursued and overtook them on the road near Dunkeld, beat them off, and rescued his friends.

During the strict scrutiny and rigorous course of punishment which followed the unhappy commotion of 1745 and 1746, Gregor, like many others, was forced to forsake his home, and take refuge among the woods and mountains of the Highlands. He was once observed lurking in the wilds of Glenlednick, and pursued across the hills to Loch Tay by a party of Campbells ; he shot one of them, and judging it unsafe to remain so near his own country, he and his only attendant, a clansman, travelled towards the braes of Athol, where they hoped to conceal themselves unmolested. Having traversed those wild and inhospitable regions for some days, they arrived at the lonely hut of a shepherd, immersed in a deep glen, surrounded with wood. The shepherd and his wife gave them a hearty welcome ; and upon hearing that they were out with the Prince, agreed to shelter them for some time. This place was so far distant from any other habitation, that the wanderers believed themselves secure. Reports, however, reached the ears of the Duke of Athol, that two suspicious men, one of them with a black mark on his knee, were concealed in this cottage ; and he found means to instruct the hind, so that his lodgers might be secured by stratagem, as the desperate bravery of Macgregor had staggered the resolution of the Athol men, and they would not openly assail him, even with superior numbers. It was accordingly agreed that six men should be concealed in the house, who were to rush upon him unaware, make him a prisoner, or effect his destruction.

It chanced that Macgregor and his lad had one day gone to kill a deer in the neighbouring forest.   The day rained so much that they were quite wet on their return.   Macgregor sat down by the fire to dry himself; and as his hair was very long and wet, the landlady offered to comb and dry it.   While in the act of doing so, she twisted her hand in it, and pulled him suddenly down upon his back to the ground.   The concealed assassins and the false shepherd immediately rushed upon him.   He called to his companion ; their strength was herculean; and in a few minutes their assailants were all either dead or maimed. The treacherous woman, with the resolution of a fiend, having opposed their departure from her house with a drawn dagger, was seized and hanged on a joist.   Gregor and his servant, who were both severely wounded, having quitted this scene of blood, returned to Glengyle ; but from the fatigue he had undergone, and the wounds he had received, Macgregor's servant only lived two days after his arrival.

When the eventful periods of Scottish history, in which those heroes flourished, had passed away, the policy of the mountains took a new and important turn.   Various arts and improvements were introduced, which speedily effected the most beneficial changes, and convinced the natives that it was possible to live

and be regarded for other qualities than those
of war ; while the removal of the long and ill-
judged proscription of the clan Gregor, though
unfeelingly opposed by a narrow-minded nobleman of their own country, turned their energies
to better purposes, and rendered them no less
respectable than other members of the state.

# NOTICES

REGARDING THE

## MYSTERIOUS HISTORY

OF

# LADY GRANGE.

"" Let it be to your glory,
To see her tears ; but be your heart to them
As unrelenting flint to drops of rain."
SHAKESPEARE.

FROM the period of the Revolution in 1688—
the most important change to which the British
constitution had been subjected in modern
times, and which established the Protestant
succession to the crown of these realms—various attempts were made by the exiled house of
Stewart and their adherents to recover the
sovereignty, from which they considered themselves to have been unjustly excluded.

In their different essays for regaining this
dignity, forfeited by a pusillanimous and precipitate retreat, they were countenanced and supported by the French nation, not only from

ancient alliance and similarity of religious principle, but from motives of sinister policy.

But, though their efforts to regain the British
throne were always unsuccessful, being defeated, in a great measure, by their own incon-
sistency, confident hopes of ultimate success
were cherished by each succeeding prince of
the family, which even their misfortunes and
frequent disappointments were not sufficient to
overcome; and it is certain, that during the
vicissitudes to which they were exposed, de-
pending on the precarious bounty of their
friends, and having their pride often mortified
by privations to which they were subjected,
they yet continued to cling to the empty title of
kings of Great Britain. Although usually bestowed in derision, it was still acceptable to
the consequence they flattered themselves they
possessed among the contemporary monarchs
of Europe, and the majority of the British
nation.

Prone to the delusions of vanity, and to the
austere yet imposing dogmas of the Romish
Church, James the Second and his family
boasted of having resigned a kingdom rather
than relinquish their religion; but in the reverse
of fortune to which this contumacy reduced

them, they experienced the painful effects of the choice which they had made.

Though the abdication of King James evinced a consciousness of his inability to withstand the just and reasonable demands of his subjects, yet a large proportion of them were instinctively led to consider his title to the throne as an unalienable and almost divine right, of which neither he nor his successors could be deprived ; and however inconsistent and tyrannical his conduct had been, they were still desirous of supporting his claim, as that of their true and natural monarch. The same spirit was manifested for several years after the expulsion of the Stewarts, and continued to influence the sentiments and actions of many virtuous and highly respectable characters.

The effects of this attachment to the cause of the family were, however, various and deplorable. It occasioned the wreck of numerous houses of distinction ; and for many years involved the whole region of the Highlands in unjust and indiscriminate suspicion—consequences which also extended widely over the Lowland districts.

Mrs Erskine of Grange, generally known by the name of Lady Grange, was a victim to the rancorous spirit to which this suspicion gave rise. She was the daughter of Cheisly of Dalry, a man of violent passions, who shot Sir George Lockhart, Lord President of the Court of Session, for having decided a law-suit against him. She was a beautiful woman ; and it was said that James Erskine of Grange, brother to the Earl of Mar, had debauched her, and that she compelled him to become her husband, by threatening his life, desiring him to remember that she was Cheisly's daughter.

James Erskine was made Lord of Session in 1707, by the title of Lord Grange, and was Lord Justice Clerk during the three last years of Queen Anne's reign. He continued on the bench for twenty-seven years ; but resigned in 1734, to join against Sir Robert Walpole, expecting to be appointed Secretary of State for Scotland. He was chosen member of Parliament for Stirling the same year, and acted as secretary to the Prince of Wales. He died at London in 1754, aged 75. He had eight children by his wife, of whom the following notices were principally collected, some time since, on a journey in the Isle of Skye.

For a considerable time previous to this lady's misfortunes, the nobility and gentry disaffected

to the Hanoverian succession were in the practice
of holding secret meetings in the city of Edin
burgh, for concerting measures to overturn the
government, and restore the Stewarts to their
ancient throne.  Many persons of large fortunes
and powerful influence joined this clandestine
association, and among them were several exalted
chieftains of the Highlands, anxious to forward
the cause.  Deputations from them were frequently sent to France and Italy, and a corre-
spondence was kept up with the Chevalier de
St George.

Lord Grange was deeply involved with the
friends of the Chevalier in this association, and
their meetings were often held at his house,
till the private and concealed manner in which
they were conducted began to excite the suspicion of his lady, lest they had some plan in
agitation that would involve him in ruin.  Her
solicitude made her eager to ascertain the
nature of these deliberations, and she applied
to her husband for information, but he declined
to give her the satisfaction she required.

The private character of Lord Grange was
far from being amiable.  He was extremely
dissipated, of a restless and intriguing disposition ; and from the manner in which he was

forced to marry his lady, was not possessed of
immaculate fidelity. His lady, on the other
hand, was violent, suspicious, and determined ;
her attachment to the reigning family was zealous in the extreme, and she became jealous of
the frequent visits of the Highland chiefs at her
house. From the opportunities she possessed,
she at length became acquainted with their purpose, though not at first with its magnitude.
Having accidentally obtained possession of some·
papers, when their schemes were developed, she
resolved to unfold the danger that seemed to
threaten the tranquillity of the nation, and of
which she received farther confirmation by concealing herself where she overheard the whole
conversation of her husband and his partisans,
respecting the manner of arming the Highlanders, and the place where a force from France
was to be landed on the coast.

She soon made her husband acquainted with
the secret she had obtained, and remonstrated
with him on the ruinous consequences that
would result from his treasonable plans ; she
entreated him to withdraw from his traitorous
associates ; pointed out the criminality of his
conduct towards the government, under which
he lived in a situation of trust and honour ; and

declared, that if he did not relinquish his principles, she would speedily disclose all she knew.

The cause of uneasiness given her by his frequent journeys to London, and his amours there,
operated at the same time upon her mind, and
rendered her determination more firm, while he,
conscious of his irregularities, and aware of her
temper, dreaded all she threatened, as her
attachment for the government appeared to sur-
pass her regard for him.   Under these impressions he lost no time in communicating to his
friends the conversation with his wife, and his
fears that her passion would lead her to follow
out her resolution.

Alarmed at this information, they did not
long deliberate on the measures to be adopted.
It was agreed that the lady should instantly be
secured, and carried away from the metropolis
to some safe and unfrequented place, where she
could be concealed till such time as the object
of their association should be accomplished ;
and Lord Grange, rather than that his life and
fortune, and those of his friends, should be in
jeopardy, and in the power of an inconsiderate
woman, as he believed her to be, readily consented to her demigration.

Everything for the removal of the lady having

been concerted, her lord took leave of her, under
pretence of going a journey for some days, but
in reality that he might not appear to have any
knowledge of the affair.

Two persons, hired for the purpose, were
charged with the execution of the plot, and received the necessary instructions, with keys for
admitting them to the house.

Lord Grange had a lodging in the city, but
the house of Grange, where his lady then resided,
was at some distance. These men arrived at
the mansion about midnight, when the silence
of the hour, and the gloom of darkness that surrounded them, accorded with the black deed in
which they were engaged. That they might not
be recognised, they were masked, and disguised
in uncouth habits. Each had in his girdle a
loaded pistol and a dirk, and they were provided
with a dark lantern, by the light of which they
were guided to a private door, which gave entrance to a back wing of the house.

The mansion was encompassed by a high
wall, erected in turbulent times as a defence
against sudden assault; but it was now partly
decayed. The architecture of the building declared its foundation to be that of a remote age,
while its internal structure was no less antique,

being fitted up in the style of the fourteenth
century. Around the house were many aged
trees, to shelter it from wintry winds, so that
the whole bore the appearance of old baronial
comfort.

When the nocturnal intruders arrived at the door
to which they had been directed, they examined
it, and were surprised that it had no appearance
of having been opened for years. They hesitated : and with a gleam of irresolution, which
must sometimes dart across the heart of the
depraved, when about to commit a lawless deed,
they looked around ; but no sound was heard to
break upon the stillness of the repose into which
all nature seemed to have been lulled. They
applied their key. The rusty lock at first
appeared to forbid their entrance ; but the bolt
at last yielded with a jerk that echoed along the
gloomy passages within, and occasioned them
some uneasiness, lest the noise had given alarm.
They hearkened, but all was quiet, and having
drawn their daggers, they proceeded. A chilling
dampness filled the space within, and dimmed
the light that issued from the lantern, yet they
went on until they came to another door, secured
with massive iron bars, but standing partly open,
and which, when they pushed it up, creaked

upon its rusty hinges with a hollow noise. They made a half turn to the right, and presently entered a spacious chamber, which appeared to be a repository for ancient armour, as they could observe coats of mail and other warlike implements hung around the walls.

From this chamber they entered the lobby; but on turning round to ascend the great stair which led to Lady Grange's bedroom, where they expected to secure her, they heard some voices whispering at a distance. Presently a flash of light crossed a long passage, from which the sound proceeded. They instantly darkened their light, and listening to the sound, more firmly grasped their daggers. After a silence of some minutes, they began to ascend the great stair on tiptoe, when a loud voice, calling out—" Robbers! robbers!  Help!"—resounded over the house, and stopped their progress. They instantly separated, and with all the haste of conscious criminality, speedily regained the door by which they had entered, and quickly locked it. The house was now in a state of alarm, a gun was fired from one of the windows, and the intruders being disappointed in their purpose, were forced to return to the city by themselves, in the chaise which stood ready to receive and carry away Lady Grange.

Her husband returned, and he and his friends were much chagrined at the failure of their project at this time.

The hatred of Grange towards his unfortunate wife seemed now to increase in a more violent degree than ever. He was as seldom at home as possible, and then he behaved to her with all the indifference in his power, till at last she seemed to have become so abhorrent to him that he wholly deserted his house, and left her a prey to melancholy reflections.

After living in this unhappy situation for some months, a separation was proposed, but she rejected it, in opposition to the solicitations of all their friends. This proposal convinced her of the extreme hatred of her husband ; and seeing no prospect of returning attention from him, she left his house and took lodgings in the town, that she might have the consolation of seeing him and her children, as they occasionally passed along the street ; every intercourse with them being forbidden her. She had not, however, remained long in this situation when she resolved to go to London, and accordingly took leave of her friends, intending to set off in two

R

days after the night on which she was carried away.

The house where she lodged belonged to a Highland woman, named Margaret Maclean, who appears to have been privy to the plan of removing her by force; for, on the night when this was effected, she ordered her servants to bed long before the usual hour, the maid-servant who attended on Lady Grange being likewise sent out of the way.

From the state of discord which now subsisted between Lord Grange and his wife, the Jacobite association became more apprehensive of her disposition to betray them, especially fearing her intended journey to London. Being determined that a second failure should not happen, they appointed two Highland gentlemen of family to conduct the business—Macdonald of Morar, and the laird of Macleod's brother.

The chief abettor of this transaction, and the great promoter of the civil commotion that ensued, was Frazer of Lovat. He had for a considerable time become notorious for the many acts of profligacy in which he had been engaged. Devoid of principle, and versed in every species of vice, his wickedness became so habitual that he could not abstain from it. Incessant views

of self-interest formed another feature in his
character, the influence of which led him alternately to befriend the Hanoverian and Stewart
cause, and to espouse the jarring principles of
Whig and Tory. He had besides repeatedly
changed his religion, and frequently fomented
rebellion ; yet hitherto had had the address to
obtain pardon for his numerous offences.

About eleven o'clock on the night of Satur-
day, the 22d of April 1732, Macdonald and Macleod, accompanied by several of their countrymen, knocked at Margaret Maclean's door, and
said they had a letter for Lady Grange. They
were admitted and shown to her chamber, where
she sat writing. She started at their appearance, and asked what they wanted at such an
improper hour. They told her that it was essential for her peace to be removed from the
capital, and that they had come to conduct her
away ; but she refused to leave the house. The
letter brought was from her husband, desiring
that she would accompany the gentlemen, who
would convey her to more comfortable lodgings.
She still resisted ; but as their purpose would
not brook any delay, they took her by the arms,
when she screamed and repeatedly cried murder. Several men then rushed in and forcibly

laid hold of her ; and in the struggle she fell upon the floor. They endeavoured to prevent her cries by covering and stuffing her mouth with cloths, but she repelled their attempts for some time with her arms, and beat on the floor with her feet to alarm the people in the house below. Exhausted with these efforts, and much hurt on the face and chest, they at length over-powered her ; and having tied a cloth over her mouth and eyes, and secured her arms, carried her down stairs, and put her into a sedan chair, on the knees of a man, who held her fast in his arms, though she made every exertion to get free. The chair was quickly carried to a field on the north of the city, where the new town is erected, and nearly on the spot where St Andrew's church now stands, where several men and horses waited its arrival. It was moon-light, which enabled her when taken from the chair to know where she was ; but all was still as the desert, and no friend was near to rescue her from her unfeeling attendants.

It was past midnight, and the drowsy city seemed hushed in slumber. While she cast a glance upon the dark turrets of the castle, the bell of St Giles' struck one with so mournful an echo, that it reverberated to her heart with a foreboding of evil that nearly overcame her. But she was not allowed time for meditation ; and though she complained severely of the harsh usage she had received, being considerably bruised, and having her clothes torn and covered with blood, the wretches paid no regard to her condition, but hastily placed her on horseback, behind Fletcher, the man on whose knees she sat in the chair, and to whom she was bound by a cloth put round her waist.

The piercing coldness of the night, with her constrained posture on horseback, produced pain in her sides and limbs, of which she often complained, requesting leave to dismount to relieve her distress ; but this indulgence was refused in terms of great barbarity and unmanly feeling, until they had travelled beyond Linlithgow, when, as the morning began to dawn, they were forced, to avoid detection, to stop at the house of Macleod, a lawyer, a zealous friend to the Stewart interest.

She was there shown into a room with a fire, and though she told two men and a woman whom she saw who she was, and that she had been torn from her friends, they paid no attention to her ; and Sandy Frazer, the most cruel ruffian of her escort, remained with her the whole day, and prevented her taking repose, or seeing any other of her own sex.

On the return of night she was again forced to leave this house on horseback as before, being told that she had still some miles to ride.

Though she remonstrated against proceeding farther, being greatly fatigued, and unaccustomed to such a mode of travelling, she was not regarded. Her conductors would not answer any question she put to them ; but they assured her that her life should be safe, if she remained quiet, and made no attempt to escape. This, however, she was not disposed to do, had she seen any prospect of being rescued, but it being Sunday night, they saw no one upon the road, her attendants taking care to travel by cross ways, avoiding the town of Falkirk, and passing through the Torwood, till they arrived at Polmaise. She was there conducted into the house through a low vault, and from that into an apartment that appeared to be a dungeon, for the window was secured with strong boards, the only light that was admitted being through a small opening from an adjoining closet. It was furnished with a miserable bed and a broken chair ; but the strength of Lady Grange was so much ex-

hausted, that she gladly reclined upon the bed,
and endeavoured to compose her disordered
spirits. After some unquiet sleep, she awoke
to painful reflections. Hurried away from her
family and friends, she was ignorant of her fate,
though she believed that her life was to be
taken away ; and convinced that her husband
was the cause, she burst into tears and sobbed
bitterly. An old man, who acted as a gardener
at the place, and his wife, entered her room,
and endeavoured to soothe her. They told her
that she was to remain with them, and that
they would be attentive to her; but that she
would not be allowed to leave the room, to
which there were two doors strongly barricaded
with iron, the keys being always kept by
Frazer, who continued in the house as a guard.
She was, however, regularly supplied with all
she wanted; but the use of writing materials
was not allowed her.

During a confinement of several weeks in
this dark and loathsome cell, to which the free
air was never admitted, and where a damp un-
wholesome vapour hung around the walls, her
mind was depressed to a state of melancholy
and despair that at times appeared to unsettle
her judgment, and she often broke out into fits

of deplorable lamentation, which greatly affected
the old gardener, George Ross, and his wife
with feelings of compassion. " I'm unco wae,
Geordie," said his wife to him one day, " for
the puir lady. I'm fear't she'll grow wud, gin
she be lang i' yon hole, for it would sconfice a
horse, forbye a body." " That's true eneugh,"
said George, " but wha dare let her out ? We
wad get our kail thro' the reek, gin we ettled
at sic a thing. An' Lord Lovat's sae mis-
lear'd a chap, that gin he kent we war kin' to
her, he wad mak whangs o' our hides to mend
his Highlan' brogues. They're no canny thae
Highlandmen." " Atweel I ken that," returned
his wife, " there was ance a fearfu' ane o' them
came to my mither's house, that they ca'd Rab
Roy, the vera look o' the fallow gar't a' the
hairs o' our heads stan' up." " Ah, Nanse,"
said George, " misken ye Rab Roy, gin he
heard o' this lady's mishanter, he wadna be
lang o' clearin the house, Lord Lovat an a', an'
lettin' her gang hame. He wadna murgullie
the howlet, or the moudiewort owther."

The health of Lady Grange was by this time
seriously affected. Forster, who lived near
Polmaise, and was factor on these lands, had
the immediate charge of her under Lovat, and

having heard this conversation of the gardener and his wife, he found that the lady was actually ill, and gave orders to remove her to a more comfortable part of the house. He did so, much against his inclination, but the people who attended her told him they would have no hand in her death. After this she was not so cruelly confined, but was allowed to walk in the court, for the benefit of air.

In this place was she detained till the 15th of August, during which period of unhappiness she made frequent inquiries for her husband and her children, but could obtain no satisfactory reply.

She was this day told to prepare for another journey ; an order which she very unwillingly heard, as she had become acquainted with her attendants, several of whom appeared to sympathise with her sufferings, and by that means expected to make her escape. About ten o'clock at night, the unrelenting guides who formerly conducted her, appeared, and forced her on horseback, when she was secured as formerly behind Forster. They travelled by Stirling, and there crossed the Forth. In passing the town, Lady Grange cried for help, but they threatened to apply a cushion to her

mouth, which they had provided for the purpose, and she was silent. They rode through
Doune towards Callander, and at the approach
of day, went off the road, and halted at a house
which appeared to be that of a gentleman.
The lady was taken into a bed-room, and the
door was locked upon her. The window had
been previously secured, and a guard was placed
at the door; for although her companions believed their charge was secure, they were not
yet in a country where they could trust the
people.

In the course of the day Macdonald and
Macleod, who had formerly accompanied her
from Edinburgh, appeared. The care of Lady
Grange was now to devolve upon them, and
two men named Frazer, while the others were
dismissed. She had here a maid to attend her,
and was provided with every comfort the house
could afford ; but comfort from a mind reduced
to such perplexity was far distant. The two
gentlemen spoke to her, and assured her of her
safety ; but cautioned her against making any
outcry, as they were only taking her to a place
of security from the plans of her husband.
They were only answered by tears and entreaties to restore her to him and her family.

They and the two guides were armed in the usual manner of their country, each with a dirk and pistol, and being all stout and resolute men, were resolved to execute their intention of carrying the lady forward. Their former precaution did not seem necessary, as they were now on the confines of the Highlands, and it was agreed that they should only travel during the day, the unformed and miserable state of the roads rendering it hazardous to proceed by night.

Lady Grange was roused the following morning before daylight, having passed an almost sleepless night. The two gentlemen were provided with horses, and she was placed behind Macleod. Their guides were on foot. The lady being wholly unacquainted with the country, it was only considered necessary to blindfold her eyes till they had passed Callander, though she believed the Highlands to be her destination. They left the house before the dawn of day; but the full moon, which shone from an unclouded sky, guided their way, and cast a melancholy lustre on the stupendous mountain scenery that began to appear, as they ascended the dark and dreary pass of Leny. The path, for it was no road, wound along this defile, by the verge of the river, which at this place rushes over vast ridges of rock with impetuous aud sullen noise, that is echoed in lonely reverberations along the hollow glens, and produces on the wayworn passenger such effects as call up feelings of reverence for the magnificent objects that form the wild sublimity of the place. Lady Grange was alarmed at the roaring of the cataract, and inquired what it was.

This entrance into the Highlands is singularly majestic and striking. A prodigious mass of rock, piled to a vast height, forms an almost impenetrable bulwark, and seems to forbid the steps of man from exploring the bleak and lofty mountains that rise behind. Our travellers now entered the wood that covers the sides of the lower mountains, whose deep shade added to the impressive awe imparted by this secluded region. As her conductors believed that Lady Grange was at length in a place to which she was a total stranger, they uncovered her eyes ; not probably actuated by feelings of pity (for it had been charity to have kept them closed a little longer), but, with a degree of cruelty unworthy of Highlanders, that she might be intimidated by the wildness of the place, and

under the impression of terror, continue unre-
sistingly submissive to their commands. If to
sport with the weakness of a woman wholly in
their power were their motive, the ruffians
succeeded to their wish. She looked around
with astonishment and dread. The appearance
of the scene, by the pale light of the moon, was
so solemn and awful, that

"A deadly cold ran shiv'ring to her heart,"

and it seemed as the harbinger of her fate. She
ejaculated a prayer, and a trembling hope arose
that gave a momentary consolation.

With fearful yet wary steps they slowly
climbed the gloomy defile. The pass was
narrow and difficult, along the edge of a precipice that jutted from the lateral declivity of
the mountain. They beheld in the ragged
chasm below, the foaming waters of the stream,
dashing over huge, dislocated fragments of the
rock, with a declivity of more than 200 feet,
and sounding like peals of thunder. Now
almost on the brink of the ravine impending
over the boiling abyss, one false step would
have precipitated them into certain destruction.
Even the hardy Highlanders, appalled at their
danger, looked with averted eyes from the

frightful gulph ; and Lady Grange, quaking in
every limb, shrieked involuntarily, shut her eyes
upon the dreadful space, and wished that they
had still been obscured.

A short time, however, carried them over
this tremendous barrier, which, in former ages,
was one of the safeguards to Caledonian independence, and opposed the daring armies of
Roman ambition.

Their guides were intimately acquainted with
all the roads and by-paths that traversed the
Highland districts, which the travellers had just
entered on.   With more composure, they now
journeyed along the banks of Lochlubnaig, upon
whose unruffled bosom the surrounding mountains were faintly reflected.   On the left, Ben-
Ledi towered pre-eminent ; but its sterile summit was hid in a cloud, from which the guides
predicted a storm, and advised a more rapid
pace.   On the borders of a beautiful lake,
enveloped by lofty hills, whose wooded sides
sloped gradually towards the water, a prospect
opened altogether delightful.   Lady Grange
had never beheld so beautiful a landscape.   She
was astonished at the variety and grandeur of
the objects before her, though they possessed a
wildness that struck her with awe ; and had her

spirits been in their wonted elevation, she would have enjoyed the sublimity of the scene.

The tract along the margin of the lake was so irregular that they travelled but slowly, and before they reached its western extremity, there appeared on its surface the dark blue belt, the certain presage of a storm ; and there being no habitation near, they beheld its approach with no agreeable sensations.

This part of the country was, in those days, infested with desperate bands of ruffians, collected from various parts of the kingdom. They lived among the fastnesses of the mountains, sheltering themselves in caves and ruined castles, and levying on the peaceable inhabitants such contributions as they thought proper ; but though they were trained to rapine and violence, despoiling the traveller of his valuable property, they were not of a sanguinary disposition, and seldom shed blood, unless they met with much resistance.

The companions of Lady Grange, aware of these banditti, felt some uneasiness lest they should come in their way ; for although part of them might be from their own country, yet the fierce manners of such people made them disregard every consideration of country or kindred, and our travellers were sure of opposition, should they chance to meet. On this account, as well as from the impending storm, they were eager to pursue their journey, that they might reach some place of shelter before the approach of night.

The guides on foot proceeded before them, to reconnoitre the glen, and as Lady Grange and the gentlemen turned the point of a rock, they observed that the guides had discovered two men on the top of a hill, one of whom sounded a horn three different times, which echoed throughout the glen, and convinced the party that they were spies from the plunderers. The lady was again blindfolded, and lest they should be surprised, they charged their pistols, in order that they might be in readiness, if attacked.

The rain now began to descend, and the wind to blow with such violence, that they were compelled to stop, and take shelter in a hut that had been erected by some goatherds. Lady Grange was wet, and trembled with cold; but as no question she asked had been attended to, she forbore speaking, and with a deep sigh, sat down in a corner of the hovel on a turf seat, to which she was led. Some refreshment being necessary, the bandage was removed from her eyes, and she partook slightly of a repast which the guides produced from a basket.

The fury of the storm having in some degree abated, they again set out, Lady Grange being furnished with a plaid by one of the guides, which partly kept off the rain.

They had not proceeded far when they met two men, who informed them that a party of soldiers was scouring the neighbouring glens in pursuit of robbers, and that they were at no great distance on the road before them.

This intelligence was not very welcome; and in order to avoid them, our travellers instantly left the beaten path, and struck into a wood, as to meet with military would overthrow the plan they had in view.

It was with considerable difficulty that they could make their way through the wood, and before they emerged from it into a valley that runs south-west into the interior of Balquhidder, the shades of evening had begun to spread over the solitary scene. They now resolved to take up their quarters at the first house they should reach ; but a dark night, rendered more dismal by the storm which beat in their faces, quickly followed, and prevented their observing the path, or ascertaining how they could be accommodated.

S

Bewildered and perplexed, they were wholly at a stand, and after some deliberation, had almost determined to remain where they were, at the mercy of the "war of elements," when they observed a light that gleamed at some distance, which revived their sinking spirits. It appeared to be on the opposite side of a rapid stream, which they, after some delay, crossed at a place where it was fordable.

When this was accomplished, however, the light had disappeared, and the storm continued with unabating rage. Lady Grange wept bitterly, and could with difficulty support herself upon the horse, she was so much overcome with fatigue and fear. Her face was now uncovered, but darkness shrouded them on all sides, and the party stood fixed to the spot, none of them knowing what to propose, or how to proceed. At this instant their dilemma was relieved by the return of the light, which, though dim from the moisture of the night, was at no great distance. They instantly set forward, and found that it issued from the window of a house that had a castellated form, although a great part of it was in a state of ruin, fragments of the wall being scattered around, intercepting the passage of the gate.

The lateness of the hour, with the decayed appearance of the building, created suspicion in their minds, and they hesitated whether they should endeavour to gain admittance, lest it might be occupied by outlaws. One of their horses, however, neighed, which seemed to alarm those within, as the light was instantly removed. In a few minutes they heard people whispering, and presently six men came forward. One of them carried a light, and demanded who they were, and what was their business.

The first part of this interrogatory Macdonald did not state, but said that they were on a journey, and had lost their way. He entreated lodging for the night, and, making use of the Gaelic language, told the man that he and his friends were passing on to St Fillan's Pool with an unfortunate lady who had lost her senses.*

* After the supposed influence of St Fillan in the victory of the Scottish army under Bruce at Bannockburn, formerly referred to, the memory of the holy man was much revered ; and among the superstitious, the water of a pool of the river, near the chapel consecrated to him by Bruce, in Braidalbane, close by the present inn of Tyndrum, was believed to cure all human maladies, particularly that of insanity. It was therefore a common practice to convey persons affected with mental derangement to this pool, into which they were repeatedly plunged, being afterwards tied in the chapel for a night. If they were found loose in the morning, it was considered a favourable omen, and showed the interposition of the saint. The practice of carrying unfortunate maniacs to this wonder-working place is still continued (1819).

The man whom he addressed said that their
habitation was indifferent, but that the lady and
her friends should be welcome to the best it
could afford ; and having led the way, they
entered by an arched gate into an open court,
and, making one turn, came to a door, where
Lady Grange dismounted, and they all went
into the house.

In going through a long passage, our travellers observed that the men who conducted them
were all armed, each having a dirk and pistol in
a leather belt they wore round the waist.  Their
wild and fierce countenances, which were now
visible, bespoke their profession, and made our
party look at each other, convinced that they
were in the hands of the outlaws of the forest.

Lady Grange was so much exhausted that
she walked with difficulty ; and though the
savage appearance of the banditti struck her
with dread, she remained silent, and allowed
herself to be conducted into a large apartment,
where blazed a fire, on which a large kettle was
boiling.  The light of the fire, which was of
wood, illumined the whole room, and allowed a
perfect inspection of its furniture, which was in
unison with the most barbarous modes of life.

The carving and stucco work, which had for-

merly decorated the walls, were still visible, and
showed that it had once been occupied by persons of consequence and taste, whose manners,'
even amidst the rude and desultory customs of
feudal ages, must have differed widely from
those of its present possessors.

The castle, for such was its style, built to repress the attacks of marauding tribes, and secure
a safe retreat in warlike times, anciently belonged to a chieftain of the Macgregors.  It was
not at this time of considerable extent, a great
portion of it having become ruinous, but what
remained preserved that massive and sombre
elegance displayed in the habitations of the
ancient barons of the Highlands.  It stood on a
peninsulated rock, washed by the waters of an
extensive lake, which defended it on one side,
while towards the land it was protected by an
embrasured wall.  For a century and a half it
had been deserted by the owners ; and having
greatly fallen into decay, it had, for some time
previous to our narrative, become the occasional
resort of banditti.

The room occupied by these people was the
great hall of the castle, where a long succession
of mighty chieftains were wont to entertain their
bold associates, and where the bards of former

times recounted the heroic deeds of the clan ;
but melancholy was now the use to which it was
appropriated. A quantity of heath, spread in
a corner, and covered with the skins of wild
animals, was used for a bed. Round the fire
were placed a few planks of wood for seats,
and some boards were coarsely put together for
a table. The walls were ornamented with the
skins and horns of various wild beasts, and with
heads, wings, and claws of eagles, while some
rusty swords and old muskets were interspersed,
and gave a barbarous uniformity to the whole.

Lady Grange was wet, and sat down near the
fire. When she looked round and saw the wildness of the place she shuddered involuntarily, as
she believed this to be the abode where she was
to be confined, perhaps murdered ; for the idea
of her being carried away in so unwarrantable a
manner for the purpose of being destroyed had
never forsaken her mind ; and certainly the
aspect of those around her, as well as the savage
arrangement of the hall, conveyed to the imagination the dread of assassination. The place
seemed fit, and the people no less capable.

The whole party, without distinction, sat in
a circle round the fire. A conversation took
place, of which Lady Grange understood not a

word ; but she supposed herself to be the subject of it, as the banditti looked at her with attention, though she could not observe that any appearance of pity was depicted in their countenances.

They were not long seated when an old woman entered the apartment, who seemed surprised at seeing one of her own sex in such a place.  She went to the fire, examined the kettle that hung upon it, and lifted it away.  It contained some venison, which she put into a wooden dish, and placed upon the table.  Our party were invited to partake.  The old woman offered some of it to Lady Grange, who thanked her, but, although much fatigued and in want of food, was not inclined to eat; she, however, took a little at the solicitation of the old woman, who spoke to her in broken English. This woman, though she lived among robbers, and her looks were haggard and forbidding, yet possessed some degree of feeling ; for she expressed great sympathy for her guest, and seemed desirous of being serviceable to her.

When the repast was at an end, Macdonald asked the man whom he took to be leader of the gang, if another room could be obtained for the lady, where she would be secure, as she might perhaps attempt to escape, if it was in her power. The leader gave orders to the old woman, and Lady Grange was conducted by a stair, so much broken as to render it difficult and dangerous, to a cold damp room in the second storey, having a window secured by iron bars, which was used by the robbers for the confinement of those they made prisoners in their depredatory excursions. A heath bed, covered with deers' skins, was the only furniture which this gloomy apartment contained, and here the unhappy lady was forced to remain—a sad reverse from the comfort to which she had been accustomed ; but at the same time, a trial which her strength of mind enabled her to support.

The old woman endeavoured to soothe and quiet her agitation ; but to Lady Grange it was a great disappointment that the language she spoke was nearly unintelligible, as the kindness of the woman led her to expect much information regarding her destiny. All she could understand was, that she was not to remain there, and that while she staid her life was safe ; but the woman could not distinctly answer these questions—" Where am I—who are the men of this house, and those who brought me here—where am I going—do they intend to

murder me—why have I.been forcibly carried
from my own home?"

Lady Grange would have put the same questions to the men she saw in the hall; but believing them to be in league with her escort, and
that remonstrance would be useless, she judged
it more prudent to desist, as she hoped a short
time would unravel the mystery. When the old
woman left her, she reclined upon her humble
bed, raising her thoughts to that Providence
who protects the virtuous and the good. The
reflections of those she had left in the hall below
were very different.

Macdonald and Macleod, with the Frazers,
were sent to occupy an empty room adjoining
the hall, upon a parcel of heather; but they
were in great perplexity at the situation in
which they were placed. Beyond a doubt they
were in the power of freebooters, and to get
away from them in safety with their charge appeared difficult, as the robbers were the more
numerous, and even should they overcome these,
others might be at hand to oppose them. While
they were thus, in low accents, considering in
what manner they should extricate themselves
from their perilous situation, their attention was
roused by a loud conversation among the rob-

bers. Apprehension, the inseparable companion
of guilt, struck upon their consciences like the
intrusive eye of a fiend, unwelcome, but imperi-
ous; and they were desirous to know what
occasioned such discourse among the outlaws.
Macleod, who was the strongest and most intrepid of his party, opened the door of the apartment to hear more distinctly, and stole softly
towards the hall, when he heard that the debate
related to himself and his company. Some of
the banditti proposed that Lady Grange and her
friends should be put to death, lest they should
betray their retreat, adding that, as they appeared to be persons of consequence, they would
have some valuable booty along with them.
But others argued that though they lived by
spoliation, which they regarded as no discreditable vocation, it would be disgraceful to take
advantage of people whom the inclemency of
the weather had thrown on their hospitality—
a consideration that was with them a cardinal
virtue. To this they at length assented, and
the debate was given up; but the fears of our
travellers were not appeased. They lay down
upon the heath that had been spread on the
floor, but not to sleep, for they expected every
moment a visit from their hosts; and being men

of great personal bravery, were resolved to die, or accomplish their object.

Everything remained quiet as the grey tints of the morning dawned upon the battlements of the castle; the screech owl that occupied the dismantled turrets ceased her discordant tones, and the daring spirits of the banditti lay stilled in slumber. Within all was silent, but without, the tempest raged in all its fury.

Loud and terrible blew the wind, quick flashed the vivid lightning, and the thunder broke in frightful peals over the towering heights of the castle, which shook even to its foundation. Lady Grange awoke from her sleep in trembling dread. Her escort, who had passed a sleepless night, heard the tempest roaring around; and even the turbulent souls of the banditti quaked within them, and the boldest shuddered for the crimes he had committed, and prayed that he might be forgiven.

The storm was so tremendous that our party were constrained to remain for some time. The robbers were also forced to stay at home; but were ready to sally forth, being in expectation of a change of weather, as they had notice of travellers who were to pass, from whom there was expected some precious booty.    Lady

Grange and her party being entirely in their power, they considered themselves sure of what money they possessed, but they had not come to any determination as to the manner of treating them, though, after several conversations among themselves, they had resolved to exact a considerable sum before they should be allowed to depart. A different resolution, however, was adopted, at the suggestion of their housekeeper, who said that she believed the lady was not out of her senses, being a person of consequence, forcibly removed from her friends, and that they would receive a large remuneration for restoring her. As this appeared likely, the leader of the gang immediately went to Lady Grange's room, unobserved by her attendants, to ascertain the truth.

This person had once seen better days, having spent some time in more polished society than that of his present companions. His name was Buchanan of Machar, whose property was situated near the Campsic Fells. He was involved in different law-suits, and had been surreptitiously deprived of his lands by the rapacity of his neighbours. In order to be revenged, he had associated himself with this gang of ruffians, and from his superior qualities,

had become their commander. Two of Rob
Roy's sons belonged originally to this association, and though not constantly along with him,
occasionally assisted with their men, when any
desperate achievement was to be undertaken.

Upon entering Lady Grange's room, Buchanan
found her still reclining on her miserable bed.
He apologised for his intrusion ; but said that
he wished to serve her, and requested to be
informed of her real situation, and why she
travelled with an armed escort. The apparent
sympathy of the brigand and his offer of service received her thanks. She told him the
whole of her story, and promised him a large
reward if he and his party would restore her to
her friends. He desired her to keep quiet and
remain where she was, saying that he would
concert measures for her relief.

He then left her, and hastening to his companions, told them what he had learned, when
the prospect of a large sum made them resolve
to set the lady at liberty. It was therefore
agreed that her attendants should be secured in
their apartment, until they had carried the lady
to such a distance that she might elude their
pursuit, and that this was to be put in execution the following night.

This conversation was interrupted by the appearance of Macdonald and Macleod, who were anxious to ascertain the state of the weather; but as it was very bad, they were urged to remain for that day. A rude breakfast was placed before them, of which all partook, while the old woman attended the lady in her room.

When the repast was finished, the brigands retired to consider how they were to effect the escape of Lady Grange, and elude the vigilance of her conductors, who kept a watchful eye over her and all their motions, as if suspicious of their purpose. They were desirous of removing her by stratagem, rather than by force, her conductors being strong, and apparently determined men, but all this was overheard by the Frazers, who communicated it to their masters. This excited in them great alarm, as a discovery seemed to have been made, that would be ruinous to their project, and their suspicions fell on the old woman; but they could find no opportunity of bribing her to be quiet.

The day passed mournfully with Lady Grange, and with her conductors in gloomy uncertainty; while the banditti were merry in the anticipation of their scheme, and frequently regaled their spirits with large potations of whisky.

As the evening approached the weather became more settled, but the anxiety of our travellers increased. The moon broke through a cloud, and prognosticated a favourable change, which they were resolved to embrace; but the arrival of a man, who was a stranger to the detained, in the meantime frustrated their purpose, the whole attention of the robbers being given to what he said, which seemed to be intelligence of importance, as they all buckled on their swords, and prepared for an expedition.

Their captain begged that our travellers would retire to their own apartment, as they wished to hold a private conference, and this they complied with; but they had no sooner entered the room, than the door was locked upon them from without, so that the hostile intention of the gang became evident, and occasioned the party great consternation. Now confined in a place which was almost a dungeon, they had no means of relief, and though they heard the banditti depart, their escape seemed impossible. They examined the door, and found it secure, though it was old. It was now near midnight, and all was silent. They tried to force open the door, but it resisted all their strength. After repeated trials, however, and applying their utmost exertion, it began to yield, and at last gave way with a great crash, which they feared might alarm the robbers.

Being once more free, they resolved instantly to leave the dreary mansion, and to oppose whoever should resist their setting out. Then unsheathing their dirks, they proceeded to the hall, where a few dying embers of the fire enabled them to light their dark lantern, by the assistance of which they discovered the old woman asleep. They aroused her, and desired to be conducted to Lady Grange; but she refused, saying that she had orders to keep her room locked, till the return of her masters. One of the guides thereupon laid hold of her, and presented a dagger to her breast, threatening her with instant death if she did not comply. The hag yielded, and they were presently in Lady Grange's room, who complained of being ill ; but as her escort believed this to be feigned, they forced her to get up, and with all haste hurried her out of the house, and placed her on horseback behind one of the guides. Meantime one of the banditti, who had been left as a

guard, awoke, and coming to the door, was surprised to see that the guests had escaped. He
did all in his power to detain them, and threatened to blow a horn he held in his hand, as a
signal to his friends, who, he said, were not far
off; but Macdonald immediately seized and
bound him, along with the housekeeper, to prevent their giving any alarm.

The party now set off with all possible expedition, to the great disappointment of Lady
Grange, who had had every expectation of being
rescued from her conductors, of whose plans she
was ignorant, but of whom she had reason to
dread the worst. They travelled with great
haste, and by daybreak were beyond the risk of
falling in the way of the freebooters.

When they left the castle, the moon had set
behind the mountains that rose to the south, and
as the morning was dark and cloudy, it was with
considerable difficulty that they found their way
across a lone and rugged muir, which extended
far to the north. The guides, however, had often
traversed those regions, and though there was
no path, they went on with tolerable accuracy.
Twice, indeed, they were wrong; but the moment
the clouds dispersed, and gave them a sight of
the polar star, they again found the proper

T

course.  By the dawn of day, they descended
from the intricate mountainous tract, to the
more level valley of Glendochart, through which
the road lay to the north and west Highlands ;
but lady Grange was so tired that they halted at
a wretched hut, denominated an inn.  She now
became very ill.  A degree of fever overpowered
her faculties, and when her companions had
again prepared to set out, she felt herself unable to proceed, and was obliged to recline
on a bed, scarcely more comfortable than that
which she occupied in the castle of Macgregor's
isle.

This detention was not agreeable to her
escort : but as the day began to overcast, they
submitted to the delay, though there appeared
but little accommodation in the house, there
being only two apartments, including that occupied by the lady, whose indisposition still continued.  The gentlemen and one of their attendants slept in a barn, the other was left to guard
lady Grange, lest her illness might be feigned
in order to deceive them.  In the morning, however, she was better, and they proceeded on their
route.

In the course of the day they met several
people of the country, to whom they mentioned

that they were going to the chapel of St Fillan, to try the virtues of that place in curing the malady which afflicted the lady.

The road passed a short way from this edifice, venerated for possessing this quality of restoring the lost faculties of the mind—an influence certainly no less ineffectual than absurd, and which often rather confirmed than removed the disorder it was supposed to cure. Whatever the miracles of the saint might have been on other occasions, his mediation was not now invoked. Our travellers had some conversation on the incongruity of such notions, and passed the sacred pile without imploring the benediction of its patron.

They travelled very slowly, from the weakness of their horses, as they had fared ill while with the banditti ; and they were forced to leave one of them to his fate. They reached the dark passes of Glencoe, as the night came on, but deemed it prudent to remain at a house of respectable appearance, which they saw at a short distance. Inns, in such sequestered regions, were not commonly established in those times, and travellers trusted to the hospitality of private families, who considered it a duty to shelter and entertain every stranger.

They accordingly stopped at the door of this house, the landlord of which came out to salute and welcome them, though he knew not who they were.

In it Lady Grange passed the most agreeable night since her departure from home ; and she would willingly have remained, as the people were kind, and seemed to feel for her situation, the true nature of which they did not know. But an arduous part of their journey was still to be accomplished, and they left their host with thanks for his kindness.

The lofty and barren mountains of Glencoe now rose around them in awful magnificence ; and frowning in gloomy silence, their rugged peaks seemed ready to fall, and entomb the passenger. Rocks rising on rocks, towered to a height which the eye could scarcely survey ; while through the fissures, produced by the incessant streams of ages, poured the foaming cataracts of the mountains. There vegetation was almost unknown, a few stunted shrubs having shot out their feeble branches from the mountain's brow, as if denied the growth of maturity. Some straggling goats, browsing on the scanty herbage, appeared amazed at the sight of human beings, while the screams of the eagle, and the croaking of the raven, declared the dreary solitude of the region.

The conductors of lady Grange, though accustomed to scenes where nature had displayed sterility and wildness, were unacquainted with so sullen an aspect as their present tract exhibited ; and Macdonald and Macleod, being both conversant with the early history of Caledonia, naturally recollected, in passing this frightful defile, the opinion which the Romans entertained of the people who inhabited so gloomy a country.

The lady being now informed where she was, and possessing an understanding highly cultivated, felt a melancholy satisfaction in contemplating such new and wonderful objects ; and while she gazed on the bold irregularity of the mountains, as the scene of the hideous massacre, a sigh of kindred horror burst from her heart, and she shuddered at the destiny that seemed to await herself. The sensations which she experienced, passed unheeded by her companions ; and though no one possessed of feeling, can pass through the mournful valley of Glencoe, without thinking of the deed which was there perpetrated, yet the escort of lady Grange proceeded with the utmost unconcern. The road was so

bad, that it had not unappropriately been named
" the devil's staircase," and it was not until the
night was far advanced, that they arrived at the
side of Lochiel.   There they were afraid to halt,
lest they might be detained by the garrison of
Fort-William, in the neighbourhood of which
they now were ; military being constantly stationed there, who were originally placed by the
angry and suspicious king William, who attempted to accomplish by force, what his temper
would not permit him to do by mildness.

The night was serene and clear, and they immediately procured a boat with an able crew,
who speedily rowed them to the head of the
loch, where they arrived by the break of day.
At this place they borrowed a horse, having left
their own with the owner of the boat, and having
placed lady Grange upon it, soon after got to
Glenfinnan, where no other shelter could be obtained, than that which an open barn could
afford.   Poor lady Grange was by this time in a
state of insensibility, the fatigue she had undergone being more than her frame could support,
so that the story which her fellow-travellers still
reported of her insanity, had more than ever the
appearance of reality.

The miserable condition to which she was

reduced, was such as to claim pity from a savage. Many days having elapsed without her having put off her clothes, she felt bruised and in great pain, and her limbs were so much swollen and be-numbed, that she was unable to walk.  When the party stopped, she was carried to a wretched hut, and laid upon a parcel of heath, there being no other bed, and there she remained some days, in such distress that she could not be removed.*

As soon as she became convalescent, though still incapable of using her limbs, she was removed, and placed in a boat brought near to the house, which conveyed her and the party down Loch-sheal; a fresh water lake, above twenty miles in length, which divides a portion of the counties of Argyll and Inverness, and has its efflux into the western sea at castle Tirum, an ancient seat of the Macdonalds.

The wind, which was adverse, greatly retarded

* At this place of Glenfinnan, not more than thirteen years thereafter, did the unfortunate prince Charles Stewart, with inconsiderate bravery, first unfurl his standard, flattered by the hopes which a few injudicious persons had excited.  To commemorate this event, an obelisk was, with classical taste, lately erected on the spot, by Mr Macdonald of Glenaladale ; which, while it is ornamental, in so desert a situation, must also be a subject of considerable interest to the future his-torian, and the descendants of those who fell in the cause of that prince.

their progress, and frequently obliged them to take shelter under the bold headlands that jut into the lake. After much labour, they arrived in the evening at a wretched hamlet on its banks. Here their accommodation was infinitely more miserable than any they had yet met with ; but they had no alternative, for it was impossible to proceed, and equally impossible to remain in the boat. Though they were within a house, it could not afford them a bed, scarcely a seat, and no victuals to allay their hunger. Lady Grange, having now given herself up to despair, regarded not the condition of so savage a habitation. She often looked around, and had it not been from the colour of the people, she could as readily have persuaded herself that she was in Africa, or the wilds of America, as in any part of her native country.

After a tedious and disagreeable night, morning at length arrived, and they again betook them to their boat. The wind had now ceased, and they soon landed at the extremity of the lake ; but the road was so bad, and the lady so weak, that the guides and boatmen were obliged to carry her in their arms to castle Tirum, a distance of three miles, where they expected to find a vessel to take her on board, and convey her to the place of her ultimate destination. In this they were disappointed, no vessel having yet arrived, and they were that night obliged to remain in the fields. Next day, an apartment being fitted up for Lady Grange in the old castle, she was conveyed thither.*

Though this fortress was deserted by the family, it was still very entire, and was the occasional residence of military, sent, after the commotion of 1715, to check the revolutionary spirit, again prevalent in the Highlands. At this time (1732) the soldiery had been removed, as the country appeared in a state of tranquillity, but there still remained a few men who had the charge of the castle.

The room appropriated to Lady Grange was situated in one of the lofty towers, commanding an extensive view of the Atlantic and a wide range of mountain scenery. It was comfortably

* Castle Tirum was erected in the thirteenth century. It is built on a peninsulated rock, formerly an island, and surrounded by the sea, at the mouth of the river Sheal, the north point of Ardnamurchan. It was the seat of a powerful chieftain of the Macdonalds, having been confirmed to his family by a charter from Robert the Bruce, still extant, and dated at Aros castle in the sound of Mull, in consideration of the assistance afforded that prince by a Macdonald at the battle of Bannockburn, when he told that chieftain that his " hope was constant in him,"—a motto still adopted by many of that name, upon their crest, which represents this castle Tirum.

furnished, though it retained the sombre appearance of its antiquities, the walls being fitted up
with pannelled oak, and adorned with various
grotesque carvings.

The day after her arrival, Frazer, one of her
guides, brought her some books; but her mind
was too much occupied by her misfortunes to
receive any consolation from extraneous subjects, and she gave vent to her grief in piteous
lamentation; yet this touched not the heart of
her guard, from whom she could obtain no information of the place where she now was, nor
as to what was to be her destiny. To her tears,
her entreaties, and the money which she offered
him, he was equally callous, and only answered
her by shaking his head.

In this solitary apartment, left to her own reflections, grief preyed more upon her spirits
than during her journey; for then some rays of
hope would brighten her mind, while now all
chance of escape seemed at an end. She sunk
into a state of utter despondency, her only
amusements being to sit at her window and
gaze on the unceasing motion of the sea, to the
surface of which a little sail would at times add
animation, or to examine the dense clouds that
floated along the hills, and mark their shapes

and changes ; at times listening to the screech-
ing sea-fowl, as they rose in the air in anticipation of a storm. These were the only objects
in nature on which she was permitted to look,
or from which she could receive any pleasure.

But she had only occupied this room a few
days when a new object claimed her attention,
and occasioned her great consternation. While
sitting at her window one evening as usual,
watching the descent of the moon, as it vanished
beneath the western main, she heard a hollow
sound, resembling a human voice in distress.
She rose from her seat and listened ; but could
not discover whence it came. It ceased, and
she again took her station at the window, thinking that it might have been the wind whistling
among the battlements, or the delusion of her
own disturbed fancy ; but she was speedily undeceived, for it returned and convinced her
that it was no deception, although she knew not
how it came.

In a state of great trepidation she went to
bed, but not to sleep. Towards morning she
again heard the voice more distinctly than
before. She instantly got out of bed, and went
to the window, from which she could observe a
human figure pacing slowly along a balcony

of the castle, at a short distance; but the moment she looked out, it disappeared with such rapidity, that she could not perceive where it went.

She had often heard of the legendary tales of the Highlands, which recorded the marvellous powers of ghosts, fairies, and witches ; nor was she herself free from a belief in supernatural agency, so that the appearance of the figure on the balcony, and its vanishing so quickly, convinced her that this castle was haunted by some malignant spirit, from which she might dread some new and unlooked-for misery. In great agitation, she lay down on her bed, where she continued till the servant who attended her entered in the morning, when she told what she had seen ; but the servant, considering her as insane, neither believed her, nor paid any attention to what she said.

With feelings of terror she beheld the approach of the following night; but she neither heard the voice, nor did the figure appear on the terrace as before. In the morning she was greatly surprised to find on her table a bit of paper, on which was written, " Lady, if you desire to escape from this place, and can face danger in the accomplishment,

knock on the panel behind your door, at midnight, and you will be heard." These words,
and their being left in her room without her
knowing how they came, agitated her so
much, that when her maid appeared, she could
scarcely articulate, and during the day continued in a state of great anxiety and fear,
without being able to bring her mind to any
decisive resolution. To escape, was her most
ardent desire; but the danger attending the
attempt, and her ignorance of the person who
made the proposal, were considerations that
staggered her fortitude. She often examined
the panel behind the door; but could not perceive that it had any particular mark: and
though the hour had now arrived when she was
directed to give the signal, her spirits failed, and
she shrank from her purpose. Perplexed and
irresolute, she sat down at the window, and
endeavoured to compose herself; but the figure
she had formerly seen on the balcony, again
appeared, and carried her attention from her
own meditations. It paced slowly about for
some time, and disappeared as quickly as
before.

Having become more collected, she summoned
all her fortitude, and at last ventured to knock

on the panel ; but all remained quiet. She repeated the signal with more confidence, and
presently the panel folded back and opened into
a passage, where a light stood upon the floor,
but no one appeared. She entered, however,
with hesitation, when the panel closed and
shut her within the passage. Her heart now
nearly failed her, and she would have returned
to her room, but could not gain admittance.
She looked round with terror, and called out to
ascertain if any person was present, but all remained silent.—Trembling with fear, and almost
in a state of distraction, she snatched the light
and proceeded along the gallery, at the end of
which was a staircase. Descending by it, she
reached a great hall, in which stood a table with
a naked dagger lying on it, and a handkerchief,
stained with what appeared to be blood. She
trembled at the sight, and hastily passed on to
a door that opened into a place which seemed
to be a dungeon. Here her light was extin-
guished, and she knew not where to proceed.
In groping about, she laid her hand upon an iron
chain hung on the wall, which rattled at her
touch, and so overcame her nerves, that she fell
on the floor, in a state of insensibility. When
her senses returned, she saw her maid and a

soldier standing beside her. The maid having found her absent from her room in the morning, had alarmed the castle, and searching, they had discovered her in the dungeon, where, some time previous, a murder had been committed ; the blood of the victim still staining the floor, and being visible on the steps that led to it.

During her stay at this place, a vessel was procured to convey her to the Hebrides : but as it lay in Lochurn, at the distance of thirty miles, she was transported from Castle Tirum in a four-oared boat, on board of which she continued during a day and night, meeting with boisterous weather in passing the various inlets of the sea that indent the coast.

While the sloop was preparing for her reception, she suffered many hardships, being removed from place to place, and often lodged in barns and sheilings, to avoid discovery. When she was put on board the vessel the weather was calm, which prevented it sailing for some days, during which, several gentlemen went on board, from motives of curiosity, to see her. She conversed with some of them, and told them all her misfortunes. One of them, who had more feeling than the others, promised to make her story known, that she might be restored to her friends ; but she never heard more of him.

The sloop was commanded by Alexander Macdonald, who was a tenant of Sir Alexander Macdonald of Sleat, and consequently under the control of that chief ; but when lady Grange told him of the treatment she had received, and that she had been carried away by force from her friends in Edinburgh, he was greatly surprised, and declared that unless Sir Alexander was concerned, he would not detain her against her inclination. He was ignorant of the cause that induced his employers to treat her in such a manner, nor did he know her destination, as future orders were to be given him when off the west coast of Skye, whither the vessel now proceeded with a gentle breeze.

When lady Grange went upon the deck, the morning after leaving Lochurn, she was astonished to behold the vast tract of mountains forming the mainland coast. The sun illumined their sides and served to display their rugged surfaces in all the wildness of their native sterility ; and the prospect was more barren and forbidding than any she had ever seen. To the north-west, the stupendous mountains of Skye reared their brown summits, on the south-east rose the black hills of Mull, and the islands of Rum and Eigg, while the immense altitudes of the north pressed upon the sight, and composed an outline the most singular in any country of Europe.

The progress of the vessel was tedious, and it was not until several days had elapsed that they reached the mouth of Loch Uig. There they lay-to for a day, when some boats went off from the shore ; but no one was allowed to go on board the sloop excepting one gentleman, who held a conversation with the master relative to lady Grange, in which it was mentioned that she was to be conveyed to Heskar, an island occupied by him, on the west coast of the Long-island, perhaps the most remote of the Hebrides.

On the passage to that place, they were over-taken by a storm, from which they were in great danger ; and lady Grange, never before having been on ship-board, was thrown into a dreadful state of alarm, while the seamen gave themselves up for lost.

Having with difficulty weathered the gale, the sloop arrived at Heskar, and lady Grange was conveyed on shore to Macdonald's house, where she experienced many hardships, and

U

barbarous treatment, suffering much from cold
and hunger. Indeed so miserable was her
situation, that for ten months she did not taste
bread, but lived on the coarse fare of Macdonald's family, who were ordered to treat her
exactly as one of themselves. After remaining
in his custody for twelve months, she became
much in want of every article of dress, and
remonstrated with him on his cruelty, in thus
depriving her of the common comforts of life ;
but he declared that he was not to blame for
her being so treated, and said that he had often
written to those from whom he received her in
charge, but that they had made him no answer.

Though of rude and unpolished deportment,
this man and his wife readily perceived that
lady Grange was born to better fortune, and
that they had no means of affording the essential
articles of apparel which she required. Macdonald now resolved to wait on his employers,
as he would no longer be accessory to such inhumanity, and accordingly set out for the isle
of Skye, where Sir Alexander Macdonald resided.

On his return, he said that the knight had
expressed contrition for having ever meddled
in such an affair, and wished to get clear of it,

if he knew in what way to do so ; but that he
still desired him not to allow lady Grange any
liberty, till he should receive farther directions.
He was ordered, he said, to treat her harshly in
every respect, and allow her no comfort he
could withhold.   In this instance, he acted up
to his instructions, and her situation daily became more intolerable.  Whether he had actually
received such directions, may be doubted ; but
he and his family, at all events, rendered her
life a burden almost insupportable to her.

   This island of Heskar is small and rocky,
situated far in the Atlantic, and at a considerable distance from any inhabited land.   Lady
Grange was here permitted to wander alone
among the rocks, and along the shore, for there
were no means by which she could escape.  Her
sole source of recreation, therefore, was a solitary walk on the sea beach, from which her only
objects of contemplation were the distant hills
of the Long Island, and the wide extent of the
ocean.   Melancholy were her thoughts on these
occasions.   Banished by the machinations of
persons combined against her, and having leisure
to reflect on the violence of the principles she
had espoused, which seemed to have deprived
her of the affections of her husband, tears of

remorse would sometimes come to her relief, and convince her that to her own imprudence much of her suffering was to be attributed ; and when thus overcome with grief, she was frequently found reclining on a rock, nearly in a state of insensibility.

While thus suffering under the agonies of despair, she often demanded writing materials to address her husband and her friends, that she might own her errors, and in contrite language, crave their forgiveness and their pity ; but her unrelenting host denied her that consolation, and she eventually fell into a settled depression of spirits, which rendered her inattentive to surrounding objects. She would scarcely answer any question ; often refused food ; and became so emaciated, that she appeared more a spectre than an inhabitant of the earth. In addition to her misery, the winter had now set in, a season attended with peculiar dreariness and gloom in the northern islands of the Hebrides.

On an evening of the second winter she spent on this island, her guardian and his man-servant having gone to secure the only boat on the island, were alarmed by vivid flashes of fire from the northern sky, which was red as blood, and alternately black. They hastily returned, expecting a storm, and it came on at midnight, accompanied by thunder, the surface of the sea seeming to be in a blaze. It continued till the following night, when it became still more dreadful. Dismay took possession of lady Grange and all in the house, which they every moment expected was to be blown down upon them. They kneeled intuitively to the Being who holds the limits of the storm, and whose nod can quiet the raging spirit of the deep, the master of the house devoutly imploring protection from the impending destruction; but before he had finished, a loud knocking was heard at the door, and a voice begged for admission. The party stood amazed. The women shrunk back, and the landlord hesitated; but no earthly being having ever appalled him, he drew his dirk, and stepped to the door. Having opened it, two men and a boy entered, who, from their dialect, seemed to be natives of Ireland. They had been shipwrecked that day on a distant reef of rocks, and of sixteen who were in the ship, they only were saved, having taken to the long boat, and with the utmost difficulty reached this island. One of them was the captain, who appeared melancholy, and expressed great regret at the loss of his crew.

During the storm, which continued for three days, they were kindly treated by Macdonald; but lady Grange was not permitted to have any intercourse with them. They were told, indeed, of her being in the house, but that she was an insane relation of the laird's. Notwithstanding this prohibition, she found means to hold a conversation with the captain, to whom she made known her situation, and who promised to assist in effecting her release.

This was the person whose figure she had seen on the balcony of castle Tirum, several months before, and who had contrived to leave the mysterious note on her table. He had been implicated for an attempt to carry off an heiress, seized on board of his own ship, then at anchor on the coast, and placed in that fortress till he could be removed to the capital; but having bribed the castle guard, he had become acquainted with all the intricate passages in it; and hearing of lady Grange's situation, had been desirous to aid her escape, as already mentioned, when she by mistake went to the dungeon. Afterwards he had got away, and returned to his own country.

A new opportunity was now presented to him to effect his generous purpose, when he hoped to be more fortunate than on the former occasion; with the characteristic warmth of his country, saying, "he would take her home, if he should die by the way."

The following night was fixed for their departure, and lady Grange having scrambled out of a back window, met the captain and his people at the appointed place. Unluckily for their project, their host had a watch dog that began to bark as they turned round the house, and alarmed his master, who instantly got out of bed ; but without any suspicion of the cause of disturbance. His first care being lady Grange, he went to her room, and discovering that she was absent, immediately called to his servant. Having equipped themselves hastily with their arms, they went in search of her, accompanied by the dog. They also ascertained that the shipwrecked seaman, who occupied an outhouse, had gone away, which convinced Macdonald of their purpose.

Highly incensed at the audacity of the men whom he had sheltered, he resolved on punishing them ; and the dog having traced their steps, Macdonald and his servant overtook them just as they had launched their boat. The captain stood in it, having an oar in his hand.

Macdonald fired at him, and he fell.   The other man and boy implored his mercy, as they could not disobey their commander ; and lady Grange, trembling on the shore, fainted on seeing what took place.

The boat was dragged on shore, when it was found that the captain was not dead, having been shot through the leg.   He craved Macdonald's pardon, saying, that he believed the lady was confined contrary to her will, though not by him, and that at her own entreaty he wished to set her free.   As he would not again intrude on Macdonald's hospitality, he and his men got into their boat, and wounded as he was, set off towards the Long Island.

After this affair, Lady Grange met with more rigid treatment than ever.   The clergyman of the parish, a Mr Maclean, was even prejudiced against her, and when she requested a visit from him, to pray with her for an alleviation of her sufferings, he refused to see her, saying that she was included in his general prayers for his parish.

In May 1734, Sir Alexander Macdonald went to Uist, and sent notice to his tenant in Heskar, that Lady Grange was to be taken from his house, as he could not afford to pay for her maintenance, and that he was to give her to any one who might be sent for her, as her presence in Skye and the mainland was known. Accordingly, on the 14th of June, a sloop arrived at Heskar, with a letter to Macdonald from the Laird of Macleod, who was now to have charge of the lady, in consequence of an agreement among the neighbouring chiefs ; and she being put on board by the crew, with great rudeness, the vessel put off. Macdonald had told her that he knew not where she was going ; but two Macleods who accompanied her, said she was going to the Orkneys. This, however, was said to deceive her, as her real destination was the distant island of St Kilda. That island, or rather barren rock, is situated in the Atlantic, upwards of twenty leagues from the nearest part of the Long Island, and was then the property of the Laird of Macleod. Being on all sides perpendicular, there is but a single landing place on it, and that a shelving rock ; so that landing can only be effected with great risk, on account of the breakers, and the tremendous swell of the sea at all seasons. The natives are, however, very dexterous in managing boats as they approach.

The surf on the shore was so awful, that

Lady Grange expected every moment to be swallowed up ; and after landing, the path to the summit of the island was so frightful, that she trembled with dread, the inhabitants flocking around her, as if she had belonged to another planet.

The houses on St Kilda were then what they still continue to be, miserable huts ; and the habitation to which Lady Grange was conducted, was of the same description. The inhabitants were primitive, simple people, the greater number of whom had never been out of the island, there being only a short period of the year in which they could venture to cross so boisterous a sea. Their principal means of living arose, as it still does, from seizing the myriads of sea-fowl that nestle on the crags, for the sake of their feathers ; an employment of the utmost hazard, each adventurer being let down by a rope over the brink of the precipice. These feathers were sent to various places at a distance, and the inhabitants, in return, were supplied with the few articles of life they required, and which their own limited sphere of existence could not produce. The errors of great and mixed communities were unknown to them. No sources of vice existed, and the ambition of the world did not disturb their peace. Every one was known to his neighbour, and no gradations existed in their society ; yet the duties of religion and morality were not neglected, a clergyman being stationed among them for their instruction.

During her voyage to this island, Lady Grange had not slept, and she no sooner took possession of her new apartment, than she went to bed wholly overcome. Labouring under poignant depression of spirits, foreboding a miserable end, far from her friends, and among people of whose language she was ignorant, she kept her bed for some days.

The men belonging to the vessel, who remained for two days, would not discover under whose authority they acted, nor tell her where she was, but having given her in charge to a man who spoke very bad English, left her in a miserable condition, nearly without clothes, and with no other food than that which the island could afford. The man to whose care she was entrusted was the only person who could speak even a word of the language she understood ; and he was so ill-tempered and savage, that a few days after her arrival, he drew his dirk in order to murder her.

Dejected and sorrowful, many months passed away in silence, as necessity alone made her speak to the wicked wretch who had threatened her life, and whom she afterwards shuddered to look at.  Her only comfort arose from the consolations of religion, which, during the dreadful season of winter that ensued, supported her broken spirits, while the roaring ocean, and the hurricanes of the north threatened even the destruction of the rock on which she was placed.  A stranger to the people, they at first regarded her as an object of curiosity, for whom they felt no sympathy ; but when she had been among them for some months, her manners became affable and agreeable ; she saw that the hauteur she was accustomed to assume, not only over her lord and family, but all her dependants, would not suit the temperament of the Highlanders, and she was now no less humble in her adversity, than she had formerly been haughty in prosperity.

There were then about two hundred inhabitants on the island, under the austere control of their laird, who were all enjoined to treat Lady Grange with indifference, and on no account to inform her where she was ; so that to the many inquiries she made, no satisfactory answers were given.

In the course of the following summer, however, her sorrows were greatly alleviated by the arrival of the clergyman and his wife, who for some time had been absent from the island. From the kindness of this couple she experienced much seasonable relief, for, in all probability she would have died of want, had they not appeared. They procured a girl to attend her, and their society and conversation tended to soften the melancholy that long had preyed upon her mind, which was now in a condition approaching to imbecility.

The minister was a devout and serious man, who, in the duties of his office, as well as in acts of humanity, paid her great attention, and she seemed to feel the full influence of his instruction.

She made frequent applications to him for writing materials ; but these he was obliged to refuse her, as he was forbidden to allow her such indulgence ; she, however, prevailed upon him to write an account of her history and sufferings, to her own dictation, but she omitted many incidents, partly from a loss of memory, and partly from a wish to conceal them.

During the long period of her exile on this
island, her principal recreation, when the
weather permitted, was a lonely walk along the
tremendous precipices that compose the inaces-
sible boundaries of its shores ; and the more
she contemplated its narrow confines, and solitary situation, amidst an immeasurable ocean,
the less she saw any prospect of being restored
to her friends and to society, regarding the
unbroken expanse of sea as an interminable
obstacle to her hopes.

She lived some years in this place, before she
could discover its name, and then it was by
accident. She had borrowed a book from the
minister, and among the leaves she found a
letter addressed to him as " Minister of St
Kilda," relating chiefly to herself, from a person
who seemed to be of the same profession, but
very unlike him in point of Christian charity ;
for he accused him " of too much attention and
care for the wicked incendiary lady Grange,
whose soul was rotten, and unworthy of being
reclaimed, and who wished evil to the whole
race of Highlanders." This discovery occasioned
the poor lady great misery. She believed herself all along to have been among barbarians ;
but she could not have supposed anything so

scandalous and unfeeling in a clergyman. Such, indeed, was the enmity and deadly hate of some of his brethren of the Long Island and other places, to the poor minister, or rather catechist, of St Kilda, on account of his Christian kindness to lady Grange, that he had reason to consider his own life in danger, and even that of his uncle.

About this time he left the island, intending to visit Edinburgh on business of his own, and while there, he promised to inform lady Grange's friends of her deplorable case, she having given him memoranda to that effect. She wished him to take the sketch of her misfortunes he had drawn up, to show them how much she stood in need of their aid ; but he would not venture to carry it, and his life being again threatened if he attempted to make any representation regarding her, he destroyed her memoranda. Ultimately, the unworthy clergyman, under whose control he acted in St Kilda, placed such obstructions in his way as prevented his journey, lest he might disclose the shameful combination entered into for her destruction :— An unmanly combination, disgraceful to those concerned in it, from the cruelty and savage treatment they sanctioned towards a helpless woman. Such was the malignity towards this good man, that, on his return to the island, he was anxious that the account he had written at lady Grange's desire should be destroyed, lest it might fall into the hands of his enemies, who would thereby easily effect his ruin. For that purpose he sent his wife to her ; but lady Grange, wishing to preserve the document, employed the subterfuge of burning another piece of paper, to allay the fears of the minister, and retained the original, which is extant at the present day.

By the kindness and industry of the minister's daughter, she found an opportunity of concealing two letters, and also the account of her misfortunes, in balls of yarn, which found their way to a confidential friend. He applied through the proper channel for the redress of the hardships to which she had been subjected ; and a ship of war was sent to remove her from St Kilda. But prior to its arrival there, an angry conference had taken place betwixt the lairds of Chisholm and Macleod, in which the former accused the latter of being the jailor of a female, and told him that he would soon unlock her prison. High words had ensued ; and such had been the dread of discovery, from the mutual

insults given on the occasion, that the persecutors of lady Grange had judged it prudent to
remove her to some other place.

It being now nearly ten years since this unfortunate lady was forced from Edinburgh, it may
well be supposed, that, in so long a period, and
suffering under so many complicated hardships,
her mental powers as well as her corporeal
appearance must have greatly decayed, and so
we learn that when the sloop which was to
transport her from St Kilda arrived, she had
nearly become indifferent to her fate, a settled
melancholy had taken possession of her mind,
and that she was carried on board the vessel
with little perception of the change.   As she was
several days on board this small sloop, confined to a miserable hole of a cabin, in a boisterous sea, with a contrary wind, she suffered
greatly from continued sickness; and when she
arrived at Assynt, on the north-west coast of
Sutherland, she was so weak that she was carried from the shore to the house of a shepherd, where she was to remain.   There she was
cenfined to bed for many days, so much en-
feebled, that the people believed she was near
her end ; yet she recovered.   She remained in

this place for several months, being allowed
every freedom she desired, as she did not
seem to have any wish to leave it, or wander
far from the hut where she resided.    There
she might have remained in quietness, and un-
noticed during the remainder of her life ; but
she was doomed to have her state of imbecility
more generally exposed to the world.

From Assynt she was again removed to the
isle of Skye, where, as her faculties became more
feeble, she was treated with greater cruelty.
She was placed in a dark and lonesome cavern,
formed in a rock by the sea shore, where just as
much of the light of day was admitted as enabled her to see the dismal abode to which her
unfeeling persecutors had conveyed her ; but it
was found troublesome to attend her in such a
place, at a great distance from any house, and
she was at last allowed to leave it, and go
where she pleased.

After this she was totally neglected, no one
appearing to take any charge of her, and wandered for years, from place to place, over a great
part of the island of Skye, in a state of idiocy
supported by the charity and humanity of the
people, until at last overcome with with disease,

and sunk to the lowest condition of human misery, she closed her life at Idrigal, in that island, seventeen years after she had been forcibly removed from Edinburgh.

At the time this ill-fated lady was carried away, it will appear remarkable, that, although the tyrannical and barbarous action was sufficiently public, no means were adopted, to the disgrace of her friends and the government, for bringing the perpetrators of it to justice, though some of them were well known. Her husband had the address to persuade the world that his wife was mad, and that she had often attempted his life, so that her confinement became a point of necessity. But what was no less extraordinary than infamous was that two of her sons, then grown to manhood, were believed to have consented to the removal of their mother. She had also a daughter married to the Earl of Kintore, besides many other respectable relations, but none of them, to their great dishonour, ever took the smallest notice of the foul and cruel transaction.—And while, on the one hand, we lament that our countrymen should have manifested such ferocity towards a female, as our sketch exhibits, we, on the other rejoice, that now there is no difference of political opinions to occasion such severe and unfeeling deeds.

TURNBULL AND SPEARS, PRINTERS EDINBURGH.

www.ingramcontent.com/pod-product-compliance
Lightning Source LLC
Chambersburg PA
CBHW031339070726
47496CB00017B/1302